Losing It

The Growing Pains of a Teenage Vampire

Losing It

The Growing Pains of a Teenage Vampire

Ross Gilfillan

**LODESTONE
BOOKS**

Winchester, UK
Washington, USA

First published by Lodestone Books, 2014
Lodestone Books is an imprint of John Hunt Publishing Ltd., Laurel House, Station Approach,
Alresford, Hants, SO24 9JH, UK
office1@jhpbooks.net
www.johnhuntpublishing.com

For distributor details and how to order please visit the 'Ordering' section on our website.

Text copyright: Ross Gilfillan 2013

ISBN: 978 1 78279 366 3

A CIP catalogue record for this book is available from the British Library.

Design: Stuart Davies
www.stuartdaviesart.com

Printed in the USA by Edwards Brothers Malloy

We operate a distinctive and ethical publishing philosophy in all
areas of our business, from our global network of authors to
production and worldwide distribution.

for Harris, Gilly and Bagel

My thanks to Lorna Read for her time and comments

By the same author:
The Snake Oil Dickens Man
The Edge of the Crowd

Prologue

I am seventeen years old and I think I am about to have sex for the first time in my life.

Oh. My. God.

'You'll have to help me with this,' she says.

Pink-painted fingernails fiddle with the brass button on the skater jeans Mum got me last Christmas.

'I can't get it undone.'

I lie there, skinny chest bared and arms outstretched like I'm about to be crucified.

She sits astride me, her shirt open and her perfect breasts jiggling as she struggles with my flies.

'Brian,' she says. 'What's the matter with you? Give me a hand here.'

Here we go, I think, and undo the button.

She shuffles down the bed and begins to pull them off. Down they go, over my thighs and knees until all I have on are my Spiderman underpants which look so cool riding up over my low-slung jeans but look painfully silly right now. I'm staring at a cobweb on the ceiling, not daring to glance down my body at what she must be looking at now. I so want this to happen. I so want to have sex. I want to go back to school with that knowing look that says you've finally got your end away. But I know it's going to come at a price.

The moment that I have always dreaded and wanted at one and the same time has arrived and it is excruciating. She takes the waistband of my Spiderman pants between her slim, cool fingers and begins to pull them down, slowly revealing my long-kept and often disguised secret if not to the world, then to the one person in it who matters right now.

Because it's all a matter of size, you know.

I close my eyes and think of England.

Going down 3-1 to Germany, probably.

Chapter 1

Get Myself Arrested

'Will you get off the fucking bonnet, Diesel? I don't want to have to beat out the imprint of your fat buttocks.'

Faruk is talking. He's done most of the work on the car.

'Bollocks. This is the warmest place my arse has been all day.'

Clive is doing a circuit of the car, looking at it the way a bomb disposal team might view an empty vehicle in a market place in Kabul. We watch him, noting the pursed lips and the little flick he gives his floppy yellow hair whenever he's unsure of something.

'Is this it? I mean, is it finished? Or haven't you started yet?'

There's a pause while Faruk and Diesel exchange glances. 'Can't you see it's finished?' Faruk says. 'That, my friend, is fine art on four wheels.'

Clive looks the car over one more time, as if he can't decide what to complain about first. 'I don't like the colour,' he says at last.

'Fuck me, Clive, what did you want, pink?' That's Diesel.

'No, of course not, but purple? And it's not even purple is it? If you look at it from another angle, it goes slime green, or a grungy grey. It's completely, irrevocally tasteless.' Clive's squeaky voice rises an octave. And the word is *irrevocably*, Clive.

'It's two-tone green, you pillock. You like it, don't you, Diesel?'

'A1 fucking babe magnet,' says Diesel, sliding heavily off the car and onto his unlaced trainers. He's bathed in the headlights and front fogs, which Faruk has flicked on to max the drama. For the same reason, *Also Sprach Zarathustra* from 2001 is blasting from the stereo. 'It's the bollocks. What do you reckon, Brian?'

The back of the two-tone Ford Escort looks like it's just been involved in a spectacular accident involving an RAF Tornado, but I'm ninety per cent sure that the enormous fin jammed on to the boot lid isn't the wing of an aircraft. Well, eighty-five percent, then.

'What's that?' I point.

'It's a spoiler.' That's Faruk.

'I can see that,' I say. 'It's totally spoiled the car. And no offence, but the interior looks like a prostitute's bedroom.'

'A dead one.' Clive, being unusually caustic.

We all peer through the windows at plastic bucket seats, an awful lot of purple felt and a pair of fuchsia furry dice hanging from the rear view mirror. 'That is truly fucking hideous,' I say.

Clive backs me up. 'It's a crime against the laws of ascetics,' he says, but I think he means *aesthetics*. Ascetics are people like hermits who abstain from life's normal pleasures and I don't think that's us.

'Fuck me,' Diesel says. 'Are you and Brian going out now or what?'

I can see we're going to have one of our differences. We spend so much time in each other's pockets that tiffs, spats and the occasional dead-leg or even a bit of a fight are inevitable. But I can't be bothered to argue. I'm too disappointed.

'Did you seriously think I would let myself be seen in that thing?' Clive says. 'While I was still *conscious*?'

He flounces over to where Faruk's brother (a Middle-Eastern Elvis, according to Clive) is spraying a Vauxhall Cavalier, orange. He looks up from his job, takes off his respirator and sticks his own oar in. 'I wouldn't get in that if it were the last taxi out of Middlesborough. And I helped build the bugger.'

Diesel says, 'Do you know how long it took to pimp that ride?' Diesel and Faruk are tight, always looking out for each other.

'Not long enough?' I say, which is a bit mean but I am seriously let down. I know that Faruk and Diesel have spent weeks making the car roadworthy, getting it through its MOT and carrying out these bonkers improvements. (Faruk and his brother did the actual work, to Diesel's specs.) In all that time, they've not let Clive or me near the project, because they wanted to surprise us, they said show us what they could do. Well, now we've seen what they can do and I'll give them this: we're both surprised.

'Fucking hell, Brian,' Diesel says (we think that swearing all the time is fucking brilliant). 'What's the matter with you? I thought Clive might have the odd minor objection, with him being a bit...'

'A bit what?'

'You know what.'

'Oh that. A bit of a rainbow warrior, you mean.'

'What?'

We've lowered our voices so that Clive, who is checking himself out in a chrome bumper hanging on the garage wall, doesn't hear what we're saying. We're not a hundred percent certain he knows he's gay yet. Always the last to know anything, Clive is.

'They have their own ideas about style,' Diesel says, hands on hips, Lady Gaga tee shirt riding up to expose his podgy white belly. 'But from you, Brian. I expected a little support, you know. I'm telling you straight, I thought you would love it. I really did. You're my mate, you know.' (Diesel can make his eyes well up at will. He's doing it now). 'I wouldn't have done it if I didn't think you'd love it. Now, come on, look at that body kit – it's the bollocks, really, isn't it?'

'No,' I say.

I turn my back on the metal monstrosity in Faruk's family garage and see a couple of girls about to enter the Casablanca, the luridly-lit kebab shop over the road. The girls are laughing like maniacs at something, our car, probably. There is nothing I can say. It's just the latest entry on a list we really should compile of. Plans We've Made Which Have Gone Tits Up.

This idea, just like all the rest, seemed brilliant, that afternoon we first heard it. We'd all passed our tests this year, all except Clive anyway, who's dragging things out because he obviously fancies his driving instructor. So clubbing together to buy a drop-dead sexy car, which we'd all use on a rotation system, seemed a spot-on idea. Diesel assured us we'd have fanny queuing up to be shagged in the back of his Uncle Lol's BMW, which he said we could buy for an amazing £600. If we got the money together by that evening.

We'd heard funny things about Diesel's uncle Lol but we'd seen the car, too, a sharp-looking black coupe with windows tinted so dark they were probably illegal. It was getting on a bit, but I had to admit, it looked the business.

What business his relative had used it for Diesel didn't specify, but there were times when Uncle Lol flashed big wads of cash, peeling off twenties or fifties when he bought his fags, or did a little business with one of the dodgy or ill-looking characters who were always turning up at Diesel's door, asking for him; and other times, like now, when he was flat broke. Diesel said he was in trouble and needed the money fast to fund some new business venture. We'd be helping out his Uncle Lol and bagging ourselves a sweet deal at the same time. We didn't need persuading. We knew that everything would be fantastic once we had bought that car. We all said that, one way or another. We'd go places together or drive off on our own, taking with us whichever bird we'd selected for the privilege that evening. How cool would that be? Could we see ourselves cruising past the girls at the bus stop in a blacked-out Beemer with drum and bass pumping from the subwoofers in the boot? Of course we could.

Me especially. Some days, I'd drive it to St Saviour's, drawing envious looks as I stepped out and fired the remote lock. I'd pretend not to care that Rosalind Chandler's eyes were burning into my back as I cut my way, like a star through paparazzi, up the (red carpeted?) steps and into the school. I'd be well endowed with confidence if nothing else.

Now all we had to find was £600, which according to the calculator on my phone, was £150 each, by that evening. It's worth repeating, this. We had a matter of hours to come up with six hundred pounds. That or we'd see the sweetest dreams we'd had all year evaporate before our eyes. Six hundred quid may not be much if you're a celebrity chef or an MP or something, but to four sixth form schoolboys, it might as well have been a lottery jackpot on rollover week. We'd all jumped at the offer, recognising a bargain and thinking the others must be able to find the cash, because they were nodding and agreeing, just like we were. How easily we had deluded ourselves. It looked like we were fucked before we had started; everyone was broke, with no one they could borrow something from.

Everyone except Clive, who spoke up now, demanding to know why we hadn't asked him if he had any money. In fact, he bragged (incautiously, in my opinion) he could come up with his share without any problem. He had £350 stashed away in the building society, which he'd apparently saved up working at the hair salon last summer. We could have the lot, he said, if we gave him 5 percent interest and one of us acted as his chauffeur until he passed his test. £350 wasn't much more than half the total we needed. But, as Faruk suggested, maybe it would make a down payment. We could pay Diesel's Uncle Lol and Clive the rest in just a few weeks, we reasoned, if we took weekend jobs.

So Clive coughed up, and armed with £350, we were soon slavering over the wax-shiny Beemer parked outside Diesel's pebble-dashed council house. Uncle Lol was staying over a few nights 'until things cooled down'. We lusted over its clean lines, fat tyres and leather upholstery while Uncle Lol himself sat in the driver's seat, gently depressing the accelerator so we could appreciate the smooth hum of the engine. It was early evening, but Lol was still wearing his vintage Ray Bans. With his shades on and dark tinted windows, I guessed that he probably relied on his sat nav more than most people. We stood there, waiting for him to say something but it seemed that Uncle Lol was the silent type. He just chewed his gum, sniffed a lot and drummed his fingers on the wing mirror. After he'd given us a chance to admire the bassy quality of his premium sound system, he switched it off, sniffed a bit more and then peered over his aviators at Diesel and me.

'Like the car, then, lads?'

We nodded dumbly. I waited for Diesel to broach the matter of our revised proposition but Diesel seemed suddenly reluctant to open the negotiations. It was left to Uncle Lol to get the ball rolling. 'Got the money?'

That was when Diesel told him we could only raise half of the agreed price.

'You are fucking kidding me' — the growl of a Rottweiler you've forgotten to feed — 'tell me you're having a laugh, Dennis?'

Diesel shook his head and stepped back from the car. Uncle Lol had visibly tensed, his knuckles white where he gripped the wheel, his expression indecipherable behind the dark sunglasses. There were probably times when he got himself like this and sprang from the car, for one reason or another. Diesel seemed to think so, because he had stepped back. Clive and Faruk had backed off too and I was edging towards them. 'It was all we could get, on my life,' Diesel said, glancing back at us to see if we were all set to back him up and then looking up the road and down the road like he was working out which way to run.

But Lol wasn't going anywhere just at the moment. In fact he appeared to be doing some complicated calculations in his head. The veins at his temple twitched like he was trying to relieve some log-jam in his bowels. He wasn't so cool now; in fact he appeared to be sweating. 'You fucking idiots,' he was muttering.

Well, that was that, I thought. I was fairly sure we had blown it with Uncle Lol, who I could see would be in no mood to contemplate taking a down payment, not unless it was made in a currency of blood and human parts, anyway. But that showed how much I knew. Diesel, being Lol's nephew, knew him much better than we did and could obviously read body language, which was inscrutable to us. When Lol had stopped growling to himself and was only hitting the steering wheel with his forehead, Diesel hitched up his jeans, went over and leaned into the Beamer, rather like a circus tamer putting his head in the lion's mouth, I thought. Negotiations went on for a while but I had no idea whether that was a good or bad sign, though I had stepped closer to the car to see if I could catch any of their conversation. Odd phrases such as *we're blood or just this one time then* and *have your bollocks* didn't mean much to me at the time.

Then it was done. Lol stepped out of the car and, amazingly, incredibly, dropped a set of keys – I could see the BMW fob hanging off them – into Diesel's waiting hand. I looked back to where Faruk and Clive were standing, gobsmacked, behind a neighbour's raggedy hedge. I watched impatiently as Diesel counted out the £350 and handed it over to Lol, who folded it into a clip and stuck it in the pocket of his leather coat. Then, just after Uncle Lol had spat on his hand and sealed the deal with a shake of Diesel's, he seemed struck by a thought. 'Fuck me,' he said, smiling ruefully. 'I'd forget my head if it wasn't screwed on! The fucking car documents. They're over at my place. Don't worry, lads, I'll just pop over and get them and be back in a twinkling.'

But we wanted to be in that car and off right now and we told him so, nicely, of course. 'I understand totally,' Uncle Lol said, plucking the keys from Diesel's open palm. 'She's a beautiful motor and you want to get your spotty arses in her as soon as. But without your V5, you've no proof of sale. The car'd still be mine, by law. I know you trust me, but I'm thinking of your peace of mind. You'll need that and the MOT, too. Stay right where you are and I'll be back in ten.'

Then, with a lazy wave from the window and a blast of Colonel Bogey on the air horn, he was gone, the car rocketing up the residential street at about sixty miles per hour before slewing around a sharp right-hand corner at the end and disappearing from view. We could hear him careening down the next couple of streets before the sound too had gone and we four were left standing on the pavement, looking at the space which had so recently contained our beautiful black Beemer. No one wanted to be the first to say it. Diesel wouldn't, of course, because Lol was family. Clive probably wasn't saying anything because he had more of a shock to deal with than we did. Faruk was usually tight with Diesel, so it was left to me to say what we all were thinking, to state the bloody obvious.

'He's fucked off with our car and Clive's money, hasn't he?'

Nobody said anything for a moment. We all looked down to the end of street, where our dreams had sashayed around the corner and out of our lives.

Then Clive said. 'Our money. You still have to pay me back.'

'How could we be so stupid?' I said.

'Whose idea was this in the first place?' someone said.

'It was Diesel's.'

'Fucking nice one, Diesel. An absolute blinder.' Faruk wasn't being tight with Diesel tonight, I noticed.

Now Diesel started getting upset, accusing all of us of having no trust in anyone and of attacking his family, which he took personally. And it had, he said, looking at his watch, only been nine minutes since Lol had left. 'He'll be back, just wait,' Diesel kept saying.

I thought this was a desperate ploy on Diesel's part, something to give us time to cool off while he thought of a better answer. But as I watched him standing on that kerb, picking his nose (something he nearly always did in times of tension), I saw that he really believed that his uncle would not let him down and that at any moment, that black BMW would reappear around the corner and cruise to the spot where we were all standing. I have to give him that: Diesel had faith in his family. For that reason, I stayed with him on that litter-strewn kerb, watching a dirty yellow sunset as Faruk and Clive shuffled uncomfortably behind us. Clive was complaining about the cold and saying we might as well go home. But Diesel showed no sign of moving, remaining stock-still, like a faithful Collie dog waiting patiently by his master's grave.

And then. Diesel saw it first, raising his chubby paw and pointing down the road like a sailor spying land. 'There!' he crowed, and we watched, sharing disbelief and mounting excitement as the familiar shiny shape of our very own black BMW cruised down the street and glided to a stop hard by the kerb. We tried to keep our cool; it was hard not to cheer. The idiotic jingle 'For Lol's a jolly good fellow!' played in my head as the window wound down and Lol looked up at us. I took a moment to admire the layout of the controls on the dash and the deep leather of the passenger seat. The back seats were leather too, from what I could see – and now there were leather bags on them. I glanced back at the other guys. They were as excited as I was, crowding around the window for a better look at our latest and greatest acquisition. I could have hugged them. Clive was, in fact, hugging Faruk.

It seemed that proper protocol was not to speak before Lol said something, which he did now, after some drumming of his fingers and more sniffing. 'I've put the beast through its paces,' he said. 'Given it a good run, tested everything. And it's all in top working order. All except the fag lighter, but who smokes, these days?'

We smiled, all of us thinking that a dodgy cigarette lighter was a small price to pay for a car in such obviously pristine condition. 'Don't worry about that, Lol,' Diesel said.

Lol was fiddling with something on his lap. Then he brought out a long, fat cigarette with a twist of paper at its tip and asked if anybody, therefore, had a light? There was a moment of confusion, with three of us searching pockets for non-existent lighters, before Faruk pulled out a Zippo and gave Lol a light. Faruk carries everything, even stuff he doesn't need.

The end of Lol's cigarette burned with a yellow flame then glowed like a red ember as he took a long pull. A deeply pungent scent filled the air. He inhaled deeply, held it for a moment and then turned his head and blew the smoke into our faces. 'Thanks, fellas,' he said and before the smoke had cleared, the BMW was once again heading off down the street, this time in the other direction. Our BMW, containing our £350, Diesel's conman uncle and what I now identified as two travel bags, on the back seat. The next time any of us saw Lol and the BMW was on *Crimewatch*, after police raided a crack house in Aberystwyth.

Which was how we ended up not with a fuck-off black BMW, but with a clapped out Ford Escort, that someone had part-exchanged with Faruk's brother and which he was more than happy for us to take off his hands. Only Diesel had thought it was a good idea, telling us he had ideas for that car which would change it beyond our wildest imaginings. We just had to leave it to him and Faruk. He promised that with his genius for design and some parts from Clive's garden, things would turn out all right yet. Well, they hadn't.

The girls are leaving the Casablanca now, carrying their kebabs and still enjoying a shared joke, probably still at our expense. Diesel's watching them as he scratches his balls. 'I've done my best,' he's saying, 'but it hasn't been good enough. Not for you. I'm telling you now, mate, you're not the only one who's disappointed tonight.' And with that, he turns and goes back into the garage, where Faruk is demonstrating the stereo's volume for the appreciation of the rest of the street. I hardly notice that Clive is at my side as I start to walk home. All I can think of is that there is no way in the world I'm going to let Rosalind Chandler see me in that car.

CHAPTER 2

It's Only Rock 'n' Roll

Rosalind Chandler.

When I first saw her I felt – I don't quite know how to say this – I felt I'd been plonked on a cloud and given a glimpse of Heaven. William Shakespeare, who is really famous with teachers, said, 'No jewel is like Rosalind', and I don't think he ever said a truer thing, not even in *Shakespeare in Love*. When I saw Rosalind – I mean, really saw her – all my other anxieties (even *that one*) vanished as she turned and, from where she stood in the middle of the dance floor, lifted her heavy black lashes and looked directly at me, her gaze so intense that I totally missed the table as I put my drink down and poured a plastic pint-glass of Sunny Delite laced with Tesco's vodka all over Andy Towse's crotch. Not an auspicious start, you'll agree.

But to tell you how I first met Rosalind, I first have to tell you how I met the other three Horsemen of the Apocalypse, because they were all there at the school Prom and played their parts in the events of that momentous evening. We didn't call ourselves The Four Horsemen of the Apocalypse then. That was the name of our ill-fated band, which we later put together on the baseless assumption that at least one of us could sing. Back then we were plain old Brian, Clive and Faruk. I hadn't met Diesel just then but I'd known Clive since he moved into the bungalow next door. Faruk was a classmate of mine. He and I had been thrown together by a mutual interest in old music, vinyl rock in particular, if that phrase means anything to you. Faruk had so many interests that there were bound to be one where we coincided.

Collectors of music must have been around ever since Edison cut his first groove and before that they probably collected sheet music, but I was no longer collecting for the sake of the music. I was collecting for collecting's sake. I mean, WTF? I had amassed fifteen thousand tracks on my old iPod, about twelve thousand of which I hadn't heard more than once and a couple of thousand I hadn't heard at all. And mostly, it was the same old rubbish that echoed between everyone else's headphones. I suppose Faruk must have felt something similar, because we had both started experimenting with other stuff at about the same time. I'd always had an interest in indie but I was like someone who'd been smoking weed for too long and needed something stronger. All those boys with cool haircuts were just that, really. I was bored.

Then it happened. Faruk showed me a YouTube clip of a band called Free playing at the Isle of Wight Festival in 1970.

'Fuck me,' I said. 'What's this shit?'

Paul Rogers, all in black, is shaking a huge mane of hair and stomping his boots as *All Right Now* thunders across the laid-back crowds on a hot summer's day, way back in hippie history. He grips two tape-bound mikes as he belts out the repetitive anthem while Paul Kossoff, a pretty boy with as much hair as Rogers, makes guitar playing look like an orgasmic experience.

'That my friend,' says Faruk, 'is rock and roll.'

'It's blinding, whatever it is,' I say. 'Play it again.'

Faruk was ahead of me. He'd dipped into all the obvious names from way back when, the Bad Companys, Creams and Led Zeps of heavy rock history. Then I came up with a handful of recordings from longer back and further away, some American stuff, and we started in on that. Me and Faruk getting into this together was like joining a secret society – no wonder we became such good mates. I don't know if it was the music we liked so much as the secretive nature of the whole business. We listened to obscure online radio stations, did some deep delving on the net and ransacked the record bins in charity shops. Faruk raved about a vinyl copy of *White Light, White Heat* by the Velvet Underground, a band that had hung out with Andy Warhol,

Brian. Warhol, he said, was an artist who had painted with soup and become famous for precisely fifteen minutes.

He was mightily impressed with some of my finds, too, which included rarities by Jefferson Airplane, The Band, Big Brother and the Holding Company and a bunch of bootlegs of some people called The Grateful Dead. What I didn't tell Faruk was that I had borrowed all of these from a box of records my granddad had left behind after his last visit. At the height of this mania, when we were spending most evenings at Faruk's, because he had the turntable, and listening to Captain Beefheart's Magic Band while we discussed Moby Grape's performance at Monterey in 1967, my granddad (or GD, as he much prefers to be called) and nana, made one of their irregular visits, much to Dad's annoyance. Nana has to attend the specialist unit at the hospital here so Dad can't very well refuse them, but it's clear there are unresolved issues between him and GD. The only one I know all about is the matter of the microbus. Dad hated having their rusting, psychedelically painted campervan parked outside our last house, in crappy old Eccleshall Crescent.

Here, on the hallowed ground of Laurel Gardens, the old heap is an excruciating, blood-vessel-busting embarrassment. And you can see Dad hates the way his parents look, with GD still having long hair at 69 and wearing denim and tie-dyed tee shirts. But what he seems to hate Nana wearing isn't her ankle length dresses or her colourful old kaftans. It's her smile. She's always smiling, unless she's in pain, of course. Dad's thinking that a woman so seriously ill has no right to smile. I love them both, but I'm only mentioning them now because it was GD who saw some of the records I'd been buying and told me to check out a record shop he knew on the other side of town.

Alice and the Caterpillar is an independent record shop hidden away in a side street. The place is tiny, but decidedly atmospheric. Back then, the main room was really gloomy because of all the posters and leaflets obscuring the shop window

– retro psychedelic artwork for '60s festivals and recent flyers advertising local raves. There was a counter buried beneath piles of records and music papers but every other inch of space was taken up by boxes and boxes of LP sleeves. Not a single CD in sight. The place reeked of burning joss sticks and the dim light, the sitar music on the nineteenth-century stereo and the mild looking old man with long silver hair and John Lennon glasses made you question reality and glance at the door, to reassure yourself that the timegate back to the 21st century was still operational. A fat boy very much from our time was helping out, pulling inner sleeves containing the records from shelves behind the counter and slipping them into the covers that customers brought to the counter. Actually, now I think about it, we only saw one other customer.

'Alright!' he'd said cheerily as we entered, like he knew us. 'Everything you want, all in them boxes there. White labels by the counter.'

Faruk had disappeared, gone to look in the small adjoining room, which was even darker than the one I was in. I flicked through a pile of sleeves and was beginning to wonder why he'd dragged me across town to see this. Everything appeared to be 12 inch dance singles, hip hop and dubstep, mainly, and if you were a DJ or just solidly into that stuff, as I had been a year ago, then you'd have loved it there. But right then, I was more than a tad pissed off. We hadn't ventured into one of Sheffield's dodgier districts for this.

'It's all fucking dance,' I said to myself as I skimmed through a box of records by the window. 'Where's the rest of it?'

The old man looked up from his paper and smiled. 'The good stuff's all in the back,' he whispered, flashing me a knowing look before he went back to his reading. He'd probably worked in a Soho porn shop before this. I found Faruk in the tiny back room, pulling out armfuls of albums and whistling at the prices. We'd never be able to afford any of it. They weren't astronomically higher than CD prices, but to music lovers who'd never paid for their music, these prices were as far beyond our reach as the magazines on the top shelf at the newsagents had once been. It looked like we'd had a wasted trip and I was seriously pissed off. There was stuff I might have been doing on that Saturday, if GD hadn't insisted on this pointless expedition. I'd planned to check out the new Chinese remedies shop on the high street, for one thing. Then I wondered if something might yet be salvaged from the day and asked the kid at the counter if they offered student discount.

'What are you after?'

'The 13th Floor Elevators,' I said.

The fat kid blew out his cheeks, like a hamster doing Maltesers.

'That's rubbish, that is,' he said, finally. 'I'm not selling you that crap.'

I must have looked like I hadn't quite heard him and I wasn't sure I had. This must be some new kind of sales technique, I was thinking. Tell them they can't have something and they'll bite your hand off.

'Look,' the fat kid, said, casting a glance at the old man, who appeared to be asleep, his wire glasses hanging off his face. 'It's very simple. Everything in that room there is shit and everything in this room is sorted. Got it? I'm trying to do you a favour. That room's for the old farts, mates of Magic Mick over there. Hippies who got themselves so ripped they think it's still the '60s. You'll find everything you should be into right here.'

Kids, these days.

'I don't think you understand how this works,' I said, in my most reasonable tone. Some people need a little patience and the fat kid was clearly one of them. 'I'm what's called the customer, I decide what I want and then you sell it to me. With me so far?'

But the kid just blew out his cheeks again.

'Excuse me,' I said, loudly addressing the man on the stool, his head drooping on his chest now, a little pool of saliva forming at the corner of his mouth. 'Can you help me?'

But the old man had begun to snore.

'Don't bother,' the fat kid said. 'He's narcoleptic. Now, if you can't afford the shit in the back and you don't want anything from my side of the shop, you might as well piss off, yes?'

Let me say here and now that I'm not a great one for confrontations of any kind. Bad service in a pizza place will still earn the chode who forgot my garlic bread and brought the wrong toppings a small tip. I make it a rule never to complain; things only seem to get worse when you do. But this fat kid had such an attitude problem that I was prepared to make an exception. Maybe it was the long drag across town, the wasted Saturday or just my time of the month. But I sort of lost it.

I can't remember what I said, it all came vomiting out. Fragments have resurfaced, though: *my money's as good as anyone else's/you're a music fascist/ overweight twat in an overpriced shop/ of course I have money/ what gives you the right to decide what I can listen to?/ wouldn't know good music if it bit you in your fat arse/ I don't care if I do wake him/ it's not an insult, it's a statement of fact/I am not a fucking hippy /I couldn't wake him if I had the Ministry of Sound's PA system/ I'll buy what I want/ he's not dead, is he?/ he looks dead/ what about the student discount?*

Just as I was coming to my senses and realising that calling a fat kid fat isn't, well, phat, I heard Faruk saying something over my shoulder. It seemed like Faruk and the fat kid already knew each other. The fat kid said something and then Faruk said something else. I can't remember what. I was too dazed, surprised and all right, ashamed of myself. Then the fat kid spoke. 'Fuck me, Faruk, you got some funny friends these days. This one's got a bigger gob on him than me!'

And so, thanks to GD, I met Dennis Dalziel. Him and Faruk'd been close mates at juniors but they'd lost touch when they went to different upper schools, Diesel to Mafeking Street and Faruk to St Saviour's. After that day at the record shop, Faruk and Diesel got all pally again and I found myself spending more time with Clive. Which was okay, because though it was now Faruk and Diesel and me and Clive, together we were The Four Horsemen of the Apocalypse, as we called ourselves when drunk – all except Faruk, of course. Now it only remains for me to tell you something about Clive and then I can introduce you, finally, to the heavenly Rosalind.

CHAPTER 3

Changing Man

'It's a f-f-flaming disgrace. Now there's rolls of playground netting in the driveway. And lead flashing on the front lawn. I wonder which church roof that's from? Somebody should f-f-flaming well report him to the council.'

My father, Charles Johnson, is peering through the small window at the top of the stairs at the side of the house, the only place from which he can get an unobstructed view of our neighbours' garden, or what's left of it.

'You did report him, dear.' That's my mum, standing a few steps below him, watching him the way a sparrow might watch a hawk. 'In fact,' she ventures, 'I think you've reported him a number of times.'

'I have reported that man,' Dad says, 'on twenty-two occasions for sixteen f-f-flagrant violations of local statutes. Six reports concerning a repeated inf-f-fringement of the same by-law.'

'Was that the one about storing work materials in your garden?'

'That's not a garden, that's Coventry after the blitz,' Dad says. 'Look at it. It's like living next door to a camp of f-f-flaming gypsies.'

'I expect he'll tidy it all up one day,' Mum says. She's looking at the world through her rose-tinted varifocals again; she has to, living with Dad. 'Then he'll probably want to have a garden just like yours, Charlie.'

'Charlie? Charlie?' says Dad. 'When in all these long years of our marriage have I ever encouraged you to call me Charlie? I hate Charlie. Charles, woman, the name is Charles.'

Mum shuts up, Dad goes on complaining. I'm waiting to go

downstairs so I can pop up town and investigate this new Chinese remedies shop on the high street but I can't because Dad is there on the bit of landing where the stair turns, standing on a short set of steps so he can see out of the unfrosted top half of the window. I'm dealing with the idea of Clive's dad having a garden like ours, where the lawn edges have been trimmed with the rigour of a military barber and every line is ruler-straight. There's not a single weed in Dad's flowerbeds and he must have used a spirit level to trim the hedge tops.

'This is too, too much,' he's saying. 'He's turned that garden into a scrapyard. Literally. Coils of wire, old engine blocks, rusty iron pipes. I tell you, Violet, that man has been a thorn in my side since the day he moved in. And now look at him, wondering around bold as brass in his swimming trunks!'

'It's a hot day, love,' Mum points out.

'But swimming trunks in Laurel Gardens! Where's his sense of decency? It lowers the tone, and the house prices too, I shouldn't wonder.'

'Don't work yourself up, love,' Mum says. 'Think about your blood pressure.'

But Dad seems to think a heart attack is worth the price of being able to stand at his post, soaking up the squalor surrounding the squat little bungalow next door. This is Clive's dad's house and, lately, his workplace, after the credit crunch obliged him to relocate his scrap metal business to his garden and down the sides of his house, and also into the knackered caravan parked by the back door.

'Look at him!' Dad says again. 'Standing there in his little red swimming trunks for all the world to see! It's disgusting. I'm going to—'

'Write to the council, I know, dear,' Mum says, and goes back downstairs, where there's a big pile of Dad's white underpants on the ironing board, waiting for her.

This was the scene *chez moi* a few days ago, but it might have been any time in the last five years. It's been played out so many times it's in danger of erasing itself. Ever since Mr Dyson and his then wife Erica moved into Number 9, there's been friction between the two houses – between Charles Johnson and Roger Dyson, anyway. Dad would happily provide you with a long list of infractions made by his neighbour against the spirit of peace and neighbourly harmony. There is the matter of borrowed tools which have yet to be returned – Dad keeps a list and reported his neighbour to the police on the occasion when his strimmer was borrowed without his permission. (Mum's permission didn't count, apparently). And then there is the fact that Roger Dyson is a Southerner, a Londoner in fact, who has come to take possession of a bungalow, a plot of land and, it is rumoured, a considerable windfall, bequeathed him by a distant relation. Dad hates Southerners, Londoners in particular and wishes Roger had stayed distant, too.

Then there are the handful of parties Roger has held since he arrived in Laurel Gardens, one with 'ghastly pop music played at a volume of 85 decibels'. Yes, Dad's got a decibel counter (85 decibels is exactly the same reading as I got when I measured the racket our own lawnmower makes when he runs it up and down his stripy back lawn, every Sunday). And then there's the issue of Flossie and Ellen, his two Rottweilers, who keep at bay nosy officials and interfering neighbours alike. They're noisy brutes, I grant you, and Dad has had to complain more than once about the barking and whining after 5.30 in the evening. They're a danger to the public, Dad has said, but in actual fact, you're only in danger of being licked to death.

Everything about Roger Dyson and his way of life repels my dad like a dreadlocked crusty with a mongrel on a string repels a Rotarian. He hates Roger's business, of course; living next door to a scrap heap has never rated highly on his list of aspirations. He hates his bad language (though this has improved since Clive persuaded him to rename one of the Rottweilers Flossie. It had been called That Fucking Dog and cries of 'Where's That Fucking Dog?' had regularly disturbed the normal tranquillity of Laurel Gardens). He hates the 'brazen Jezebels' who show up in the evenings and leave in the morning 'looking like the unmade bed they've just rolled out of'. He hates Roger's many tattoos, which he sometimes examines with the aid of binoculars when Roger takes off his shirt to unload his truck or to work in his yard. He doesn't hate Clive but he has his doubts about him. But fair play to him, we all have those.

Most of all, he hates the idea that he bought our house on the firm understanding that the long-dilapidated wreck next door was scheduled for imminent demolition. He'd understood that planning permissions had already been approved for two neat semi-detached town houses to be built on the site. But it's five years on and somehow the eyesore is still standing, pretty much unchanged and now the property of someone who no more suits the tone of Laurel Gardens than the bungalow itself does. To say that Dad finds all of this very trying is an understatement of epic precautions, as Clive might have said.

Before we moved into Laurel Gardens, we lived in a crappy pebble-dashed semi on Eccleshall Crescent. A crappy monkey-puzzle tree blocked almost all the light from the front windows, while the back was overshadowed by crappy '60s hi-rise flats, every one of whose occupants could, even without their telescopes, enjoy whatever was happening in our kitchen and back bedrooms. We'd bought the house as a temporary measure when Dad's employer, GirdEx, relocated here. All we needed was a base from which Dad could go to work in the week and spend his weekends looking for somewhere more befitting the status of an up-and-coming middle manager.

Then the bottom fell out of ladies' girdles, GirdEx went into receivership and Dad had to take a job as under manager of the haberdashery department in the amazingly old-fashioned Victoria department store, where he still works, selling knitting patterns, balls of wool and buttons, mainly. That was when he was visited by the crushing realisation that we might be stuck in Eccleshall Crescent for the foreseeable future, if not longer. He'd disliked it before but now he began to loathe the street and everyone on it, himself included, I think. According to Dad, we lived in a road full of people who had climbed the promotional ladder only to find the last rungs missing and then had settled back into lives of resigned obscurity. He dreaded a similar fate.

We'd been living in Eccleshall Crescent for nearly three years when two things happened. One, a new estate of executive homes started going up on a big plot of land about half a mile from where we were living. Two, Mum's dad Roy became seriously ill and eventually died, leaving Mum quite well off. Mum might have seized that moment and changed her life; she could have opened a florist's shop, like she had always dreamed of doing. But there was never any real chance of that, not with Dad being as keenly interested in the development of the new estate as a paedophile in the building of a new junior school.

Dad had gone sniffing around early on, spending hours up on the estate, coming back with mud on his shoes and tales of gravel driveways, double-glazed patio windows and brick-built barbecues. Mention of breakfast bars, fitted wardrobes, en suites with bidets and as someone called Helen suggested he had been looking over the show home too. As Roy's illness got progressively worse, so Dad's visits to the new plots increased. Soon whole rows of alternately identical houses had been completed and the first ones sold. People moved in. I expect Dad gnashed his teeth as he watched those early adopters put up their curtains, plant their gardens and wash their Ford Mondeos in their drives. More and more houses were being completed and sold, but Mum's father, instead of being considerate and dying quickly, lingered on and Dad could only watch helplessly as "Sold" signs were planted outside the last few executive-style homes. By the time Mum's dad finally died, only one house was left, the show home which he must have traipsed around a hundred times already, much to the bemusement of the site agent.

But the show house had always been high on Dad's wish list. He loved that house inside and out and already, its fixtures and fittings, soft furnishings and décor were as familiar to him as if he had been living there for the last twelve months – which he very nearly had. On the afternoon of the day on which Mum's dad had died, his idea of 'a little jaunt to take your mind off things, Vi', was to drive us up to the estate and give us a guided tour of the show house, Mum sobbing quietly as he led us through the kitchen, pointing out the fitted oven and marble-effect worktops and then up the stairs to show off the frilly-valanced beds and swagged floral curtains.

These builders knew how to furnish a house, he told us, nothing mismatched, everything nice, neat and clean as new pin. Lovely pictures on the walls, natty ornaments on the windowsills and even a row of realistic fake books on the living room shelves. On the day Mum's inheritance came through we were looking around the house again, but not for very long. 'We'll take the place, Helen,' my dad told the site agent, with whom he was now on first name terms. 'And everything in it.' Mum was sobbing again, but whether she was still crying for the loss of her dad or the death of her dream, I'll never know.

But every Eden has its snake, as Dad discovered when he approached the council about the projected demolition of 13, Laurel Gardens – Clive's dad's bungalow – and was met with a lot of humming and hawing and not a few blank looks. Yes, the house was supposed to have been torn down, but there had been problems, legal ones, and there were reasons why a compulsory purchase order could not be issued. The matter was far from settled, they told him, but, just for the moment, it was all up in the air. Different departments gave him different answers. Yes, they knew about the scrap business in his garden but for the moment, the matter 'fell, unfortunately, between two stools'. He wrote, he called and presented himself regularly at the council offices, but lately he had found that the person he needed to see was usually in a meeting which was expected to last all day, or at lunch, which was often a very late, or an unusually early one. And while he waited for something to be done about what he called the horror next door, he built sturdy fences and dreamed of unexplained gas explosions or uncontrollable conflagrations.

This was how the Dysons came to rule Dad's life, how they become his passion, his obsession. It's got to the stage now where nothing happens without reference to the Dysons and by 'the Dysons', he means Roger. If it rains then the piles of scrap metal next door will get even rustier and make the place even more unsightly. If the wrong politician wins a local election, it's because people like the Dysons have voted him in or were too lazy to go out and vote anyway. The states of the roads, the railways, the NHS, and Britain itself are all, somehow, Roger Dyson's fault. I sometimes wonder what Dad would do without the Dysons. With no Dysons, he'd be hard put to fill all the time he uses up writing complaining letters, making angry phone calls and knocking on doors trying to enlist support for his campaign to get the Dysons moved on (as if they were travellers who were squatting there illegally). In some ways the Dysons have done Dad a lot of good; he's finally got a purpose beyond his little empire of buttons and begonias.

For Dad, the Dysons' land is East Berlin before the Wall came down, with him standing 24-hour guard at Checkpoint Charlie; the difference being that anyone escaping into his sector would be shot on sight. But for me the Dysons' house has always been a much-needed refuge from my regimented life at Stalag Johnson. And if I complain about Dad's strict timetabling of my bedtime, bath time and getting home pissed time (as if!) then his own daily life is even more controlled. His alarm rings at 06.50, the toaster pops at 07.35, his shaver buzzes from 07.45 to 07.49, the toilet flushes at 08.00 and the key turns in the ignition of his Rover at 08.10. He says this means he is always at work by 08.29, in plenty of time to make a cup of tea, straighten his tie and be at his counter by 08.55 precisely.

His life runs on rails. Everything has an allotted time and duration. He has one of those diaries where each day is divided into half-hour slots and most spaces are filled in with his neat but rather girlie handwriting, even if the entry for Thursday at 17.30 is only the drive home. It seems a miracle that he ever found a slot for making me. A miracle he found the slot, period. Sick making as it is, my mind has sometimes ignored the *Verboten!* signs with skulls and crossbones on them and drifted over the invisible line, and I have visualized their wedding night. 'Rightoh,' he'd have said, as he folded his trousers into the Corby Press at the Travelodge they stayed in, en route to their honeymoon in Eastbourne, an erection of indeterminate size tenting his Yfronts. 'The sooner this is done and dusted, the better for everyone.'

Mum and Dad aren't Heathcliff and Cathy, theirs wasn't a wind-blown romance. It couldn't have been. I can't imagine Mum filling Dad's thoughts the way Rosalind has filled mine. I can't imagine why he proposed to her or why she accepted, but I can imagine that convenience came into it somewhere. But that's not to say that theirs hasn't been a successful marriage. It's lasted nearly twenty years and it's produced me, for one thing, though the fact I've no siblings suggests they weren't keen to repeat the experience. And in a way, it does work. Dad decides how they will live their lives and Mum goes along with it. I don't know if she actually regrets marrying Dad or whether she wonders how her life might have turned out without him. I don't know if this is the life Dad has always wanted or whether he once had his own, secret, dreams. It doesn't look like a marriage made in heaven, but they've stayed together this long – perhaps because they can't see an alternative, maybe for my sake or, just possibly, because they really love each other. I have no way of knowing.

I don't know what I would have done back then if I hadn't been able to go next door. Gone mad, I expect. Clive's house wasn't run on timetables, his dad didn't complain if Clive played his music too loud and he didn't much mind when he came and went. Not that Roger Dyson didn't care about his son's well-being. In fact, there was something Clive's dad cared very much about regarding his son, but we'll come to that in a moment.

When I first got to know Clive, we would play outside. Clive liked catch and tag and wrestling, so long as I didn't play rough, but as Roger seeded the garden with more potential mantraps, jagged bits of metal or rolls of barbed wire, we confined ourselves to playing in Clive's bedroom, where there was plenty to play with. Roger had sorted his son with an awesome range of toys and sports stuff. There was a PC with *Tomb Raider* and *Grand Theft Auto* and an internet connection with no parental controls, which can be of enormous educational value when you're twelve. There was a pair of boxing gloves and a four foot pro punch bag hanging from a fixing in his ceiling. Other sports goods included a football signed by the entire Millwall team, two rugby balls, a cricket bat and a half set of golf clubs. In a chest of drawers I found an arsenal of cap guns, plastic daggers, catapults and everything you might need for re-enacting the assault on Baghdad. All brilliant stuff, but Clive never wanted to play with any of it. Instead, we would spend whole days dressing and undressing his Action Man figures.

I didn't think anything of it at the time. It didn't seem to matter that Clive didn't like football but quite liked dressing up in Roger's girlfriends' clothing. I was only too pleased to have a friend with a bolt-hole I could escape to whenever I liked. As far as Dad was concerned, I wasn't supposed to be going round Clive's at all but Mum would tip me the wink and so long as I was back before he was, that was all right. I had spent so much time round at Clive's that I hardly noticed that he was getting progressively less like my other friends and more like Jane Gallacher, whose parents were our other neighbours. Now I think about it, there was a phase when he seemed to be copying her hairstyle.

To Roger Dyson, Clive's blossoming gayness was particularly galling. Being a shaven-headed scrap dealer who had until recently used flags of St George for curtains and kept a pair of Rottweilers (even if they too were a bit gay), he could not 'for the life of him' understand how he had sired an offspring with less than the full complement of masculine attributes. What had he done, he asked me once, to deserve a son with a voice like Alan Carr and a walk like Barbara Windsor in a tight dress? Not that Clive hadn't been aware of these original characteristics himself. For a while – and probably because he'd taken some stick at school – he'd done his best to disguise them, adopting a Mockney accent that would have made Lily Allen blush and a gait like wading through treacle instead of dancing on hot coals.

Roger Dyson had, after a period of denial, seen where things might be going with Clive and had equipped him with every masculine accoutrement he could think of. He took him to boxing evenings, where Clive had been shocked by every punch thrown, covering his face and complaining loudly, 'That must have really hurt, Dad!' or 'I like those shorts!' After that, he took him to watch Millwall play at home, but Clive had spent the game flicking through a homewares catalogue and politely clapping when a goal was scored – by either team. Or, like a bird teaching a fledgeling how to fly, Roger had tenderly pointed out gorgeous babes on TV or one of his stronger DVDs and had nudged his son in the ribs, saying, 'Couldn't you just slip her one, eh, son?' He'd also made sure that his collection of hard core porn magazines were piled just under his bed, where Clive would be sure to come across them (if only!) in the course of his cleaning.

I haven't mentioned the cleaning? This, as much as Clive's posters of Barbra Streisand and a recent tendency to use just a little eye-shadow, was what made everything so much worse for Roger Dyson. Not only was his son homosexual, a condition apparent to everyone except the boy himself, it seemed, but he was a compulsive cleaner too and was developing a mania in this department that bordered on OCD. He was never happier than when armed with a packet of Jay cloths and a bucket of homemade cleaning product, he attacked some corner of his home which had presumed itself safe from incursions of this kind.

While Clive could do nothing about the forgotten battlefield outside, he waged his own war on dirt and dishevelment inside. He cleaned the place top to bottom – okay, not so hard in a bungalow – leaving only the kitchen untouched. 'You'd need someone who cleans up murder scenes to tackle that,' he'd said. Then he started haranguing his dad about buying whatever was necessary to smarten the place up. Roger might have been severely disappointed about his boy's sexuality but he was still his father and still as likely to cave in to requests regularly and winningly made. And the boy had a point, he admitted; the place, now you looked at it, was a bit of a tip.

This didn't mean that Roger felt any more comfortable being dragged around Habitat or Laura Ashley while Clive looked for some 'nice pastel throws' to cover his tatty furniture. It was funny how there weren't other blokes in Laura Ashley wearing England shirts, he'd thought. With the patience of a saint, Clive's dad had considered the merits of chenille covers, cinnamon fabrics and special edition wallpapers. In time, something was bound to rub off on the one-time terror of the New Den. I was with them when Roger caused a little scene by the counter where Clive had laid some scatter cushions. Their colours would set off Roger's new bed linen perfectly, he explained. But Roger was of a different opinion. 'Cerise and aubergine? Together?' he'd exploded, holding up two of the cushions. 'Fuck me, Clive, you're having a laugh! Go and get the burgundy, like I told you.'

About this time, Roger's latest girlfriend Nerys, who thought a few filled ashtrays and empty bottles made a place homely, moved out.

And slowly, little by little, the bungalow was transformed from the sort of place where a bloke could put his boots up on the sofa after a knackering day in the yard, sink a few beers with his takeaway and clear everything away in the morning (or not) into something you might've seen in the pages of Ideal Home magazine. In fact Roger said that Clive had obviously drawn some of his inspiration from the June issue they'd shared in the dentist's waiting room. My own dad would have been gobsmacked to see the difference between the house's exterior and its interior. He'd have had that slack-jawed expression The Doctor's assistants wear when they first enter the Tardis. It was the look Roger used still when he came in from outside smiling about something, having momentarily forgotten that his son was a fairy who had just transformed his drum into something he would never feel entirely comfortable in again. He didn't think his old London mates would, either. He could just imagine Clive bustling about in his pinny and dusting their Doc Marts off the coffee table.

Clive was turning his father's life upside down and inside out. He even had him wearing shirts at weekends, not his England shirt or the Millwall home strip, but proper shirts with collars and cuffs. I caught him one day looking at himself in the mirror and deciding whether or not he had the bottle for a shopping trip up the high street wearing cream chinos, brown brogues and a *not-fucking-lilac, it's purple* shirt. If Dad knew half of the misery Roger was enduring, he'd have lightened up considerably. I don't know what he'd have said if he knew that I was the only person Roger could turn to about his troubles – his mates weren't the sorts you could talk to in much depth about incipient homosexuality and the design ideas of Laurence Llewelyn Bowen.

'Brian,' he said to me in the kitchen one day, while Clive was in the front room, flicking his feather duster over a signed portrait of Nick Griffin which he'd reframed in a lively Kath Kidston rose-pattern, 'you're a man of the world.'

I shrugged, looked man-of-the-worldly.

'Can't you do something about Clive?'

'Like what, Mr Dyson?'

'Like take him out, get him drunk and, you know, sort him out with some fanny? All that boy needs is a taste of cunt, I'm sure of it. This' —he swept a hand around the newly wallpapered front room (a delicate black fern motif on a light grey ground) and over the chenille-covered armchair and sofa, the sprays of flowers in vases, the pink rope tiebacks on the new curtains— 'is probably only a phase.'

Self-deception, I was thinking, might be a sort of safety feature, something the brain does when it can't take in the information the eyes are sending it.

'I don't think that would be easy,' I said.

'Look, Brian,' he said, softly, with one eye on his son, who was drip feeding a bonsai tree on the mantelpiece. 'When I was his age I had a life of drinking, fighting and shagging anything with a pulse. It was a man's life, normal, you know what I mean?'

I nodded, meaning that I'd drunk and had fights and shagged a lot of birds too.

'You've put it about a bit, eh, Brian?'

'Use it or lose it, Rog,' I agreed. He's a big bloke with a serrated line tattooed around his neck, with the words 'Cut here'. I wouldn't want to upset him, even if he has taken to wearing fuchsia shirts.

'So you'll help me, won't you? Get him shagged, Brian, and the sooner the better. Once he's wet his wick he'll be a different boy. He'll be man, I'm telling you.'

'I don't know, Rog,' I said. 'You can lead a horse to water…'

'I'm not talking about whores,' said Roger, who had misheard me. 'Just find him someone nice who won't mind fucking a fairy.'

'I'll give it a go,' I said. 'But don't—'

'Good lad, that's settled then. I've always appreciated your friendship with Clive, Brian,' he said, a big, meaty fist on my shoulder. 'I can't tell you how important this is to me. You won't let me down, will you?'

My menace-detector was going into overdrive: hard to tell if this was a friendly request for a favour, or an ultimatum with bruising consequences.

'Of course I won't, Rog,' I said, and we both turned to watch Clive, who was humming a tune from Billy Elliot as he emptied a bag of pot pourri into a little bowl on the windowsill. Get Clive laid? Some chance. I hadn't even been able to get myself laid. And yet here I was, suddenly elevated to Roger's great shining hope, who would successfully pimp his son and return his life to normal.

Oh. My. God.

And Roger wasn't the only one thinking about match-making. Roger didn't know it then, but all Clive's work in sorting out the house, and then his father himself was being done with a similar object in mind – which was to get Roger fixed up with a better sort of girlfriend, not another brassy tart who left her hair in the shower and her knickers in the toilet but a nicer sort of girl altogether. One Clive could talk to about clothes and go shopping with. One who might, who knew, make a nice mother.

CHAPTER 4

Dancing Queen

'You'd have to be quick, or you'd be up my arse.'

Diesel, who else? He joined the sixth form of St Saviour's this year.

The Four Horsemen of the Apocalypse are sitting on orange moulded-plastic chairs with our feet up on four more plastic moulded chairs, in a dark corner of the assembly hall, discussing whether we'd choose to perform the sacred act of sexual intercourse with Shelly Lark, who is wearing a strappy silver top which shows off her boobs amazingly and 'takes all comers', or Kirsty Stephenson, whose designer-jeaned arse with its faintly visible thong line, is to die for. Faruk belches loudly and says he wouldn't kick Holly McManus out of bed, either. She's the one in the thigh boots who's dancing a little too closely with Kelly Jordan, who shouldn't be here anyway, as she's in the year below.

'I'd fucking have the lot,' Clive says. He's having one of his self-denying butch phases, which piss us off more than when he's being camp. 'Fucking Shelly Lark could suck my cock any day.'

Faruk belches again, as if he's had a pint too many. 'Shelly Lark'd blow you out in bubbles,' he says shortly.

We're all a bit annoyed with Clive. We know he's gay. Everyone knows he's gay. No one cares. We want him to come out, mainly because we all think it will be fucking spectacular when he does, like a peacock fanning its feathers. But tonight, at the Prom, he thinks he's Gene Simmons or Iggy Pop. 'I'd fuck her and all,' he says of a Year 9 who's only come with her parents to collect her elder sister, the girl who was sick at the feet of the saint whose plaster image stands between the doors to the boys' and the girls' toilets. Saint Upchuck, she's called now.

Clive's behaviour is partly my fault. 'Take him out and get him drunk,' his father had said and I really don't like to argue with Roger. Half a bottle of Tesco Value Vodka has disappeared into Clive's Sunny D already and he's nudging me to top him up under the table again.

Diesel is showing us a pill he's found on the floor. 'Ecstasy. It has to be ecstasy.'

'Could be a contraceptive,' Faruk offers.

'Or Viagra,' I say.

Diesel considers his options.

'So that's an uncontrollable erection, a big hit of female hormones or getting so loved up I grope Lauren Sykes.' The word minger was coined for Lauren Sykes.

'Do I feel lucky?'

He swallows the pill with a big hit from Clive's plastic beaker and I watch him as he waddles off to check out the table of flapjacks and brownies provided by food tech. I'm looking for Rosalind Chandler, of course. I've clocked her once or twice already, easy to pick out amongst the bunches of upper sixers decked out in penguin suits and Prom frocks. She's wearing some kind of vintage black dress with lace edges but her same old bag, stuffed with books, is hanging off her shoulder. Her hair is like a bunch of ruffled black feathers with coloured beads and plastic mirrors and things in it, totally unique. The next time I saw her, she was standing in the middle of the dance floor staring at the coloured lights with that look she sometimes has, like she's listening to an imaginary iPod, then I lost her behind a crowd of Prommers zombie dancing to Michael Jackson's *Thriller*. Needless to say, she looked totally, gobsmackingly gorgeous, a bohemian cocktail two parts Helena Bonham Carter to one part Ally Sheedy in *Breakfast Club*. Tonight I will speak to her, I thought, tonight she will know I exist.

Prom night. Our latest American import and one which is fast becoming as ubiquitous as a Big Mac. It's the new rite of passage for upper sixth formers about to go off to university to encounter a whole new world of opportunity, drugs and debt. Like the long wedding scene in a DVD I saw called *The Deer Hunter* before Robert de Niro and Christopher Walken go off to get fucked up in Vietnam. But the lower sixth, that's us, are here tonight to make up numbers and add to the takings on the door. The Prommers have to look the part, but we can go as we want. We're not dressed up as headwaiters and their wives like they are, not this year at least, but that isn't to say that we have spent any less time with our preparations for this big night. Maybe more, in fact. It's all been about hitting the right note.

I've really gone for it tonight, wanting to look my absolute best in case I end up (in some separate universe with two suns and a World Cup winning England squad) actually talking to Rosalind. It's not something I've managed yet, though. She seems so beyond anyone I've ever known. She reads, for one thing. According to a glance I stole at the contents of her shoulder bag – it was hanging off the chair in front of my desk – she's into writers whose names begin with the letter K, Kafka, Kesey and Kerouac it looked like, so I'm beginning to think she's almost halfway through a very long reading list. She's different, special. You can tell that from the space the other girls give her. And tonight, with a bit of luck and quite a lot of Tesco's Value Vodka, I'm going to make her aware of Brian Johnson. I can't see Rosalind and I'm thinking about the phone calls I've been getting from Clive's dad. 'Regarding Clive, Bri?' he'll say. 'Any news on the cunt front?'

He's not threatening, but he's persistent and he's big and he has tattoos and it would show willing if I could somehow send Clive home with a girl tonight. Even an unconscious one would be something. I need to talk to Clive, who has been in a world of his own this evening. As an icebreaker, I compliment him on his decorating.

'Fucking nice job,' I say. 'Like what you did with the

windows.'

'Yeah, I had a right fucking time trying to team those fucking Designers Guild curtains with that fucking Farrow and Ball shade on the fucking walls,' Clive says. 'And trying to find fucking decent modular furniture within the budget of your average scrap dealer can be a right pain in the arse too.'

I try to read Clive's geezer performance as a hopeful sign and direct his attention to some girls in our class who are almost unrecognisable in their party clothes and slap. Cheryl Park's red satin miniskirt, which only just covers her bum, draws an encouraging reaction from Clive. 'Fuck me!' he says. This is good, but it would be better if he weren't looking at Patrick Nally's well-stuffed packet.

'I can have a word with her if you like,' I tell him. 'See if she's up for it.'

'Nah,' says Clive. 'You're all right. There's plenty of pussy here. I'll make my mind up later.'

The Prommers have had a couple of hours to get into party mode. Mr Stevens has relinquished the turntables to Andy Ottewell, who's now amping the mood nicely. Mr Bembridge and Mrs Rochard have gamely taken to the floor to demonstrate how totally uncool dancing was in their day. Diesel is looking fairly uncool himself as he idiot-dances with Lauren Sykes, a silly grin spread across his face – not something that might be produced by oestrogen or Viagra, I decide. Faruk, who hasn't had a drink in his life, is serving up his party trick: pretending to be blind drunk. This is something he does very well, becoming alternately belligerent, funny, morose and sometimes falling over. (The dead giveaway is that he hasn't yet mastered the art of puking in the street and being abusive to taxi drivers.)

Kids have collected in their little groups. The uber cool boys, ironically and not so ironically called the Gods, hang around like bulls in the field. You know that lame old joke? The old bull and the young bull clocking a field full of cows? The young bull says,

'Let's charge down there and fuck one.' But the experienced, older bull replies, 'No, let's walk down and fuck them all.' I actually get the joke now that I watch Dave Fletcher and his mates coolly appraising the available fanny, which for them is most of it. The kids who want to be cool but aren't, hang out in another clique, each with one eye on the fanny and another on the Gods. They don't have the easy, relaxed style of the Gods; everything they wear is this year's brand, the latest style and the rips in their jeans look freshly made.

There are the geeks, whose standing is now higher than the nerds, thanks to their expertise with technology and also to their heavily-framed glasses, which are finally cool. Then there are the loners, the wall-flowers, at least three gatecrashers from Mafeking Street, two nuns who are dancing together and us: the fat kid wasted on E, the Muslim drunk on Appletise, the gay kid who claims to have shagged every bird in the place and Brian Johnson, who has a complex about the size of his penis and may be hopelessly in love with Rosalind Chandler.

It's over two hours into the Prom and cracks are beginning to appear. It's not only the kids who have smuggled in secret supplies of alcohol: Mr Crowley is sitting inappropriately close to Sarah Payne and Lisa Moreton on the next table to us and he's telling them how his wife doesn't understand him, that there's more to him than being a teacher and something about 'releasing the animal inside'. Sarah and Lisa are nodding and giggling and probably recording it all on their phones for wider consumption later. Smeggy Cleggy, our deputy head, looks terminally stressed as he tries to separate Dave Fletcher and Jennifer Davies, who are enjoying a grope behind the piano while he shouts noiselessly at an unidentified group in the darkness beyond the windows, betrayed by the dancing fireflies of their cigarette ends. He hasn't noticed that Andy Ottewell is now playing some totally obscene mixes.

Over by the fire exit, Diesel is dancing dangerously closely with Lauren Sykes, his porky hands stretched over her bum while Faruk lurches about the room with a plastic glass of apple juice assuring everyone that he's not drunk, he can handle it. 'I love you, man,' he tells me, as he passes. Then I see Rosalind again, her eyes aglow, skin bathed in orange and blue light, a puzzled frown on her face. Unusually, she's on her own. It's not often I see her without that other girl in tow – Teresa someone, she's called and she hangs on to Ros like a terrier with a bone.

But now Rosalind Chandler is by herself and actually looking like she might welcome some company. This is my moment and being a man – and a little drunk – I seize it. I begin to push through the jostling, bouncing bodies towards the place I think I saw her last. Various potentially disastrous chat-up lines are rushing through my head, Is it hot here, or is it just you? Fuck me if I'm wrong, but haven't we met somewhere before? Do you come here often? (Why not come at my place instead?) None of the above must even begin to form on my lips when we meet. But I have confidence born of the finest cheap vodka and I'm certain I'll know exactly what to say as soon as we're face to face.

Just then there's a commotion in the crowd, which has begun to draw away from its centre, like the ripples from a shopping trolley dropped in a canal. The music I'm hearing is something old and iconic and DJ Andy O has pumped up the volume. Of course, it's the intro to the Bee Gees' *Staying Alive*, always a crowd pleaser, but never more so than tonight. Something is happening in the middle of things and suddenly that's where I am, just in time to see Clive, for fuck's sake, dancing the most perfect interpretation of this song I've ever seen – and I've seen a lot. I know he spends hours in his bedroom dancing to records, but up until now I haven't paid it much attention. It was just something Clive did while I played GTA on his computer.

But here is now, our own John Travolta, launching himself across the floor, hair flopping, groin thrusting and hand-jiving, as the crowd claps to the beat, everyone full of respect, loving his moves, no- one taking the piss. It's an A-starred performance. Is this Clive's dancing twin? He jumps, he struts, he strikes poses, he whirls his jacket above his head before throwing it into the crowd. He pirouettes, adds a break dance where he falls on his hands, flips over twice, spins on his back and leaps back on his feet. Some girls in our year push in front of me, desperate to catch it all on their iPhones, totally floored, like everyone else, by this secret side that Clive has decided to showcase tonight. Tomorrow he'll have a hangover the size of Japan, but tonight there's no stopping him. The record is ending but Andy segues the last seconds into *You Should Be Dancing* and Clive takes off again, adding a crotch-splitting slide across the floor on his knees before an audience which is whooping and calling for more. Fuck me, I think, if I can't get him laid tonight then it won't be my fault. I can see half a dozen damply excited girls who'd go home with him right now.

Which reminds me, I'm trying to find Rosalind and who knows, maybe take a step or two towards getting myself laid too. I scan the gel-shiny and wax-spiky heads of the crowd and spot something flashing in the lights. It looks like one of the tiny mirrors that Ros has woven into her hair tonight. The crowd pulses to the beat like a huge collective organism, gaps appearing and then closing up again. I get a tantalising glimpse of her, then my view is blocked by a swaying wall of torsos with upraised arms. I'm standing by some chairs on which a boy with hair like Jesus appears to have passed out, when the crowd opens for me like the Red Sea parting for Moses.

It's like this has been decreed by fate, that nothing shall obscure the moment when she lifts her face and looks directly at mine. Which is when I tip my glass of Sunny D&V all over Andy Towse's crotch. She's looking at me, there can be no doubt about this. Yes, me, Rosalind Chandler is looking directly into the eyes of Brian Johnson. And not just looking, but staring. Staring directly at me. I feel kind of faint, but excited too. I hold her gaze, savouring the moment. I try to look cool, as if this were no more than my due, that it was only a matter of time before she recognised me for what I am, a sex god.

I'm thinking things are going to pan out. I'm going to go across to her, start a conversation. We'll find somewhere quieter where we can talk. We'll chat and we'll laugh and we'll wonder how we never connected before and there will be that look again, the one she's giving me still. It's true, then, I think. Time really does stand still at moments like this. It has to, because she's been standing there gazing intently at me, not moving a muscle for what must be ages. Something isn't quite right. The gears in my brain, which have temporarily seized up, begin to grind and turn once more. I become aware of the music again – it's *Night Fever* now and the crowd is still clapping and chanting Clive's name, but Rosalind Chandler is oblivious to everything, as she holds that look. The look of love, I thought it was at first, but it's starting to look a little odd and even disturbing. Then the bag of books falls from her shoulder and her eyes roll back. Everyone else is watching Clive and only I see what is happening and I run towards her, colliding with a girl carrying a tray of Diet Cokes and just miss catching Rosalind as she collapses to the floor and lies there, perfectly still.

The following moments are a chaos of sights and sounds. Someone is shouting like a maniac, then I realise it's me, crying for help and ordering people to 'stand back and give her some air.' I'm taking charge, kneeling by Rosalind, checking her airways, looking for vital signs. I've seen this done a thousand times, but all of them have been on TV. She's breathing, thank God. Her head is in my lap as her eyes open and there's that perplexed frown again. I tell her not to move and ask the ring of concerned and confused faces, where the hell is that ambulance? I'm talking, shouting rather, to Rosalind, asking her what's the matter, where does she hurt, has she eaten something, taken anything?

Her eyes flutter and for a moment I think she's going to answer me but then something unexpected happens: she sneezes, a real tsunami of a sneeze, spraying my face with atomised snot. Mr Clegg is with me now, but he doesn't know what to do, he's reached stress overload. He's asking me what is it, is it an overdose? I don't know what I tell him, I can't even hear myself think because no one has told Andy O to kill the music and some of the concerned onlookers are tapping their feet and one or two are starting to shuffle about to *More Than a Woman*.

I make Ros as comfortable as I can, folding my jacket under her head and telling her now- unconscious form not to worry, I have everything under control. Time passes, then, thank fuck, the paramedics are there, with their rucksacks of equipment and bottles of oxygen and they're asking me stuff and I'm nodding. They might be asking me if she has taken something, whether, as Mr Clegg is now asserting, she has overdosed. She's back with us now and trying to say something, but I am in charge, I am saving her. I tell her not to waste her breath, that she will be all right, she's in good hands. Then we're outside and there's the flashing blue light and the brightly lit interior of the ambulance. Rosalind is on the gurney, still trying to say something but the paramedics are holding an oxygen mask over her face and her arms are restrained by straps and a red blanket. The doors are closing and then Rosalind has gone. It's been a horrible experience but the ambulance men have assured me she will be okay. At least I had been there, ready to take control, ready to show what I was made of. My prompt actions may even have saved a life and not just any life. Yes, it has indeed been a horrible experience but, looking at it another way, it's one which will probably have earned me Rosalind Chandler's undying gratitude. Result.

Chapter 5

People Are Strange

It's funny how things never seem to turn out like you expect them to, isn't it? Not funny, but you know what I mean. Adolf Hitler probably said something like that to Eva Braun before blowing his brains out and I expect much the same kind of thought was occurring to Julius Caesar when Brutus stuck the knife in. The best laid plans and all that. Well, that was me and Prom night all over. There was the way things were supposed to have gone and then there was the way they actually panned out, pan as in toilet.

Now, in an ideal world (that one with the multiple suns and an England side with a sense of direction) the night might have gone like this:

Clive would have taken home Shelly Lark or any of the other fanny suddenly available to him and given her one on his Linda Barker duvet. This would, of course, have cured him of his homosexuality and given him something to think about other than designer decorating. A grateful Roger would probably have slipped me a bunch of used tenners, or at least a dodgy roll of roof leading.

The pill Diesel found and swallowed would have been merely Viagra and given the amount of sizzling pussy about that night, would have provided several bulbous inches of riotous entertainment for anyone checking him out.

Faruk would have amused everyone with his impression of a schoolboy only slightly drunk and would have been ready and available to drive us home in the Green Dragon, our suspect Escort.

I would have hooked up with Rosalind, this night marking the beginning of a long, beautiful and highly sexual relationship.

Was that really so much to ask? That we might all have stayed sober and out of trouble for just one evening? Partly, I blame Tesco. Had their Value Vodka not been so cheap and so easily available to anyone who knew Billy Fairchild, who's old enough to pop in and buy it, then maybe things would have been different. But compare and contrast what actually did happen, the full horror of it all, which was this:

Diesel necks a tab of E and goes off to the bandstand in the park with Lauren 'the gob' Sykes.

Faruk pretends to be drunk so convincingly that he starts a fight with Dave Fletcher and needs three stitches to his bottom lip.

Clive doesn't get off with Shelly Lark, but gets off instead with her brother Kevin. They are found by Miss Hogg 'practising Greek wrestling' Clive says, in the girls' changing room.

And me? Well, according to a tempestuous Teresa Davenport, who's Rosalind Chandler's best friend and protector from creeps and idiots like me, what I do is this:

a) comprehensively mistake Rosalind's symptoms;

b) refuse to listen to her when she tries to correct me; and

c) assure teachers and paramedics that this is a classic case of overdose, so that Rosalind is rushed to casualty and immediately stomach pumped, when all she has, from what I've been hearing, is a virulent type of flu.

Well, nice one, Brian, you played a blinder. You finally meet Rosalind Chandler, *the* Rosalind Chandler, the girl of your dreams, but rather than making small talk and showing her how intelligent and interesting you are, you have her sent to casualty and unnecessarily stomach pumped. AFB. Absolutely Fucking Brilliant. Of course, I offered to go to the hospital, where they're keeping her in for observations, but Teresa tells me that I am the very last person Rosalind wants to set eyes on now. As I said before, *result*.

And now it's the day after the prom and for want of something better to do, I'm standing in front of the big, plate glass window of Foo's Quality Asian Remedies, the new shop on the high street which is quickly becoming known, at least among the town's culturally challenged, as Foo Q's. Through the glass I can see potted plants and on the walls, bamboo mats with paintings of mountains and waterfalls. There's a polished wooden counter with hundreds of little wooden pigeonholes behind it, each containing a labelled packet. There are little pyramids of packets on the counter, where the owner or maybe the shop manager is weighing a quantity of grey powder on a set of scales. It's much like the back of my local pharmacy, really, but everything looks a little more interesting, exotic, more likely to help someone suffering from a very particular condition.

I'm running an eye down a sort of menu which is printed in large and small lettering on the window. I once saw a documentary on TV about how Oriental medicine was treating conditions we weren't even looking at. Could hundreds of millions of users be wrong, it asked? The printing on the window suggests there may indeed be something for me here; there seems to be a remedy for everything. I scan down the list hopefully, occasionally looking up to see Mr Foo, presumably, leaning on his counter and watching me with a dull curiosity. I start with Acne, Anxiety, and Asthma. Then there's Backache, Balding and Breast Cancer, Diabetes, Depression and Diarrhoea. Further down – I notice that Mr Foo has straightened up and is watching me with interest now – there's Hangover, Hepatitis and Haemorrhoids. Under Sexual Matters, they have something for impotence, loss of libido – I'm getting warm now – erectile dysfunction and what must be a polite term for premature ejaculation.

I scan right down to the bottom of the long list, unwilling to believe that I haven't come across what I'm looking for, then I start again at the top in case I have missed it. Perhaps there's another name for what I want curing, some special medical term for having a small cock. Or perhaps it's not the sort of thing you'd print on your window and the cure has to be kept under the counter. I wonder what the cure will involve. Pills, probably, and powdered rhino horn will almost certainly be involved. I see a notice threatening acupuncture and allow for the possibility of a physical cure. They might use a system of small weights attached by wires to the foreskin which pull and stretch the penis, I'm thinking, but then I realise I have this all mixed up with some weird porn we were watching at Diesel's the other night. But still I can't find any mention of what I'm after in the window, so I peer through the glass, using a hand to provide shade from the reflective glare of sunlight as I try to read the notices and advertisements on the walls inside. I don't notice Mr Foo opening the door.

He pops his head out and beckons me in. He's not saying anything, probably doesn't speak English. So I speak slowly and loudly, and use my own sign language to thank him for his kind invitation (I bow once) to inspect his new shop (a sweep of my hand indicating his premises) but tell him that I am only a curious (forefinger to temple) passer-by (two fingers walking across the other palm) who is naturally interested (two taps of my temple) by the phenomenon of an Asian (point to Mr Foo) remedies shop on our High Street, but (flat hand over my eyes like a sailor searching for land) am only looking.

Mr Foo looks like he is having trouble understanding me. I bow once more, and I'm about to go when Mr Foo utters something that sounds intensely foreign, a strange, alien noise which reminds me of how little I know of either China's Mandarin or Cantonese dialects. For a moment I can't make head nor tail of it, but now I think about it, what he said to me was – if I have this right, 'Hey up, me duck, if there's owt tha' wants that's not in 'window, chances are, we'll have the bugger inside. Pop in for a butcher's and a warm – by heck, it'd freeze the knackers off a brass monkey today. Call this summer?' And I'm inside before I've worked out that if Mr Foo's from the far East, it's the far East of Yorkshire.

Mr Foo can see that this is all new to me and helpfully explains many of the practises and procedures of Chinese medicine. Soon I am about as clued up as I ever will be on the holistic theories of TCM (Traditional Chinese Medicine), 'how tha' has to balance t' yin and t' yang', given a smattering of Taoism and Confucianism and asked if I know what I might be (he does my sailor thing with his hand) looking for? I'm examining everything, reading labels, hoping to stumble on what I want without asking for it. There is literature in Chinese and diagnostic charts unlike anything I've seen at my GP practice, where I've been having treatment for a verucca. Everything, in fact, apart from Mr Foo himself, is so exotic that I can't help feeling that my answer must lie here, if I can only find it.

There's a black door behind the counter marked Private and I wouldn't be at all surprised if the real secrets of this place, the cures for cancer and stunted cocks and so on, are all kept in that room. But knowing what you need is one thing and telling a Yorkshireman, even a Chinese one, that you have a small todger is quite another. I make a mental note to return soon armed with a totally credible story about an unfortunate mate of mine who, poor sod, has a deficiency in the dick department and wants to know if Foo Q's has a remedy for this? My friend will say that he doesn't want to overdo it and that just an extra two or three inches would probably be all right.

Meanwhile, I pick up a packet from the counter top at random, pay more than I can afford and leave quickly, clutching, I discover when I'm safely around the corner and standing in the entrance of the Golden Days retirement home, a paper bag containing a Number One remedy for Alzheimer's. I pop it through the letterbox.

'Someone called for you,' Mum says when I get home.

'Who was it?' I'm feeling a little under the weather, nothing much, just a bit of a head, which is probably down to last night's Sunny D&V. I can't be bothered to go up to my room, so I slump on the sofa in the living room, where Mum's ironing Dad's vests and watching Jeremy Kyle with the sound off.

'That man, the one your father doesn't much like. He wants to talk to you about little Clive next door.'

'That'll be his dad,' I say. 'I expect Clive brought his new bum buddy Kevin back last night and gave him one up the arse, Mum, when I was supposed to be fixing him up with some fanny. So now Roger'll be wanting to know what time I want to come round to be castrated with a Doc Marten's toe cap.'

Actually, most of this was unspoken, but it was what I was thinking.

A pile of ironed golfing sweaters (not mine) makes a useful pillow as I stare out through the new conservatory windows at Dad's ordered universe, his stripy lawn and square goldfish pond, his shed where all his garden tools have their places on the wall outlined in marker pen and the only thing that's missing from this scene is a little 'Keep Off the Grass' sign planted in the lawn. He's out there now, despite the rain that's started, in a collar and tie and sharply-creased M&S slacks, fixing a trellis to the top of our already quite high fence with that slightly maniacal look he gets whenever his routine has been interrupted, or when we have unexpected visitors. This will mean we now have the tallest fence on our street, if not the entire district, but it also means we are that much more insulated from the disorder and God Knows What Else that lurks just over it, on Roger Dyson's land.

Again I wonder what it must be like for Mum, to have lived with Dad this long. My parents met in their teens at a scout jamboree, to which the girl guides had been invited, to give the scouts a better idea of what girls were. What an innocent world they must have lived in. But times have moved on and I expect even the scouts have changed now. They'll get badges for rolling a joint or blowing the scout leader, I expect. Woah! Where are these thoughts coming from? How can I think such things in front of Mum? I've always worried she might tune in somehow, so I've tried to keep my more degenerate streams of consciousness for the bedroom or bathroom. I'm not even sure I didn't say all that about Clive and Roger out loud. If I did, Mum doesn't appear to have noticed, she's too busy ironing the daisy-patterned curtains from the toilet window. But like I say, I've not been feeling myself. It could be down to Tesco and their cheap vodka but I'm beginning to think it's the poisonous concoction of bitter disappointment and lacerating guilt I'm feeling about that fiasco with Rosalind. I doubt she'll ever speak to me again.

But Mum and Dad getting their ging gang goolies off while other kids were raving in Madchester and popping E's to the Stone Roses and the Happy Mondays? From the photos I've seen, the only thing baggy about Dad in those days was his cardigan. But Dad's always been like that, staking a tenuous claim on normality with his buttoned-down attitude, short hair, crisp shirts, knife edge creases and, in this day and age, polished shoes. Dad imposes order on things and people; he gave up on me the day after The Party To End All Parties but he still makes Mum march to his tune and she's always been too meek to object. I can imagine him proposing to her. 'The correct thing to do, Violet, would be to get married,' he'll have said, or maybe it was just, '11.00 at St Just's. White dress. Be there.' She must have gone to the altar like a lamb to sacrifice.

Sometimes when she's had a Bailey's, which is at Christmas, she'll tell me about the flower shop she wanted and how she has dreams about Russell Crowe. She likes men who make her laugh too, which is why she likes Diesel. The only time Dad made her laugh was when he fell off the ladder installing his CCTV system. I was there watching and there was the crash of ladder and Dad and then these weird noises. For a second, I thought it was Dad's chest caving in, and these were the choking convulsions of a dying man. But it was Mum, laughing quietly at Dad as he opened his eyes, got up and shook himself off.

I'm thinking so intently about my parents' strange relationship, that I haven't noticed that Mum is waving a pair of my own underpants in front of my face, trying to get my attention.

'Have you said hello to Nana?'

'Nana and GD? They're here?' This is news to me.

'They came this afternoon while you were out,' Mum says, looking at the rain spattering on the windows. 'That's why your father's still out in the garden.'

Nana smiles as I enter the back bedroom where they always stay when they visit. Despite her condition, Nana can still get upstairs thanks to the stair lift Dad installed. I've always suspected it wasn't put in so much as an aid for her, as a far-thinking precaution against his own old age. There was a closing down sale at the mobility shop, so he bought that, some handgrips for the bath and a wheelchair ramp for the kitchen steps. The house now has everything it needs to see him through to his death, in about 45 years time.

Nana and GD always look out of place and a little uncomfortable in this room, its fussy neatness clashing with Nana's flowing skirts and GD's tie-dyed tee shirts, but it's the only place in the whole house that Nana can abide because if she looks through the gap between the rows of new and identical houses that climb the hill behind us, she can just make out the dark shape of the moorland ridge and almost see the towering rock on which GD knelt so many years ago and asked her to be his bride.

'How are you?' I ask and sit down on the nearest of the twin beds. There's just Nana. GD must have gone to see his old friend in the town, as he often does when he's here. Garcia will have gone with him.

'I'm okay, Brian. Don't look so glum! I'm here for more treatment, of course, but lately I've been feeling much better. I've even started to write again.'

Nana is a poet. I ask if she wrote the book of poetry she has open on her lap. She shakes her head and picks it up and reads me something about death and eternity sitting in a carriage together. It sounds so morbid but she obviously likes it.

'It's good,' I say. I never know quite what to say to her these days. She's so ill and each time I see her, it's like a little bit more of the Nana I loved has disappeared. She's thinner, her face is more lined, her eyes sort of poppy.

'I was just thinking,' she's saying, 'of when you spent a fortnight with us when you were younger? You remember that?'

This was the summer Dad dragged Mum up North to watch the Scottish Open at Loch Lomond and to spend a few days touring the Travelodges and garden centres of Scotland and all points South. That's what Dad does whenever we go anywhere. But for me it was the best outcome possible. I stayed with GD and Nana in their little cottage in the hills, the place I called Narnia, because it sounded like Nana. Narnia was everything Laurel Gardens has never been. There was always music, GD's records or people playing guitars, mandolins or whatever. Because they always had friends staying over, people from the college where Nana taught English, or GD's friends from his vague and colourful past.

I was only ten at the time and I hardly knew what to make of them. They were old, of course, but not in the way that Dad is old, at just past 40. They were old with experience and appeared to have learned the secret of enjoying life. They would wake me in the early morning hours and take me with them onto the hill to watch the dawn break over the distant castle. We would tramp through the knee-high and dew-laden grass to a spot which commanded a view of the world. They talked, joked and sometimes sang as the sun pushed itself up from the distant horizon. At the time I thought they might be botanists or scientists because they took such an interest in the world about them, the petals of flowers, the bark of trees, the intricate patterns on a leaf. Later, I realised that they were all off their heads on acid. GD was still working as a carpenter then and I sometimes wonder what his work would have been like, on those long days that began like these.

'Yes,' I say, holding the thin, blue-cheese hand she's stretching out to me. 'I remember it all, Nana.'

I ring the bell and Clive answers the door while the dogs are still barking and Rule Britannia's not finished chiming in the hallway. I hadn't noticed he was wearing makeup last night – he's very subtle with it these days – but there's black streaks all over his cheeks. His hair's a mess and he looks like he's spent the night nesting in the rust heaps in the yard. 'Oh, it's you,' he says without much enthusiasm while he takes a squint up the street. 'I thought it might be someone else.'

'What happened to you last night?' I say, though I'm not sure I want to know.

'I was up a friend's,' he says ambiguously. 'Didn't get in 'til two.'

'In where?' I can't help saying, but it passes over Clive's head without damage.

'I tell you, Bri, I was completely fucked last night.'

Does he know he's doing this, I wonder?

'Dad's somewhere. I think he wants some help with the scrap metal scruncher.'

'Not the compactor?' My worst fears, etc.

'That's the thingy,' Clive says cheerfully, closing the door. 'I'd do it myself, but I've got the new floors to think about.' I'm seriously considering ignoring the call I got from Roger while I was talking to Nana, and returning home on health and safety grounds, but that's the moment when Roger appears from around the corner, wearing nothing but his red Speedos, a pair of flip flops and a lot of tattoos. It's an unnerving sight at the best

LOSING IT

of times.

'I thought I heard you,' he says. 'Come on round the back.'

We sit by Roger's new compactor, on sun-warmed bales of metal made from written-off cars and Roger opens a plastic cooler box and fishes out two tins of Tennent's Super. He chucks me one, but the way he's sizing me up, he might be wondering if I would gum up the works if he fed me into the compactor.

'Have you seen the state of him?' he asks, finally.

I have.

'I'm still up when he gets home, watching some old cobblers on cable – *Changing Rooms*, it might have been,' and as he warms to his subject, he sounds a little friendlier, I think. 'Fuck me, the way things change, eh, Brian? All that MDF wouldn't get a look-in these days, not in my gaff anyway. That Laurence Llewellyn-Bowen still wants a slap, though.' Roger takes a long sip of his lager and I can see that in his mind's eye he has LLB's throat in his meaty grasp as he tells him where he can shove his MDF, adding that Anna Ryder Richardson could dump all over his idea of style and she's crumpet and all. Then he wakes from his reverie. 'Sorry, where was I?'

'Still up when Clive got home,' I say, though my mind's still on Anna Ryder Richardson.

'So I was. And in comes Clive, looking like he's been in a car crash, but also like the cat that got the cream, know what I mean? Maybe it had run in front of an electric milk float and caused a pile-up, I dunno. So I ask him about it and he's telling me this wild story about all the skirt just gagging to take him home. Well, chip off the old block, I'm thinking! Perhaps we've all been wrong about him. So – here's the million-dollar question, Brian, have you fixed it for me? Has Clive finally got his end away?'

The easy bit is telling Roger all about Clive being the star of the Prom and how other blokes weren't getting a look-in while his son was wowing them all on the dance floor. Then comes the hard bit, telling him that, as far as I know, Clive didn't avail

52

himself of all that snatch on tap, but spent the rest of the night up a mate's'. I'm more than a little nervous about how Roger will take this.

But Roger only sighs, adjusts his hefty balls and opens another beer. 'I don't fucking know, Brian, I really don't. It wasn't like that in my day.'

And Roger tells me how it was in his day, how he only had to rub up against some bird in a disco and then it was, wham, bam, thank you ma'am – unless she screamed and it all kicked off, of course. And then I tell him how it is in my day, how it was for me last night, anyway. And this is where it all gets a bit unexpected. I start talking and soon I find that I'm telling him way more than I intended to, personal stuff about my feelings for Ros that I haven't told my best mates. And I'm telling him all this because he's not one of my mates and I know that whatever he says, it won't be the kind of spaccy reaction I'd get from Diesel, for instance.

I tell him what I'd tell my dad, if I could actually talk to him about something other than the price of lawn feeds and how racy The Archers is getting these days. Still, standing outside my body, as I sometimes do on such occasions, I'm amazed to see myself telling Roger Dyson that I'm in love with Rosalind Chandler and in language that I've no memory of ever using before. She is, I tell him, hardly noticing his eyebrows cocking, 'beguiling'. She has, I say, an 'ethereal, other-worldly charm', and 'hidden depths'. *Ethereal*? Where did that come from? There's more along similar lines and I probably sound like Oz Clarke describing a glass of, what is it, Chateau Petrus? And because I'm talking to Roger, who is very blokey and probably a bit thick, and because I can be a patronising git at times, I punctuate all this with *know what I mean*?

Roger listens politely and nods and scratches his balls a lot. Then he asks me how far I've got with Rosalind. First or second base, he asks, or a home run? Then he *gruckles*, which is the only way to describe the sort of grunting chuckle he does, and asks me if I struck out (for a Millwall fan, he seems to know a lot about baseball). I have to tell him I've never actually spoken to her. 'Fuck me,' he says: for some reason, he seems to find this appalling. It's all beyond his comprehension, though perhaps the fault's with my crap situation, rather than his IQ.

I tell him I have no idea what to do now.

Where other people might signify cogitation by stroking their chin, Roger's equivalent is to slip a hand inside his Speedos and sort out the lie of his tackle. He seems oblivious to the shuffling movements of his hand inside his trunks as he leans back and blows out his cheeks.

'It's hard,' he says, worryingly.

We sit there soaking up the sun for what seems like ages and despite Roger's alarming appearance – he may have a shaven head and Love and Hate tattooed on his knuckles, but the Speedos are scarier – I feel oddly at ease talking with him about Ros and reckon I could probably talk to Roger about all kinds of stuff. Not that of course, but maybe anything else. Is it the effect of drinking strong lager in the sun or is it because I really am being patronising and think that maybe he won't properly under-stand it all? I dismiss that thought – I can be an arrogant sod as well, but not that arrogant. Maybe, I'm wondering, as Roger hawks up something chewy from the deepest recesses of his lungs and spits it against the metal side of the compactor, where it begins to loop downwards like a phlegmy Mexican bean, maybe it's because there's actually something fatherly about him, just like there once was with my dad, before his mind became fixed on others things, like Roger's scrap business, Roger's dogs, Roger's swimming trunks, etc, etc.

'What you and this bird need, my son,' Roger says at last, 'is a mutual interest. Common ground. That'll get you into her knickers, if anything will.'

'It's a thought,' I say.

'Of course it is. Clive's mum and me had a mutual interest and that's what made it all work for us.'

'What was it?'

'Shagging, mainly. She fucked me for two years before fucking off herself. But you know what I mean. It works with other stuff, too.'

'Does it?'

'Take Trudy, I mean. She was the bird in the boots going out as you were coming in last week. We had a mutual interest and you know what it was?'

Roger grins and gives his balls a squeeze. I try not to look, and suggest, 'Shagging, again?'

'Eventually, yes. And she is the business, I have to say. Squeezes your cock like a python digesting a live mouse. But no, it wasn't that, not at first.'

'So what was it?' I'm imagining everything sexual short of cross-dressing – which produces a disturbing image on the back of my eyelids, which is Roger in a light, summer dress and a pair of sling-backs.

'Fucking quiz machines,' Roger says. 'I was playing one down the Barley Mow one night and I got stuck on the wotsits, the picture questions. Who painted *The Haywain* and all that bollocks. Trudy had been playing the machine since they put the fucker in, so she knew them all. But I was fucked if I knew who won last year's Turner Prize.'

'Art not your subject?' I say, allowing myself a superior little smirk. By this time, I was beginning to think I almost liked Roger. I was grateful for the interest he had taken in my problem and was even beginning to think he wasn't so scary after all – but I didn't see him sitting by his compactor with a Tennents in one hand and a copy of Gombrich's *Story of Art* in the other.

'It's bollocks, what they call art these days, innit?'

'Yeah,' I say.

'Fucking Damien Hirst? Pickled cows? Tracey fucking Emin

and her dirty knickers?'

'It's all shit, isn't it?' I say, and belch amicably.

'Cunts, the lot of them,' Roger pronounces. He raises himself from his seat to expel a loud, whining fart. 'Compared, I mean, with your Leonardo or your Michelangelo.'

It seems our chat is taking a strange turn, but I can go with a flow.

'Fuck, I was a big Turtles fan too,' I say, keeping up nicely. ''Course, no way should they have changed their names from Ninja to Hero. That fucking sucked.'

'And your Raphael,' Roger goes on, seeming not to have heard me. 'Though Fra Angelico had his moments and Giotto too, obviously. No, your actual masters of the Quattrocento piss all over those modern cunts. But the secret is to see the fuckers in situ. In the chapels where they was painted. Or at least in the fucking Uffizi, you know?'

'Right,' I say. When Clive told me him and his dad'd been to Italy, I thought he'd meant Rimini, somewhere with a beach, not Florence, ground zero of the Italian Renaissance.

'Yeah, I can see you're surprised,' Roger says. 'There I was, in Michelangelo's fucking library wearing Union Jack shorts and a Millwall shirt. But I won it, you see, two weeks in fucking Florence. Competition in one of Trudy's magazines.'

'Fucking Florence,' I say, as I don't know what else to say.

'But they give you headphones and these recorded guides. All in English, too. Soon get to know your way around, know what I mean?'

Is he taking the piss?

'So,' I say, while I think about that. 'You were able to help this Trudy on the quiz machine?'

'Help her? We emptied it that night. Then we went home and she emptied me. So what I'm saying is, you and this bird have to find something you both know a bit about, something you can rabbit about with her. You do that, she'll think you're on her wavelength then and that's half your battle won.'

'Half? What's the rest?'

'Well, getting her pissed won't hurt.'

'So how would you suggest I go about this?'

'Well, to start with, what's she's into? Has she got interests?'

'I'm not sure. Reading, maybe. She's always got a bag full of books.'

'And what do you know about books?'

'Not a lot,' I say, truthfully. The last book I read without having to was probably something by Roald Dahl.

'Well, find out what she likes and read that. Then it's a couple of drinks, some old pony about Harry Potter or whatever and it'll be all systems go for the old pink Polaris.'

'Will it work?'

'Of course it will. You're on your own with the fucking books though.'

Roger pushes the button on the compactor, which starts rumbling and clanking. Now he has to shout to make himself heard over the grinding and mangling of metal going on in the belly of the machine. 'Only things I ever read are Millwall programmes,' he says, then there's something I can't quite make sense of, but it sounds like, 'And fucking Vasari.'

I can't just sit there, so I get up and start helping him feed the compactor from a tangled heap of rusting scrap. I'm quite enjoying the mechanical nature of the job as we both take an end of something heavy and drop it into the hungry jaws of the machine. I'm knackered after about three minutes, but I'm liking that feeling which all manual workers must get when they work up a sweat from honest toil. And I'm thinking how noble it is to work with your hands and satisfying to have your muscles ache at the end of the day, when Roger stops the machine to clear an obstruction.

'That's helped you, has it?' he says.

'It's certainly an idea,' I say.

'Good,' he says. 'And now I've helped you, you'll remember to help me, won't you?'

I look around at the patch of flattened earth where one of the many heaps of scrap had been. It's now reduced to a couple of neatly compacted bundles. 'Not with that,' Roger says. 'With Clive. You'll stand by your promise?'

'Promise?' I say. Had I actually promised anything?

'You know what I mean,' he says. Roger sees something in the long grass and picks it up. It's one of Clive's old Action Man figures, now naked and headless. 'I don't mind you, Brian, so we'll forget about last night and start over. I know you won't let me down again.'

He drops the little figure into the machine. Any thoughts I'd had about Roger actually being 'a bit of a pussycat when you got to know him' wither entirely as he nails me with a loaded look.

'Of course I won't,' I say. 'You can count on me.'

'That's what I thought,' Roger says, and digs his hand into his Speedos to offer another imaginative configuration of his cock and balls.

CHAPTER 6

Do You Remember the First Time?

'We used to play this, remember?'

That's Faruk, who can use the jukebox for free.

He sits down and begins to rattle his teaspoon on his coffee cup to the sound of Motorhead's *Ace of Spades* while his sister Deniz shoots him looks from the other side of the counter.

'To be accurate,' says Clive. 'We tried to play this.'

Clive has remained tight-lipped about last night, all the way from his house to the Casablanca.

'We weren't bad,' says Faruk. 'Just different. And that's no bad thing, innit?'

I'm remembering The Four Horsemen of the Apocalypse's debut gig, also our farewell gig, as it turned out.

'We were different,' says Clive, 'in the way that being good is different from being crap.'

Faruk messes with his kebab, opens it up, injects more sauce.

'It's not an easy song,' he says.

'It's three chords,' Clive says. 'How much easier could it be? How could we balls that up?'

'The audience was expecting a Craig David covers band,' Faruk says.

Faruk finishes his kebab while Clive watches people passing up and down a rainy street. The girls who are giggling in the corner booth look like the ones who were giggling at our car the other night.

'Well, at least we know Paranoid doesn't work as an *a cappella* version now,' I offer.

'No,' Clive says. 'We know that it doesn't work when we do it.'

'I said the Masons' PA would be dodgy,' Faruk says.

'It wasn't the amps, it was the wiring wotsits,' Clive says. 'It won't have powered anything more serious than a three valve radio since the war.'

'And that was one tough audience,' I say.

Everyone nods, lost in thought.

'Did you see the looks we got when we played *Last Handjob Before I Die*?' Faruk says.

'I didn't think Masons could be so rude,' Clive says.

'That stamping they did,' I say.

'The slow hand clap,' says Faruk, shaking his head.

'Even your dad was shouting, "Get off!"' Clive says.

The girls start giggling again. Perhaps they can hear us.

I'm remembering how Dad's Masonic lodge had been blown out by the band they'd hired to give one of their fundraisers some youth appeal. (The accordionist and the xylophonist had contracted flu and the singer was 'feeling poorly'.) Dad was in charge of entertainments and it was down to him to find a replacement act at short notice – not easy, with the money the Masons were offering.

As a last resort, he asked me what I'd been up to with that guitar of mine. He'd seen me taking it in and out of the house and might have heard me practising *Smoke on the Water* or *Seven Nation Army* once or twice in my bedroom. 'So, Brian,' he said to me one day, as I was headed out the door for band practise in Faruk's garage. 'Am I right in thinking you've joined a musical combo – you know,' and here he winked, conspiratorially, 'a band?' He's not often right in what he's thinking and his idea of a band (which, ten to one, will be three Brylcreemed boys and a cheeky drummer), would not have been Donny Tourette's, for example.

But I nodded and smiled, pleased that he was taking an interest in me, for a change. 'I thought as much,' he said. 'Now what do you say to this? Your old dad has only gone and got you your first engagement!' Like playing for a lot of old knackers with funny handshakes was doing us the favour, and not him. And like Faruk's saying now, loudly enough to earn him disapproving looks from his sister and one more burst of giggles from the party ordering the nitrous oxide in the corner, that gig was 'a fucking disaster.'

The career of the Four Horsemen was one marked by frequent differences of opinion regarding the group's identity and future direction. And now, months after the disbanding of *Britain's Most Exiting Newcomers* (I quote from the flyers Clive printed up, complete with prophetic misprint), we're at it again.

'The problem was your keyboards, really,' Faruk is saying.

'What was wrong with them? At least I got my grade three piano.'

'We were a death metal band. There's not even supposed be keyboards. And definitely not Liberace playing them.'

'What do you mean?'

'That silver jacket you wore. With the sequins. That quiff. You know.'

'But we weren't a death metal band,' Clive protests. 'I wasn't in a death metal band.'

'What were you, then?'

'I don't know. Indie, maybe. With a hint of early Abba.'

'You were death metal, weren't you, Brian?'

'Well, yeah, sort of,' I say. 'With other stuff thrown in, you know?'

And that was The Four Horsemen of the Apocalypse, murdered by musical differences before we'd even begun. Well, not only musical differences – while Faruk had his own guitar, Clive, Diesel and me had taken summer jobs at Henshaw's Chickens to pay off our second-hand instruments. Nigel Henshaw is head honcho at the Masonic Lodge and shifts at his factory became rarer than hens' teeth after our gig and our instruments were duly repo'd.

What was most annoying about this was the waste of hours of

preparation that had been put into the project. I'm not talking about rehearsal time, I'm talking about the time and effort I put into writing and designing our album covers, in case we got a record deal. They were bloody good, though I say so myself. We all got dressed up in leather jackets (borrowed from Faruk's cousins, who are in a motorcycle gang called Allah's Angels), persuaded my neighbour Jane Gallacher to do our make up and spent an afternoon taking photographs of each other jumping off walls, leaning over balconies, pointing menacingly at camera, striking phallic poses with our axes and generally looking like death metal hombres about to kick musical ass. I Photoshopped the best of these onto a series of mocked up album covers for CD and, to add retro appeal, old-style vinyl gatefolds too. We foresaw a multiple album deal once we were discovered, so I was working flat out for several weeks before the sleeves were completed and I was happy with the result.

The first album's front cover featured a black and white shot of The Four Horsemen in a grimy alley, which looks like it might be somewhere in the Bronx but is actually the one where the Casablanca keeps its bins. We look appropriately mean and moody. Diesel manages an Elvis lip-curl and stands, hands on hips, snarling at the camera. Behind him, Faruk, Stratocaster copy over his shoulder and a fag smouldering between his lips, is plainly looking for trouble. Clive leans against a wall wearing sunglasses and trimming his nails with what might be a flick knife but is actually only a nail file. He's always doing that. And me, I'm in there too, sporting fake designer stubble thanks to a bit of pointillism from Jane Gallacher's eyebrow pen and I'm wearing a seen-it-all, fucked-it-all expression. We look the business. In fiery contrast to the grainy monochrome image is the splash of blood-red lettering spelling out the band's name and along the bottom is the title of the album, Slaves to Sex.

The back cover features the other pictures we took on the afternoon's shoot, one or two with the camera's self-timer feature, some others taken by random passers-by. All these images, which for the sake of contrast were in colour, had been exposed to the full range of available effects and filters. Particularly effective is the one where we're shaking our fists at a nuclear holocaust sky, the environmental message as clear as day. And in a text box on the right of these is the track listing:

1 *Dog's Bollocks* (Dalziel/Dyson/Osman/Johnson)
2 *I've Had Her* (Dalziel/Osman)
3 *Death's Handmaiden* (Dalziel)
4 *Gonna Make It Big Tonight* (Johnson)
5 *Teenage Gunman* (Dalziel/Osman)
6 *Black Death in Mordor* (Dalziel/Johnson)
7 *Apostles of the Apocalypse* (Dalziel/Osman)
8 *Acne Carriage* (Dyson/Johnson)
9 *Pox on your House* (Dalziel/Johnson)
10 *A Last Handjob Before I Die* (Dalziel/Dyson/Osman/Johnson)
11 *Larger Than Life* – bonus track (Johnson/Dyson)

And beneath them, in another text box imposed over police mugshots of the band members (bits of blackboard/chalked names/photo booth) were the sleeve notes, some provisional copy which would promote us with interested record companies and to which minor adjustments and updates could be made for sake of veracity, at a later date:

Every so often a band comes along which blows away everything in its path and changes the course of rock music forever. The Beatles, Led Zeppelin and The Sex Pistols were all such bands. Now comes The Four Horsemen of the Apocalypse, an outfit of such raw energy and startling originality that the music press has not only sat up and taken note, it has prostrated itself before them. The Four Horsemen pride themselves on well-crafted songs, delivered with all the power of an Airbus A-380 on takeoff. Their recent barnstorming British tour, which culminated in a show-stopping performance at the Wembley Arena, has confirmed the

Horsemen as the UK's No 1 rock act. Their forthcoming tour of the United States and Asia is expected to take Britain's best to the next level.

Then there are some faked-up clippings looking like they've been torn from newspapers and pasted into any spare spaces. These aren't actually the clippings I used on the versions I showed the band, but ones that I personally prefer:

Horsemen Ride On!

Success won't spoil four local lads from South Yorkshire. Although their single "Broken on the Wheel" has hogged the number one spot for six weeks, charismatic bass player Brian Johnson (17) says that the band have kept their feet firmly on the ground. "We're all about bringing death metal to the average man on the street," Brian says. "We're into the music, not the trappings of success. Obviously, we've all got new cars and I've bought my mum and dad a new house which is five miles from the nearest neighbour but apart from that and the tour jet, we've not changed a bit."

Horsemen Voted Sexiest Band

Chart-toppers The Four Horsemen of the Apocalypse have been voted the Sexiest Band of All Time. All members of this amazing four piece polled votes, but attention has of course focussed on bassist Brian "Sex on Stage" Johnson, whose pelvic grindings and thrustings have put Elvis in the shade and have caused many an excited female fan to speculate on just how appropriate Johnson's name might be. He's a sex god on stage but is it all just part of the act, we asked? Johnson smiles knowingly. "It's rock'n'roll," he says. "Sure, there are groupies, and God knows, we're only human. But there's only one girl for me and I dedicate every performance to her." He's sexy, he's romantic, but sorry, girls, he's spoken for! We wonder which very lucky lady can be the object of Brian "BJ" Johnson's affections?

And another one, about how things might develop, given time…

Peace in our Time

BoJo (aka Brian Johnson) has issued a warning to warring factions in the Middle East. "Chill out," says the heart-throb frontman of smash-hit rockers '4H' (previously The Four Horsemen of the Apocalypse). Says Brian, "There's always stuff on the news about people being uncool with each other and I'm asking both sides to come together over 4H's new download, *Fuck Your Enemy*, in the cause of peace, love and indie death metal." BoJo made his announcement following meetings with local leaders prior to flying to Washington for top-level talks with President Obama. The President, who is reported to be a big 4H fan, has said that if the world had a few more people like BoJo, it would basically be a better place.

I'm still thinking of how things might have been when Clive puts down his Cherry Coke and points at something in the street, where the rain is coming down like sackfuls of silver nails. 'Is that who I think it is?'

We wipe spaces in the fogged window to see someone in a bright red, hooded sweatshirt dodging traffic as he crosses the road and trots briskly towards the Casablanca, casting furtive glances over his shoulder as he approaches.

'Teletubby coming,' Faruk says.

'Eh oh!' Clive says, as Diesel opens the door and pulls off his hood.

He sits down, picks up the laminated menu and calls out, 'Usual, please, Deniz, with an extra sausage and a slice on the side.'

'What's that?' says Clive.

'What?'

'That red thing?'

'It's not mine. Have you finished with those chips?'

'It's no excuse.'

Clive has firm ideas on fashion.

'How long for that special, Deniz?' Diesel calls, his mouth already full with Clive's cold chips.

'It's hideous,' Clive proclaims, of Diesel's sweatshirt.

'You're like Red Riding Hood. Only redder and more of a twat,' Faruk offers.

'In case you haven't noticed, it's completely hosing it down out there,' Diesel says. Deniz, long brown hair pinned beneath a white cap, voluptuous arse encased in a tight pair of black jeans, parks Diesel's recommended calorific intake for the week in front of him: two eggs, three sausages, beans, mushrooms, extra chips and a doorstep of bread and butter. Watching Diesel eat is an acknowledged source of free entertainment. We're still amazed and genuinely impressed at the speed of the operation: the grey blur of the fork as he scoops up monumental piles of food like a souped-up JCB clearing hardcore. Today's is a bravura performance, probably knocking five or six seconds off his record and that's with the extra sausage. The rest of us exchange looks, privileged to have witnessed this special moment together. While Diesel mops his plate with the slice of bread and butter, Faruk tells him what we've just been talking about.

'Great days,' Diesel agrees, still chewing. 'The band and all the other stuff too.'

'It's like we've all known each other for years,' I say, apropos of not much.

'I've known Faruk for thirteen years,' Diesel says.

'Though we didn't see each other for the last six of them,' Faruk reminds him.

'Brian and me go way back,' Clive says, opening the Faruk and

Diesel, me and Clive division which sometimes shows itself in our doings together.

'But the fact is that together, the Four Horsemen, by which I don't mean our cruelly received musical partnership, but us four as mates, go back only a few months. A few months! But I feel like I've known you lot all of my life, you know?'

Am I imagining it or is Diesel starting to well up?

'It's true, my friends, we've lived it large,' Faruk says.

Why is everyone getting so wistful?

Someone asks if we remember getting caught by security guards as we skateboarded through the shopping centre, then someone else remembers the first wrap of hash we ever bought, which turned out to be Oxo cube. Then other priceless stuff is brought up, like Faruk surprising Clive with Trudy's dildo stuck up his bum (Clive still says he fell on it, getting out of the bath). Then there was the night Diesel and Faruk used a loudhailer and scared the shit out of shagging couples at a remote picnic site. None of this happened more than a matter of weeks ago and yet Diesel's talking about it nostalgically, like it's all in the distant past and such days won't be coming again. It's like he's suddenly grown up. he's suddenly grown up.

But the rest of us are still top-trumping each other with reminiscences of good times, or times that look good now that a decent interval has been allowed to elapse since they occurred. Diesel's injuries after he tried to skate down the department store escalator weren't actually funny at the time. But Faruk and me bonding over all those old records; Clive getting pissed and going shopping in Trudy's clothes; our graffiti period, torpedoed by Clive's spelling and Faruk's colour blindness; our urban adventure phase, when we were marooned on the library roof the whole of a cool summer's night after the decorator returned for his ladders: we all agree that those were good times.

Then the other plans we've made are revisited, especially The Road Trip, the pipe dream of pipe dreams in which we celebrate finishing school next July by taking off somewhere together. Amsterdam. Barcelona. Marrakech. Wherever. How cool would that be, we ask, for the hundredth time? We all know it'll probably come to nothing, but it's always great to talk about. There's no doubt about it, these last few weeks have bonded us as real friends and right at this moment, it is hard to envisage a time when universities, girlfriends, changes of location and finally, marriage and kids will ever tear us apart.

The Four Horsemen have been built around these things and an unspoken other, which is our shared virginity. So we all see the threat to our tight little unit when Diesel pushes away his plate at last and says, flatly, 'I had it off with Lauren Sykes last night.'

And no one knows what to say or even what expression to assume.

The natural reaction would be to say 'No way?' and to crack up. Not Lauren Sykes, we should have said, 'Lauren Sykes with the legs like skittles and the lunar complexion?' Who'd be desperate enough to fuck lardy Lauren Sykes of all people, in the bushes behind the bandstand in the park? Surely not Diesel Dalziel, who's just 'fessed' up to exactly that? But none of us says a thing.

It is an earth-shattering announcement. Yet for reasons which will become clear, we all nod or shake our heads, mould our features into knowing grins and take the news like it's the most commonplace thing in the world. I had it off with Lauren Sykes. We are amazed, appalled and secretly jealous.

It breaks down like this: the same thoughts are going through my head, Faruk's and Clive's heads, with one or two fairly crucial differences. Faruk, never mind that he's subject to an arranged marriage with a girl called Rashida, who lives in a suburb of Istanbul, whose photographs I have seen on numerous occasions and about whom Faruk has mixed feelings, has told us on numerous occasions that he lost his virginity with exchange student Donato Epifano, on the night before she went back to Italy. Clive popped his cherry, supposedly, during a weekend in Brighton 'with mates'. And, as I remember graphically, I assumed the mantle of manhood after fucking 'some dirty little blonde' after a party in a house down the road. Needless to say, the family moved almost straight afterwards and I've completely lost touch with her since. Diesel was supposed to have lost his virginity with 'Serena', a cousin who supposedly lived on the Isle of Wight.

We used to be four secret virgins. Virgins with stories, which were repeated and embroidered upon whenever necessary, but virgins all the same. It was something we had in common that bound us, something else that had forged our identity as The Four Horsemen or, more simply, as four close friends. Could we ever be the same again? How could we be three virgins and Diesel? How will this affect the dynamics? How can we ever pretend to be other than virgins now – not when Diesel already has the knowing look that seems to say to everyone, 'Yes, I've done it. I've actually shagged a girl. So what?' It is a period for reflection. Clive is playing with his phone while Faruk gazes over the road where his brother is fiddling with the carburettor of our car. I'm sneaking stealthy glances at the girls who giggle. They're actually just about fuckable, I decide. All about our age, one with the most enormous tits which she's showing off with a low top and the others a bit overweight but fit enough to be cocksure of themselves. I only wish I was. When Diesel orders a plate of baklava, I notice he winks at Deniz. Does he always do that? I'm not sure.

As for the sex itself, of course we all want to ask him what it was like but that would blow our covers out of the water. Whenever we glance his way, Faruk and I are piecing together the details of Diesel's amorous encounter with Lauren Sykes – what Clive's thinking is harder to say. Did they kiss, I'm wondering? How many clothes did she take off? What would she look like naked? What does Diesel look like naked? Eurrgh! Don't go there! Did he feel her up, tits first, then fanny? Did he get a hard-on right away or did she have to suck him? What must it have felt like, even with Lauren Sykes, as his fat little cock (I actually have no idea how big Diesel's cock is) slid slowly into a warm, wet cunt? Was he on top or was Lauren? Did she make a lot of noise as he thrust into her? How long did it take? Is it exactly like you imagine, when you come inside a woman? Did he come inside her? Is she on the pill? Did he use a condom?

These and a million other messages are chasing about my cerebral cortex as I watch Diesel apply himself to the dessert like a man with a well-earned appetite. I don't know how many hours have elapsed since he made his announcement, it seems like hundreds and no one has said anything except for Faruk, who has managed, 'Fuck me, Lauren Sykes,' to which Diesel has replied, 'No, fuck *me*, Lauren Sykes.' This has broken the ice and slowly, as if it doesn't matter to us, we prise out little details. 'Back of the bandstand, under the rhododendrons,' he says. 'Where Tony the tramp sleeps. No, he wasn't there, what d'you think, I wanted a threesome?'

He sounds so experienced.

And then he tells us everything, about how they had been going back to Lauren's where her mum was out, when she stopped to snog him in the park. She started to rub herself up against him, he said, actually placed his hand on her tits and in the dark she's actually all right, is Lauren, with a nicely shaped body. She stuck her tongue in his mouth and he slipped his fingers under her bra and felt her hot, hard nipples and that was when he knew he wasn't going to make it to Lauren's house. If it was going to happen, he said, it'd happen there or in his pants. And he might have told us about how he fucked her like a stud, going on for ages, making her beg for more, but he didn't. I think it was out of consideration for our feelings that he told us the less-than glorious truth. 'I came as soon as I got inside her,' he says. 'And that was pretty much it, really.'

Faruk shakes his head and says, 'Fuck me, Lauren Sykes,' again, while Clive mutters, 'Rather yours than mine' as he watches boys in leather mounting motorbikes outside. I'd like to know a little more, in fact I'd like to know a lot more, but that would be uncool and besides, I'm still not feeling well, which is the thought inside my head as my whole body convulses with a seismic jerk and I sneeze loudly, uncontrollably and incredibly messily, all over Diesel's dessert. The comic chorus in the corner has never, ever seen a funnier thing.

CHAPTER 7

One More Saturday Night

It's late when I turn into Laurel Gardens and see GD's camper van parked directly under a streetlight, so that its time-warped patterning of skulls and roses, weird dancing teddy bears and the huge, white-painted decal on the front – which I'd thought was Volkswagen branding gone mad but is actually a Ban the Bomb sign – can be easily enjoyed by anyone taking a nosy peek from their front windows. It's late because after we'd taken the Green Dragon for another test drive and then had to return it yet again to Faruk's brother's garage (the car is throwing up a mechanic's alphabet of problems: Alternator, then Bearings and now the Carburettor), Diesel insisted I went back to his. Apparently, in Diesel's eyes I am sensitive and intelligent and someone he can talk to about a problem he's got.

The problem is Lauren Sykes, who is full on for Diesel. This morning she called for him before lunch and when he said he had to go out, she made him wear her bright red hooded sweatshirt because it was raining and even then he hadn't been sure she wasn't following him to the Casablanca. And we all heard him fielding her phone calls when we were road testing the Green Dragon: call 1) she wants him to come round for tea at hers to meet her mum, 2) there's a rom-com she's dying to see at the Odeon, 3) she's seen a snuggly pullover she wants to buy him but needs him to come with her to try it on, 4) she wants him to tell her that he loves her, out loud, on his mobile phone.

'All I wanted was a shag,' Diesel complains, as we saddle up our video game horses to ride out of town. 'Not my life mapped out for me.'

'It's that bad?'

'Worse. We're going shopping at Meadowhall tomorrow.'

Meadowhall is Sheffield's busiest shopping centre.

I scope some hombre taking a bead on us from the roof of the saloon and my Winchester cracks out two shots; the dude is coyote meat before he hits the dirt. 'That's real tough, pardner,' I say, but secretly I'm wondering if I don't see the hand of justice in this. Diesel's been led on by his cock. He's not thought about how this irresponsible act might affect The Four Horsemen – who appear now to be galloping towards us, guns blazing – and what's more, he's not committed his crime with somebody who would actually be worth it, Rosalind Chandler for example, but with The Minger, Lauren Sykes. I try to offer what advice and consolation I can, but there's not a lot I can say. Diesel has made his bed and now he'll just have to lie in it. With Lauren Sykes, it looks like. It's a lesson for us all.

At the back of the house the kitchen light is illuminating a trapezoid of stripy lawn and Garcia, who is sitting in the middle of it, licking his balls. This might be a good time to mention that Garcia is GD's black and white collie dog. In the bright kitchen GD and Dad appear to be arguing. It's not unusual and it's not surprising: in terms of dress and lifestyle, likes and dislikes, they're as different as chalk and chutney. I think it might be down to genes, the ones that skip a generation especially. Or maybe it's just a matter of one generation rebelling against the last. GD's own rebellion was as wild as his upbringing was strict. And maybe because of that, my dad's made sure he's as different from GD as possible. Maybe.

'That dog stays out of this house,' my father – nattily attired in a new beige dressing gown and his crisply-ironed green striped pyjamas – is saying, 'until it has learned not to, ah, do his business in the f-f-flaming shoe cupboard.'

GD, wearing his big old jeans and the starburst tee shirt which pulls focus to his considerable paunch, is making a hot drink for Nana. He takes her one up before he retires to the camper for the night. He can't sleep in this house, where everything is in its place and the only part which hasn't had the life sucked out of it is my bedroom, an agreed no-go area for parents in which there is plenty of life, even if most of it may be growing on unwashed plates and old pizza boxes.

'He can stay with me in the van,' GD is saying. 'At least he won't feel unwanted there.'

They take no notice of me as I check out the fridge before helping myself to a bowl of Dad's All-Bran and sitting down at the kitchen table. 'This is not about the dog,' Dad's saying. 'And it's not about that blasted monstrosity you insist on parking in front of the house. It's time we talked about Mum.'

'Ruth is where she wants to be, and that's at home, with me,' GD says. 'I thought this was all settled. I'll bring her in for treatment but the hospital is not going to have her, Charlie.'

Dad has started to unload the dishwasher. He can't just talk and he can't just watch TV for that matter, he always has to be doing something else as well. God knows what he does while he has sex. Mental note: really must stop thinking about parents having sex. He's sorting cutlery into the drawer as he says, 'But, Dad, you must see that's not right?' (With GD being so young at heart and Dad so old before his time, it seems arse-about-face whenever Charles Johnson calls GD, Dad.) 'She needs a proper, supervised medical regimen, close observation, palliative care.'

'And waking every four hours for her obs and poked and prodded and talked about like she was just an interesting case? That's not what I want for my Ruth, Charlie, and it's not what you should want, either. And if you knew your mother like I do, you'd appreciate that.'

'But you can't keep her at home, you just can't,' Dad says. He runs himself a glass of water from the tap and peers out into the blackness of his garden. 'I don't think that you realise how very demanding her home care will become. You simply don't have the f-f-facilities or the skills to deal with what is going to happen.'

'We do, as it happens,' GD says. 'There's a nurse on tap, she'll be in and out and there's a tame doctor in the village. She'll have friends dropping by to see her. She'll have me. This is what Ruth wants, more than anything else. And this is what she will have.'

Dad waits for GD to calm down before he clears his throat and says, 'There's a very decent place I know about, set in lovely gardens, with a man-made lake she can sit beside. I have a little money put by and—'

'She's not going to die in a hospice either,' GD explodes. I haven't seen the normally peaceful GD angry before, but right now, he is furious. 'Ruth is not going to a Centre Parcs for the dying. She doesn't want a nicely packaged death, Charlie.'

Stop. Stop. Stop.

It's like a flash has gone off and everything freezes for an instant, Dad tightening the cord on his dressing gown, GD with the kettle in his hand. They know I've heard. Suddenly we've all stopped pretending. I know Nana's very ill and maybe I haven't thought she'd get much better, but no one has said out loud that she's going to die. It's been easier to imagine Nana and GD going on turning up here for Nana's hospital visits and Dad going on complaining about GD's camper van and the hundred other things that annoy him about his parents' chosen way of life. But now the truth is out and it's ugly as fuck. Nana the poet, Nana the person I've always gone to for wise words instead of the platitudes which Dad would trot out or the helpless looks and *best ask your father*s which was often all Mum could offer, is dying. Nana is going to die. It's like the floor has dropped away and beneath me is a bottomless abyss. And that's what it must be like for her, only a million times worse.

I know she's not religious, not in the sense the nuns at St Saviour's are religious. She doesn't go to church and I'm not sure she believes in God. I know she doesn't believe in a life after death, because she told me so once, when we walked past the churchyard in the village where people were gathered around a hole in the ground as they buried Mr Simpson, who had managed the post office. 'We're just brief flashes of light in the darkness,' Nana had said, and then she told me to shine brightly while I was here, whatever that meant. What can it be like for her, standing on the edge of that empty black hole knowing that any time soon she'll topple in and be falling, endlessly? And that pit will have no bottom, because death has no end, you die and you die and you die.

No one I have ever known has died. No one at school, none of my relatives. I'm only seventeen and though I sometimes panic about being struck by some terrible illness like those kids in the paper, the ones with bald heads who now go to Disneyworld instead of Lourdes, and though I know how dangerous and unpredictable modern life can be – people at bus stops mown down by lorries, the house fires and disasters at football matches, bombs on trains and aeroplanes falling out of the sky, I've always thought of death as something too vague and too distant to waste much time thinking about.

But now death is in my house. Nana is actually dying. When is she going to die? Does anyone know? Why wasn't I told about this sooner? Is she dying now, in the room above my head? I feel faint, cold and queasy. I have been looking at the last twigs of All-Bran in my bowl, like a fortune teller reading tea leaves and when I look up I see that GD has left the room, taking up Nana's hot drink, I suppose, and Dad is being all brisk and efficient, washing out the milk bottles and acting as if nothing has happened. The only telltale oddness about his behaviour is that when he puts out the bottles, he lets in Garcia and gives his coat a bit of a ruffle before settling him in his basket by the door. 'Well, Brian,' he says. 'Sunday tomorrow, big day in the garden, so I'll say goodnight!' And off he goes. I hear him checking the locks on the front door, unplugging the television and then mumbling something to someone, GD presumably, at the top of the stairs.

When GD appears in the kitchen and says Nana is asking for me, it is all I can do to get my arse off the chair. But I do and I tread softly upstairs and open her door. Sometimes Nana seems well, at other times she's not so good. After what I've just heard, I'm expecting her to look awful. But tonight, Nana's sitting up in bed looking at a bookmarked collection of poems, her night light throwing out a soft pink glow. The hot chocolate is on the bedside table, next to a framed photograph of herself and GD, which is so old that the people in it both have long, dark and shiny hair. She looks okay and I can't quite believe what I have just heard, that she really is dying.

'Is that you, Brian?' Nana finishes what she is reading before she turns to me and smiles. 'Have they been quarrelling again?'

'Yes.'

'I do wish they wouldn't. But they're each as pig-headed as the other. Neither of them wants to give an inch about anything. It's such a shame.'

I sit on the end of her bed and say, 'I wish Dad could be more like GD.'

There's a lengthy pause and I'm thinking that Nana has dozed off. But then she says, 'We all have to be true to ourselves, Brian.' She puts down her book and folds her spectacles. 'And if that's what your father is doing, then we must respect that.'

'Is that what he's doing?'

Nana sips her drink before she offers a reply.

'I think your father's shielding himself from what he sees as a threatening world. He's had his ups and downs, has our Charlie. Life has disappointed him. Frightened him too.'

'Frightened him?'

She won't let me help as she shakes up her pillow, settles back into it and turns to me.

'We've frightened him, Arty and me. We didn't mean to, of course, but ours was never the life for a strange little boy like Charlie was. We tried to bring him up the way we thought a boy should be brought up. We wanted him to question everything, to be happy and out-going, to live for the moment, not for some far-off day that never comes. But none of this was for Charlie and he began to retreat from us, to spend more time in his room doing his own things. It wasn't our idea he joined the boy scouts. You remember the way we lived at the cottage?'

Dawn strolls, music making, shrieks from bedrooms, anarchic disorder.

'I can't imagine Dad being there.'

'He wasn't, not in spirit. And the fault was ours, Brian. He didn't like the lack of restraint, he was frightened of our freedoms. I don't know what we could or should have done for your father. He didn't fit in and there was an end of it. He couldn't wait to leave home and he did, at the first opportunity.'

'That's terrible,' I say. 'I can't imagine you and GD being bad parents.'

'Irresponsible parents, that's what we were. Too intent on having fun, always thinking that our way was right and so Charlie must turn out right in the end.'

It's hard for me to envisage anyone not liking living with GD and Nana. I've spent as much time with them as I can and I know they've been a bigger influence in my life than my own parents.

'Is he happier now, do you think?' I say.

'With Violet and you, of course he is. And he's happy to have his garden, where he has complete control and is lord and master of all he rotovates.'

I have to laugh: it's so true. Nana smiles.

'Your father's done a better job with you than we did with him. So don't think any better of me than I deserve, Brian. Think of me as someone who had a lot of good intentions that she often buggered up.'

She's sounding like she's writing her own epitaph.

'Arty thinks I should have a word with you.'

'About what?'

'About me. He thinks he may have shocked you this evening. Wants me to talk to you about the pickle I'm in. I think you're old enough to talk about such things?'

I nod dumbly, because what can I say? I can't refuse her anything, now that I know.

'It's funny, you know,' she says, with a little chuckle. 'But once you know you're on your way to the check out, you can get taken much too seriously. It's like everything you say must contain a pearl of wisdom. GD has started treating me like an old, wise woman.'

'You are,' I say. 'Wise, I mean.'

'Wisdom is just common sense tempered by experience,' Nana says. 'And I'm no wiser and certainly no more sensible than when I was well. So don't start taking what I say as profound. Arty thinks we should have told you about my prognosis before this, but your father worried about how you would take it and to be honest, we thought there was more time.' She must have seen my face fall because then she says, 'But death is the most natural thing in the world, Brian, as natural as being born, as having your own babies, as growing older. People regard these events as beautiful, but if you saw a birth you'd probably think it was anything but beautiful. There's blood and tissue and you can't always control your own bodily functions and you scream and you swear. And then you can give birth to a corpse, a stillborn child. There's nothing beautiful about that, let me tell you. And yet people persist in the illusion that these are magical moments always to be treasured, whereas death is always ugly, always to be feared.'

'It's the survival instinct, isn't it?' I suggest, though I'm getting out of my depth here.

'That and the fear of the unknown and more besides. But death is no more to be feared than life. I'm sure that if we were to know every trial and discomfort that awaited us at the bright end of the alimentary canal, we would all stay put.'

Then she says, 'Come here, let me feel your forehead. You're not well, are you?'

I feel the irony. Nana is dying, she's just told me so and yet here she is, worried about the heavy cold I'm brewing. 'I'm fine,' I tell her, though I'm beginning to think in terms of a slow day tomorrow and maybe even throwing a sickie from school on Monday. Nana strokes my brow again.

'You're worried about something, Brian.'

'I'm worried about you, I say.

'Thank you, dear. But it's not that. Tell me?'

And when I've told her about Ros and how I want to share the only interest I know that Ros has, which is books, I ask Nana what I should read if I want to impress her. As someone who has taught English in colleges, I think she should be able to rattle off a handful of names for me to check out online without me having to actually read all the books themselves. But I'm not sure I want to do that after she says, 'Choose for yourself. Find books which mean something to you, personally.' Always a jump ahead of me, she adds, 'And read every page, Brian. Enjoy what you read. Understand what you read. Whether reading well is going to help you with the young lady I really couldn't say, but it'll help you, Brian.'

I want to ask how reading books will help me but now she's reaching for the light switch, saying she's in need of her beauty sleep. She looks tired too, and I am afraid that I have exhausted her. I bend down and kiss her lightly. 'Goodnight Brian,' she says softly, already three parts asleep. 'Look after your dad.'

High upon the monolithic edge of millstone grit which you can just about see if you stand on the bed I should be tucked up in now, and thirty feet above the shadowy shapes of giant boulders strewn in the bracken below, GD is about to tell me something important about my dad.

But I need to rewind twenty minutes or so: it's three in the morning and I'm being driven out of town, past stumbling drunks and clubbers fighting over taxis, by a long haired, 69-

year-old night owl in a psychedelically-painted Volkswagen camper van.

'I thought we might have a bit of a chat,' GD says, by way of an explanation.

All I can think about is my bed. We leave the last suburbs and head for the hills.

GD takes drives like these almost every night. Just when the traffic's died down and you're about to drop off, the old camper van will fart, belch and rattle off up the road, taking him no one knew where, up until now. Now I know: it's Nana's Rock, where we perch precariously, a crescent moon only faintly marking the edge of the precipice, with a few bright-eyed cars snaking along the road in the valley bottom, and a startling heaven above. It's cool, I mean in the sense of being cold, but GD doesn't seem to notice the temperature, as he sits cross-legged on the stone, fiddling with something in his lap.

On the way here GD has been talking about Garcia, who clearly has hidden talents, over and above his proven ability to shit in a shoe cupboard. However, I find it hard to believe that he fronted a legendary rock band, along with its various offshoots, for nearly thirty years (I didn't think collies lived that long) and when I hear about the prodigious amounts of acid he is reputed to have taken, I have to wonder if we are talking about the same dog.

According to GD, Garcia can play a number of instruments and his favoured genres are country, folk, jazz, bluegrass, space rock and whatever can be broken down into a freeform jam lasting anything up to an hour. But well before GD has finished speaking, I've worked out that it's not Garcia the collie we're talking about, but Jerry Garcia, lead singer of the Grateful Dead, GD's number one passion – after Nana.

But now, sitting on this great rock in the cool night air, GD's got something else on his mind. He fumbles in his lap again and a match flares, his face blossoming from the gloom. After inhaling noisily, he passes me a spliff. It's an old-school five-skin filled, I discover, with some very excellent old-school dope. I'm blazing with my grandfather, I think – this is so random. But GD isn't your average grandfather. To hear him speak, it's like listening to every adman's ideal grandfather, a kindly, Northern voice with the faintest of lisps. You'd sooner imagine him sucking on a Werther's Original than a fat old dooby.

'I want to talk to you about your dad,' he says at last.

I can't imagine what he can have to say about my dad that I don't already know, but when GD says, 'It's something important,' I give him my complete attention.

'When your father, Charlie, was six years old, he was in the back seat of a car that was involved in an accident. A bad one. Some fellow in a lorry had fallen asleep at the wheel and smashed into the car Charlie was riding in. His parents were both killed, instantly.'

'His parents? But you and Nana…'

'Wait and I'll tell you. The shock of losing both of his parents traumatized the boy and he lost his memory, not only of the event itself but also of the life he had lived, right up to that point. Even now Charlie's got no memory of his early years, none whatsoever. He certainly has no idea that Ruth and I aren't his natural parents.'

This isn't my dad, it can't be, I'm thinking, and yet—

'A couple of years before that, Ruth had found out that she couldn't have children. She got pregnant all right, but then the foetus was stillborn and they said it would be very dangerous to try again. And that was that, for a while. Then some friends of ours adopted a child and it seemed to be working out so well we thought we'd have a crack at it too. It was a right old palaver, I'm telling you, but the worst bit was making a choice. That was heartbreaking. There was this one kid no one ever considered because of his amnesia. It made him an oddity, a bit of a freak. But Ruth and I talked it over and we thought he might be all right with us.'

I'm making a thousand mental adjustments to my long-held picture of my dad. And then comes the massive aftershock as I realise that GD and Nana, my life's anchors, aren't really my grandparents. It must be a mistake, I'm thinking, surely GD has it wrong? I'm starting to panic. I'm feeling like I just got cut loose from everything and if someone doesn't hold me down I could float away into the cold black night. It's dreadful – but then I feel GD's big hand grasping my shoulder, squeezing hard. 'It's okay,' he's saying, 'nothing has changed, nothing at all,' and I'm no longer the smart-arsed teenager old enough to smoke weed and chase girls. I'm just a kid who needs a whole world of reassurance and I throw myself into GD's open arms and hold him as tightly as I can and hope he doesn't notice that I'm bawling my eyes out. And now, my face buried in the warm, wet wool, I can't help wondering if my real grandparents, whoever they were, could ever have been half so good to me as GD and Nana have been.

When I have got myself together and have pushed him away like it was all a joke or something, GD waits for the right moment to tell me more. 'We tried to bring him up as we saw fit,' he says. 'His name had been Graham when he was with his parents, but we thought a clean break with the past would be best and so I called him Charlie – after Cosmic Charlie, the song.'

'By the Grateful Dead?' I ask. Already, he has me smiling again.

'Naturally.'

'He's always loathed being called Charlie. He uses Charles.'

'Charlie doesn't know how lucky he was. My first choice was China Cat Sunflower, but Ruth made her displeasure known, as they say.'

I'm still smiling. GD is such good medicine.

GD gets up slowly and dusts himself off. The far side of the valley is edged with light as we start to retrace out steps, down the sandy track to the van.

'We knew raising him wouldn't be easy, they had told us that much,' GD is saying. 'But we didn't think it would be quite as hard as it was. There was too much ingrained of his past life. He wasn't conscious of any of it but it was still there, this life which was at total variance with our own. It confused him, frightened him. He was unable to adjust.'

'I still can't see anyone having an unhappy childhood with you and Nana,' I say.

'Not unhappy, as such. There were times when it looked like he was going to fit in and it was all going to turn out fine and these times were like bursts of sunshine on a cloudy day. But Charlie seemed to sense there was something missing, something not right. You don't grow up with no knowledge of the first six years of your life without doing a lot of thinking and coming to all kinds of wrong conclusions.'

'Then why didn't you tell him he was adopted?'

'How do you tell a child he's not yours after spending every day of every year trying to convince him that he is? To have told him that would have robbed him of what security he has. Once he was grown there seemed no point in brewing up another lot of trouble, let sleeping dogs lie, we thought. But now that Ruth is—'

'It's all right,' I say, quickly. 'Nana's told me all about it.'

'Has she? Well, that's as well, I think. No more secrets. This just makes it all the more necessary that your father knows the truth. He needs to know that as much as we love him as a son, he's not ours. He needs to know that he hasn't failed us by being unable to go along with our ways. And I think he needs to hear it from someone he loves and trusts. Nana and me have talked it over and—'

I think I know what's coming.

'—we want you to tell him. Not now. Maybe not even soon. But when the time is right.'

'Wouldn't it be better coming from Mum?' I say, weakly.

'I think that right now, this could be as shocking for her as it will be for him. She's going to find out that the husband she's known so long isn't the man she thought he was.'

'And I have to break the news?' As if there might be some other way.

He puts a heavy arm around my shoulder. 'You're the man for this job, Brian. You know that there are some ties that are stronger than blood.'

Nothing has changed, he's saying. I can at least do this for him and for Nana, of course.

'I'll help you in any way I can,' I promise. 'But how will I know when the time's right to tell him?'

'You're a bright lad, Brian. You'll know.'

GD opens the door for me and I climb into the camper van, which smells of damp leather and stale smoke. As he starts the car, the new sun is showing golden over the distant crags. GD fumbles beneath his big arse and pulls out a cassette case, which he opens with one hand and slips the tape into the player.

'Attics of My Life,' he says, sounding tired, but content. 'Finest thing ever committed to hot wax.'

I look at the image on the plastic box. It's the Grateful Dead's *American Beauty* but in this light, the hippie lettering spells out Reality as well.

'You like this band a lot, don't you?' I say.

GD chuckles and taps his old fingers on the wheel.

'You think GD stands for Granddad?'

I do, actually.

Chapter 8

You Can't Always Get What You Want

According to my phone, it's 2.30 in the afternoon when I wake and I'm not feeling my best. It's a real effort to go for a pee, change my mind, sit down, take a dump and drag myself back to my foul-smelling room. What did I do in here last night? It smells like the venue for a national farting contest. I collapse back onto the bed and pull up the covers. My head is throbbing like a porn star's dick and I ache all over.

Mum has heard me lumbering around and pops in to see if I'm okay. I'm not, obviously, and the two paracetamol she gives me aren't going to help much. Nor does the news that Roger Dyson has been calling up all morning; I'd know what it was about, he'd said. 'At least you've got dressed,' Mum says cheerily. Then she opens the windows, 'to let in some light.'

I need rest and lots of it, but it appears that I'm still wearing yesterday's clothes. I pull off a sweat- soaked tee shirt and kick off my jeans. I'm surprised, under the circumstances, to find I have a hard on requiring my urgent attention. I lie on sweaty, damp sheets and think about Ros doing the sort of things Ros probably wouldn't do outside her regular contracted roles in my fantasies. I'm running on my reserve energy tank, trying to bring our latest shagfest to an eruptive conclusion, when I'm ambushed by a horrible thought, a boorish gatecrasher barging in to announce that Nana is dying. I pause for a moment, but only for a moment – life goes on even in the midst of death, I argue – and Ros, wearing a pair of liquorice and blackcurrant knickers and nothing else, once more bends over my bed, her full lips parting in a perfect "O".

But it's no good. I lie back, exhausted and stare at the picture of Katie Melhua pinned to the ceiling. I wonder if all it's a waste of time anyway, this fantasising about what I'd do if Ros and I hooked up. I lift the sheet and look down, wondering what she would make of such a pathetic specimen. Admittedly, the only real life cocks I've been able to compare it with have been those I've seen in the showers at school and that was a while back, when we were all in developmental stages, genitally speaking. And now the shower block has been rebuilt and we all get private shower stalls I have no way of measuring just how far short I fall of the average dimensions. All I have to compare it with are the cocks I see on the internet porn we all watch.

All the guys in porn have cocks like fire-hoses and clearly get enough action to look thoroughly bored with the proceedings. The girls look bored, too. A big cock is nothing new for them, it's what they expect. They'd probably think mine was some kind of mutated wart. I've no way of knowing whether some of the biggest specimens, the ones which look like a sheep's heart mounted on a Pringles tube, are freaks of nature or not. It's going to be a terrible life if what they've got turn out to be bog-standard todgers.

But, the hopefully, non-representative world of porn apart, what other references do I have? The postcards of Michelangelo's David on Clive's bedroom wall are reassuring – such a big man, such a small cock – but except for those and photographs of naked tribesmen in Dad's *National Geographics*, there hasn't been much else to go on. The internet will show you very big and extremely small, but who wants to see pictures of Mr Average? There is, of course, Biggleow's Chart, but how much stock you should accord the graphic scrawls of a schoolboy sex-fiend is highly debatable.

Biggleow's Chart is a standard reference for boys at St Saviour's. This venerable document, the prototype etched on the inside of a box-file lid, has been handed down, copied and improved upon by successive generations since it was first conceived and drawn up, in (carbon-dating suggests) AD 1983.

The original, which is treated with similar reverence to the Turin Shroud, is kept under lock and key by whichever boy is nominated to be this year's Holder of the Chart (actually, I just made that bit up, but it gives an accurate idea of its holiness). But if you aren't a recent alumni of St Saviour's, you'll just be wondering what this thing actually is. Quite simply, Biggleow's Chart is the graphic representation of every shape and size of cock, if not known to man, then to a one-time student at St Saviour's, and now the youngish and thrusting, up and coming, Tory MP for Sheffield South Central, Martin Biggleow.

Before embarking on his master work, Martin had done a lot of useful preparatory work, mostly executed on the back of Trap 3's door in the boys' toilets. Here can still be found examples of his finest penmanship, flying cocks that even the most accomplished of flying cock draughtsmen would have to concede the quality of. That this defaced piece of school property has never been repainted is tacit acknowledgement of the sheer excellence of the work, I think. Boldly inked and carefully crosshatched on a series of door panels are fantastically-detailed flying cocks which aren't just cocks with feathery wings in a featureless sky, but fully-armed fighter cocks, shown engaged in aerial conflict. Plucky British cocks, sporting the familiar RAF roundels, fire off streams of globular tracer at swarms of invading German dicks (*Fliegendikken*, the legend reads), while vast, lumbering flights of heavily-loaded bomber-cocks crowd the skies as they take the war to the Hun. Particularly fetching is a flight of Spitcocks with testicular wheels awaiting their scantily-dressed female pilots, who are scrambling across the field, eager to bestride their purple-nosed aircraft.

Biggleow's cocks featured detail on a Leonardo scale, some anatomically correct, much invented, but all superior to the humorous pictures of men wheeling gargantuan examples in wheelbarrows that Uncle Michael had once slipped from his briefcase to show me. With Biggleow's chart, a cock can be compared with an illustrated example and awarded a proper species name, compared to others in shape and size and given its proper place in, and I think I have the correct word here, the taxonomy of cocks. I'm not sure I remember all the gradations, as you can never find Biggleow's chart when you need it – some chode is always using it to make scientific measurements and comparisons of his own and "forgets" to return it to its proper place.

And chode is good a place to kick off, this being a cock which is actually bigger in girth than it is in length. Other featured types included on the list are the Tom's Thumb, explained as being little larger than the teat of a baby's dummy, the Asparagus (thin, with a spear-like tip), the Angry Python (long and thick) and the Billy Club (like a baby's arm with clenched fist). Under this are some impressively realistic depictions of a rather veiny, bulbous member at various angles of erection with each stage properly labelled, from the standard semi up to the full *Seig Heil*! But much as I appreciate the ingenuity and artistry of Martin Biggleow's work, I can't really say that it has helped me to see where my own cock stands in the scheme of things.

I'm hot, my whole body aches and despite sleeping soundly for several hours, I'm still incredibly tired. I need to sleep some more but it's like I'm in a greenhouse in the middle of a heat wave and I can't stop thinking, my mind going round in dizzying circles as I think about Ros and whether I will ever get anywhere near her – she can get someone better than me, she can get someone bigger than me – and about what I would do, what I could do, if I had a big cock, and I'm thinking about Roger and Clive and Clive and Roger and Diesel and Lauren and the car which looks stupid and needs more work. I'm thinking about Nana down the hall and about the man who turned into an insect in a story I read. And I'm thinking about Dad not knowing that Nana and GD aren't his parents and how I will tell him and what Mum will make of all this, after thinking she knew him inside out. I'm thinking about the girls in the Casablanca, who are laughing again, laughing at us, laughing at me especially, as I sink into my pillow, my whole hot body sinking deeper into the bed, a bed which has no bottom, a bed through which I'm falling, falling…

Oh. My. God.

I keep still. Very still.

But I can't help twitching and that's when I feel it again, halfway down my right thigh.

There is something in the bed with me. Something alive.

I don't want to move in case it stings or bites me. A scratch from a sharp talon could be nasty, too. As I slept naked last night, I'm feeling doubly vulnerable.

My heart is racing and I'm trying my hardest to control my breathing in case I disturb whatever is down there beneath the sheets and cause it to bite or sting or scratch. In my loudest whisper, I call out, Mum! But there's no answer. My phone is in my jeans, which are on the floor by the door, and I can't reach them. Not without disturbing it.

I decide to give it another minute by my bedside clock and if it hasn't moved in that time, I'm going to take a look under the sheets. The minute passes ponderously but I'm encouraged by the lack of any movements, sudden or otherwise, down below. No fangs piercing my scrotum, no panicked animal trying to tear its way out of the predicament it has found itself in. Perhaps it is sleeping, I think. By the forty-five second mark, there has still been no action, no rippling in the bedclothes, no squeal of something frightened and therefore dangerous. In fact, I'm beginning to wonder if whatever it is, might be dead, suffocated by my heavy duvet or my noxious farts.

It's time to take a look. With all the delicacy of a bomb disposal team dismantling an IED, I lift a corner of my Stig duvet and peer cautiously into the foetid gloom.

Which is when I get the kind of shock normally set aside for people carrying TV aerials in electrical storms.

I don't believe it, not at first, or at second, either. I rub my eyes and look again. It can't be right, it's not possible, it must be a trick of the light. I drop Stig and stare upwards at Katie Melhua, who's wearing a blue blouse and a beatific smile and seems to be mouthing, 'It's true, Brian, look again, it's true!' I look again and, fuck me, it is true. I throw back Stig in his entirety and haul myself up on my elbows to better look down on what must be the biggest, fattest penis I have seen outside of some truly atrocious porn I once downloaded. There, with the dimensions of a chip shop's family-sized serving of saveloy and two scotch eggs, is my genitalia, now miraculously enhanced. And how! It is fucking enormous. Thank you, thank you, God, Jesus and Katie Melhua – or whoever else was responsible for this.

Thank you!

But that aforementioned trinity aside, I don't know how this can possibly have happened, whether such freakish growth spurts are known to medical science, or whether they might even be common. I just know that I've never heard of such a thing myself and I'm having difficulty accepting the evidence of my own eyes. Perhaps it is a proper miracle, one just for me. I prayed an awful lot and extremely hard, for just this result. How soon do you get an answer to your prayers, anyway? God must get billions of prayers every day and half of them are probably just spam, so maybe he's only just got around to answering mine. It's possible. If what's happened to me today is possible, then anything is.

I extend a hand towards my new penis, tentatively is the adverb I want. I'm still not sure that this big, fleshy thing actually belongs to me. I flash the thought that I got extremely drunk last night and ended up in bed with a man, that he's lying beneath me now and that these are his bits poking up between my legs. But no, it's just my own malodorous mattress beneath me, I'm sure. My hand approaches its object like a zookeeper about to pick up a highly venomous snake. I would only be half-surprised if it didn't suddenly rear up and sink a pair of fangs into me. There is more hair too, a regular rain forest going on down there, which will have to be negotiated before I have got to grips with the problem, so to speak.

But I am soon able to confirm that it is indeed attached to me and that I can feel no evidence of recent surgery. I pick it up and it's heavy in my hands – way heavy! I wonder if it'd be possible to weigh it with the scales my Uncle Michael uses when he goes fishing? After admiring it and guesstimating its length and girth, I flop it from side to side, letting the bulbous end thwack against both thighs. Sweet as! My testicles, I decide, look less like scotch eggs and more like a pair of pocketed snooker balls.

'Oh, fuck!' I say. 'Fuckity fuckity fuck!' (Though if I am ever celebrated as a medical original, I'll remember saying something much more profound.) I sit on the bed (it droops over the edge!) and then stand in front of the mirror on my wardrobe, legs apart, arms folded, impressive new cock a-dangle. Oh, yes, no doubt about it, that is big. That boy is hung. I move my hips and it swings from right to left and back again. I do it again and then, with a forward thrust of the hips, I'm able to set it swinging front to back, flapping against my stomach, smacking against my arse. This amuses me for a while, as does striking a series of poses before the glass. I offer my new-found friend to Katie, Pixie, Jessica and others whose images have pride of place on my walls and ceiling.

I still have no idea how this has happened. Nothing suggests itself as a reason why I should wake up with a ma-hoos-ively big cock – not even the principles of natural justice. I have an indistinct memory of returning to Foo Q's quite recently and run that tape. I see myself entering the shop and hear myself saying, 'This is all very rum.' (Which is odd in itself, as I have never in my life said anything is 'all very rum'. A bit fucked up, yes, but rum, never). It's rum because when previously I was there, Mr Foo hadn't appeared out of a cloud of smoke, for instance and I'm fairly sure his accent was broad Yorkshire, rather than stage-Chinese.

However, I let such details go as I follow him into the room marked Private and sit before him as he fumbles with something in his lap. *Many are the mysteries of the mysterious East,* he alliterates. *And sundry are the searchers seeking enlightenment,* I find myself replying. Mr Foo nods and crushes various curious items in a stone mortar with a thick, pink pestle before handing me a sacred wrap. No payment is required, he tells me. I ask only that you use this gift with wisdom. To abuse the gift will bring a plague upon your house. I'll make a note of that, I say, as Mr Foo rolls back his eyes and disappears into his cloud of smoke.

As I start to dress, I begin to think that this strange episode might indeed be connected with my new and amazingly improved manhood. But questions can come later, there are other pressing matters to consider now, such as whether my pants will stretch to accommodate such a serpentine beast? I consider going commando, but I can see immediately that creating a really good packet to be admired by all depends on the wearing of a pair of pants. It's all a matter of support. I select my lucky black briefs, which have never actually been lucky for me up to now (though all that is surely set to change very soon) and slip them on, coiling my new appendage into them. I pull on my jeans but then I can't resist doing something I've always found amusing in pictures, which is to liberate my cock from my flies, pull my pockets inside out and perch a pair of sunglasses on the top of my penis, so that it now looks like the trunk of a very cool pink elephant, with an afro.

And then I'm walking down the high street, no, strutting is the better word, and meeting every glance with a cocky grin that says yes, get over it, I've got a big one. My sense of balance is affected: it feels like I'm wearing a heavily-filled bumbag or a front bustle. I also find myself in the grip of an exhibitionist urge I've never had before. What's the point of having the goods, I'm thinking, if you can't put them on display? But it's hard to see how I can advertise my wares without becoming an all-out flasher and I don't know where you can get a dirty old raincoat these days – not since Oxfam went upmarket, anyway. I think about all kinds of new possibilities which have suddenly opened up for me: I might become a model for men's underwear, Homme or someone like that. I rather fancy seeing myself and the bulge adorning a massive billboard. This pleasant thought lasts as long as it takes me to realise it's not all a matter of bulge. It's also bronzed skin and flat stomach, a six-pack too, usually. And though I've got the packet, I haven't so much got a six-pack as a party seven.

Or maybe I could become a male stripper. How hard would that be? The equipment is cheap and probably tax-deductible. All I'd need would be a few cans of whipped cream and a capacious thong. But dangling my bits in front of sex-starved hen parties sounds dangerously like throwing a sausage to a pack of hungry dogs. Or I could be a life model in an art lesson; that sounds much classier. I could be Rodin's Thinker. (No chance of being Michelangelo's David now!) But having a lot of arty girls who will probably look a bit like Ros staring at my penis, could easily have unexpected results. And do I really want blokes with beards taking a studied interest in my tackle? Maybe I should just find a public place and streak, like they did in the seventies. At Wimbledon, possibly: I could leap the net on Centre Court and be escorted off with a policeman's helmet covering my bits and appear in all the papers the next day. But there's the cost of a Centre Court ticket these days and besides, I'd probably end up with Andy Murray's racket up my arse – he looks a bit handy, for a tennis player.

As I near the Casablanca, I realise that no one has actually given me a second look. There have been no furtive glances at my prominent package, no eyes popping or tongues lolling, even though I spent over five minutes at Tesco's big plate-glass windows pretending to read the special offers while waiting for the checkout girls to turn and check me out, which they didn't. Now I'm hoping the girls who sit in the corner will be at the cafe today, the two dumpy blondes, the cute little one with red hair and big tits and Carole, I think she's called, who has the dirty laugh and shows her thong whenever she reaches across the table. Perhaps they'll check me out when I walk in: *Hey, big boy* (that'll be Carole), *what are you packing?* And I'll tell them I could show them but I'm like a Gurkha who never unsheathes his weapon without using it, at which they'll shriek with laughter, and then ask me what a Gurkha is.

But the only person in the Casablanca today is Faruk's sister Deniz, who is sitting at a table by the counter, having a fag beneath the No Smoking sign. She looks up from her copy of *Chat* long enough to mutter 'All right, Brian?' And though I'm standing there right in front of her, on the pretext of asking her if she's seen Faruk, she isn't giving my big new packet a second look. From where I'm standing, I can see right down her low cut top and I'm sure I can feel stirrings down below, but when Deniz looks up again, it's just to say, tetchily, 'Are you still here?'

The rest of the day is no better. I go down the leisure centre, ostensibly for a swim but really to try out an old pair of Speedos which I bought rashly one summer, wore once and never wore again. But now, seeing my reflection in the mirror in the changing room, I have to say, I'm well pleased. But not as pleased as a middle-aged bloke who sidles up to me, squeezes my bicep and says I'm a very big boy for my age, aren't I?

Then I run into Diesel with Faruk at Faruk's brother's garage, but they're more interested in seeing the new carburettor installed in the Green Dragon than life-changing enhancements to their best mate's physique. Clive checks me out as I pass his dad's yard but he always does, bless him, and he doesn't seem to

see anything out of the ordinary. Maybe if I jogged across town
with my dick hanging out of my jeans I might get some attention.
If I got arrested, it would at least mean someone had bothered to
take notice. This is not at all how I imagined the world of big
dick.

Then it gets worse. I arrive home to find that Mum is holding
one of her teas for the Church Roof Funding Committee. Mum's
a member, but only because she finds it impossible to turn down
a request from anyone wearing his collar back to front. The
geriatric committee takes turns to hold teas at each other's
homes, both domestic and institutional, where they talk about –
well, you can work it out for yourself. Today Father Patrick, in his
familiar threadbare tweed jacket and equally threadbare bonce, is
sitting at the head of our dining table, where four very elderly
ladies are gathered, awaiting starter's orders to devour a plate of
French fancies and a Battenberg cake. Iris Alsop and Minnie
Middleton, who used to play tuba and cornet respectively in the
Salvation Army brass band – you've probably paid them to fuck
off at Christmas – are shaking their heads and tut-tutting about
something.

Father Patrick is passing cups of tea down the table and saying
that it, whatever it is today, is a very sorry state of affairs indeed.
Aggie Sharpe, who volunteers in Oxfam and has put on some airs
and graces since, as I mentioned, it went upmarket, says that they
– whoever they are today – want punishing the way her generation was punished, when she was a girl. There's much nodding
of grey and blue-rinsed heads and rattling of beads and bones,
and teaspoons in Mum's best china. It's only taken me a moment
to see all this and I'm ducking out in favour of my room and my
Xbox when Aggie Sharpe says, 'Can you spare us a moment,
Brian? We need a young person's opinion.'

'I've got a ton of homework to do,' I lie. 'I've got my exams
soon.'

'Fiddlesticks!' Aggie says. 'This won't take a moment. Come

and sit by me, dearie.'

'Yes, Master Johnson, do take a pew,' Father Patrick says, smiling at his little witticism as he jerks out the spare chair between himself and Ancient Aggie. The others eye the cakes hungrily and wave me to my seat. I flash Mum a 'do I have to?' glance, but she just gives me a sympathetic smile and I know I'm stuck here for the duration.

'We're talking about the dreadful blight of vandalism that's hit the neighbourhood,' Father Patrick tells me.

'Terrible, terrible,' Iris and Minnie say together.

'It's not nice,' says Doris Binder, who's learning to live with dementia. 'Is it?'

'It is a plague on our house,' Father Patrick says, which sounds familiar to me, somehow.

'It's sheer, wanton destruction,' Aggie says. She has a face like Satan's scrotum, I notice.

'The devil,' says Father Patrick, seeming to pick up on my thought, 'has found work for idle hands.'

'What vandalism is that, exactly?' I ask. I'd be quite interested to know. There aren't any more phone boxes to trash and the Eccleshall estate looks like it's been trashed already. Anything being broken in Laurel Gardens would be fixed before a vandal had finished breaking it.

'Those horrible daubings on the bus shelter,' Iris says.

'Terrible, terrible.'

'It's the writing on the wall,' Doris says, tapping her nose.

'And in the gentlemen's toilets by the bus station,' Father Patrick says.

'And on the side wall of Trollope's the bookshop,' Iris says.

'I think that's a mural,' Mum says. 'I think that's art.'

'And the words they use!' Minnie says. 'I was shocked, shocked!'

'It's the young generation,' Father Patrick says. 'When they have too much time they are but tools in the hands of Satan.'

'They want tools in their hands,' Aggie says, conjuring up an entirely inappropriate image. 'Apprenticeships, that's what they want. That'd keep them off the street corners.'

'Bring back National Service,' says Minnie.

'And hanging,' Iris says.

'That's right, some of them should be hung,' agrees Minnie.

Some of them are, I can't help thinking.

'And what does our own young man say?' asks Father Patrick.

But I'm too busy trying to remember which were our graffs and which were the work of chodes from the estate. About the time Banksy started making money from drawing on other people's property, we Four Horsemen started to develop our own interest in street art. Well, actually, I don't think any of us could claim to have elevated what we did to that status, but we all felt that when we went out with our spray cans and our stencils and tagged something, that we were making a statement of some kind. Mostly, the statement had to do with being bored and too lazy to think of something more constructive to do, but, hey, it rocked while it lasted.

What makes me sure that the Committee is talking about the work of rivals is that we never had the bottle to do our graffing anywhere very public. Our work, which generally was executed on a small scale anyway, can be found on the underside of bridges and culverts, on walls in obscure alleys and on the backs of some forgotten sheds in a corner of the park. The other thing that assures me I'm on safe ground is the spelling. I know the bus shelter graff and the one in the toilets too, though I only go there in emergencies, as it's a bit notorious. Both of these very basic apprentice pieces have omitted the "k" in the word "knob". Because of an elemental error worthy of Clive, Jack D is a nob just looks like someone whinging about Jack D's social status, while Jack D likes Nob End might conceivably be saying that the same person takes an interest in the Nob End lock system on the Manchester, Bolton and Bury canal. (Seriously, that's what it's called, as you'd know if you had Googled as many dirty words and phrases as Diesel and I did one afternoon.)

'Brian?' someone interrupts. 'Are you listening?'

'We were just saying that young people seem to lack a purpose these days,' Father Patrick tells me.

'They need a taste of what we got when we were naughty,' Minnie says.

'We were spanked,' Iris Alsop says. 'Soundly.'

'My father used to take his belt to me,' Minnie says.

'And teachers weren't afraid to use the cane.'

'Six of the best,' Father Patrick says. 'Never hurt anyone.'

'What do you think, Brian?' Mum says.

It's time for my expert witness look. If I wore glasses, now is the time I would take them off and polish them. 'I think we have to be aware of the widely varying socio-economic backgrounds these young people spring from,' I say. 'And of how certain environments will inevitably produce an underclass who feel very much alienated from mainstream society and who can make their plight known to the rest of us only by resorting to what we mistakenly interpret as meaningless acts of violence and destruction.'

Well, this is the sort of thing I would have said if they'd given me a little more time to prepare.

As it is, I have to make do with, 'I dunno, it's all so random.'

This earns me a round of uncertain looks and maybe the flicker of a smile from Mum, who goes off to the kitchen, saying something about a Viennetta in the freezer. Thinking I've offered a solid contribution here, I try to rise, but Aggie sinks her bony fingers into my thigh and says, 'You stay where you are, young man.' And so I sit there, bored out of my tree as they rattle on about young people today, how it was in their day, what cats won't eat and whatever's become of someone called Paul Daniels. Fuck all about the church roof, you notice. And my mind begins to wander, as it will always do under such circumstances.

Once my neighbour's claws have released my thigh in favour of another cup of tea, I'm looking around the table at these envoys from another time and I'm trying to imagine what each of them might have been like at my age. Hard to unwrinkle that skin, re-colour the hair, add a few more marbles in Doris's case and a couple of inches in stature in Minnie's, and reinvent them as real people who must once have been objects of desire and about whom the blokes of their generation must actually have fantasised. It is an appalling thought, but no matter, I've had worse. I wonder which of them would have been the fit one? If I had to say, and I'm bored enough to accept my own challenge, I'd say it was Iris. I bet she was a fox back in the day, in her nylons and suspenders, the naughty little minx.

And what about Aggie? I steal a glance at Aggie's craggy profile. She does have a little sparkle left in her eye – actually, now I look closely, it's only the left one, which looks like it's glass anyway – but her legs aren't too bad, from a non-medical perspective, anyway, and of course she wouldn't always have had the zimmer. Doris is three parts bonkers and her cheeks look like they've been rouged by a drunken mortician but even she must once have had something to trouble the trousers of whoever used to slip her the sausage. Thinking of that, I have a funny, familiar feeling which seems somehow wrong and which I can't quite identify.

I dismiss the thought that there might be trouble in my own trousers – impossible under the circs – and try to pay attention to the conversation, which now seems to be cribbed entirely from naughty postcards. I've not had any for years. My Dick was big. You need something wet and warm inside you. My pussy hates getting wet. And in my mind, I'm putting each of these volatile phrases into the scarlet-lipsticked mouths of the past lives I've created for each of the girls at the table: Aggie the slim, haughty babe who fucked more Spitfire pilots than the Luftwaffe; Doris the busty blonde with the big arse who gave knee tremblers in the black-out; Iris the voluptuous brunette who went like a train after a couple of port and lemons; and Minnie, the hot little redhead who was always being slipped a little extra meat by the butcher. I stop suddenly, a cold, clammy horror creeping through me: I'm not mistaken, there is something going on in my pants. Against every natural law, I am getting a hard-on, and a big one at that. This is so wrong. I try desperately to divert my train of thought into the sidings. 'I see they are getting on with the new church roof,' I say.

'Yes,' says Iris. 'But it's costing a huge packet.'

It hears *huge packet* and immediately puts on another couple of inches. I look down and I can see the bulge in my jeans growing and twitching violently. If you've ever seen a snake struggling in a muslin bag, you'll have an idea of what I'm dealing with here. I sit at the table trying to summon as many cock-shrivelling thoughts as I can but not even the image of a naked Margaret Thatcher pole dancing or Mum and Dad shagging in my bed has the slightest effect. The monster keeps on growing. It's bigger than it was this morning, it's bigger than it's been all day. When I woke and discovered my new, improved length, I thought that was it: I'd no idea it was just my starter for ten. And now it's not only bigger and thicker, it's fully erect and about as flexible as an iron bollard. Unless I ease down my zipper, it's going to burst out of my jeans like the Incredible Hulk from his shirt.

I decide to get up and clear out the room as fast as I can. As I stand, I try to cover my embarrassment with my hands, but they just aren't big enough for the job and now it looks like I'm trying to hold it. And anyway, the minute I rise, they've all seen it. Minnie's glasses fall off her nose but she rams them back in an instant while Doris licks her lips like a famished wolverine and I can feel Aggie's claw again, though this time it's not on my thigh. 'Oh, my dear God,' Father Patrick says, as Iris mounts her zimmer and starts to shuffle around the table towards me. There's nothing for me to do now but to run for the door and the safety of the hall. They're like Daleks – they can't follow me up stairs. I prise Aggie's claws from my voluminous bulge and push past Minnie and Doris and make for open floor. But now it's like the room has suddenly expanded and the door is hundreds of metres away and behind me are the zimmer frames, rattling like Triffids on the attack and a glance over my shoulder confirms that the women are closing in fast. It looks like a scene they cut from Day of the Dead because it was way too scary and now the cry goes up, 'Get him, girls!'

I don't stand a chance. I hadn't noticed my bed had been brought downstairs but there it is, in the middle of the room and Aggie is throwing me down upon it, a slice of Battenberg doing for her what a can of spinach does for Popeye. Like sex-starved succubi, they rip off my clothes until I lie there naked and vulnerable, with that awful thing sticking straight up between my legs like a fleshy belisha beacon, flashing pink and purple as she works the foreskin up and down. Then I hear ominous splashes, the sounds of a succession of objects being dropped into water. Straining to look up, I see a row of wine glasses sitting on the sideboard, each containing a set of false teeth. Father Patrick is removing his own now, as Minnie, Doris, Aggie and Iris, dressed only in bright red bloomers, their withered tits pointing south, stand at each corner of the bed, grasping an arm or a leg so tightly that it hurts. Father Patrick is taking off his shabby jacket and undoing his dog collar. Doris, dribbling from a corner of her puckered mouth, makes a sudden grab for my cock but Father Patrick shoves her back, much too roughly. 'Not so fast, lady,' he growls. 'Wait your fucking turn.'

He turns to give me a sickly smile. Then he looks up and down my helpless, prostrate body and his eyes, fixing upon my cock, light up, they really do: bright pink and blood red. For what I am about to receive, he says, as he cranes over my helpless body, his cracked, thin lips opening wider, and then wider still…

I open my eyes suddenly to find that Mum has hold of one of my arms and Dad has the other. 'He's awake!' Mum says, as she and Dad let go of my limbs, which she says were flailing about all over the place. My eyes are sticky, I feel like I'm floating on a leaky waterbed and my mouth tastes like I've been chewing on sandpaper.

'Looked like you were f-f-fighting with a monster, old son,' Dad says, as he pours something cold into a glass.

I take a sip of chilled lemonade while Mum shakes a thermometer before popping it under my tongue.

'A monster!' Dad says again and reflexively I jerk up my knees, hoping to disguise that monstrous erection.

Oddly, there's no sign on their faces that they've just discovered that their son has suddenly grown the biggest, thickest and most ungovernable penis known to man. With my knees up, Mum can't see the movement of my hand which is making exploratory moves beneath the sheets. I'm expecting to find it coiled up on its two big pink cushions, sleeping like a well-fed anaconda, but my fingers find no sign of it at first. I wonder if it has taken itself off hunting somewhere. Then I do find it, well, not it as such, but the cock I had known and worried about for so long, the cock I had thought was so abnormal but now feels reassuringly normal, if still very much on the small side. Dad wipes my forehead with a cold, wet flannel. 'We were worried about you, old son,' he says. 'That was a high old f-f-fever you were running.'

A fever?

'But he's all right now,' Mum says after she's read the thermometer. 'The doctor says you can get up in a day or two, but St Saviour's won't want you back just yet. Not if you've just had a nasty strain of the flu.'

Flu?

Thank God.

I have a long cold drink and I go straight back to sleep and this time, there are no more dreams.

CHAPTER 9

Stuck in the Middle With You

'It's fucked.'

Some sheep have ambled across the meadow to see us.

'How do you know it's fucked?'

They huddle in the corner of the dry stone wall and watch us.

'I can see it's fucked.'

On the ridge high above, ramblers in bright jackets are looking at us through binoculars.

'How's it fucked?'

The sheep start bleating, possibly offering advice.

'What sort of fucked is it this time?'

'Is it carburettor fucked?'

A distant rambler wearing red is pointing, just possibly at a loose spark plug lead.

'Or alternator fucked?'

More bleating, which may translate as fuel line fucked?

'Or out of petrol fucked?'

Faruk stares at lumps of metal, plastic bottles of liquid, some wires, tubes and what is clearly the battery. 'I can't say, exactly,' he says. 'Not at this stage.'

'Then how do you know it's fucked?'

Faruk ducks out from under the bonnet and slams it shut. Peevishly, I think.

'It won't go,' he says.

'Brilliant,' Diesel says.

Seventeen years of living in a flat above a garage owned by his family and now operated by his brother have yet to equip Faruk with a mechanical mind. He's tried to mend the car before, when it broke down on the Chatsworth estate, where its two-tone grungy paint job and flying fin made an exciting contrast for anyone photographing the big house behind it. He couldn't do anything with it then, though he did manage to dismantle a few parts. Now, like last time, we'll be at the mercy of the AA, who can take anything up to five hours to arrive, depending on how far we got before we broke down and what more-urgent jobs he's got on that day. The AA is Abdullah Aslan, Faruk's brother. The brother who was really good about helping us out with the car, completing Diesel's bonkers custom job and getting it on the road but who, since we've been driving it and breaking it, is revealing a much darker side to his character.

'I can't call the AA,' Faruk says. 'Not again. He'll fucking kill me.'

'You have to.'

'Why?'

'It is your duty.'

And so we wait, while Faruk decides whether he will risk the wrath of Abdullah.

We are not alone. For a narrow lane in the wilds of Derbyshire, a surprising number of cars have passed by, many slowing down to show a friendly interest in what we are doing. It's almost worth pausing to enjoy Faruk cursing and hitting his head on the bonnet, while the rest of us mill around looking not quite as clued up as the sheep. It's quite possible that some drivers have been sufficiently interested to raise the subject of our predicament with other travellers, at a petrol station a few miles down the road, and these curious motorists have driven up here to take a look for themselves.

Whatever the reason, cars have been passing us this last hour or more and though no one has actually offered to help, a great many drivers have at least wound down their window to ask what was the trouble. I suppose we might have interested them more if any of us had half a clue as to why the car had just stopped. And now, we need help. Black clouds are piling up across the distant valley tops, it only stopped raining half an hour ago and it looks like we're in for more. It's late afternoon now, so if Faruk doesn't call the AA soon, we may, like the car, be a little bit fucked.

At least I know where we are. I used to ride my BMX at astonishing speed down these steep hills until it clicked that one fast ride downwards equalled one long and tiring push back to the top. That was when I was staying with GD and Nana, at Narnia, which isn't that far from where we're stranded now. As it was supposed to be a day out in aid of my recuperation from the flu, I got to choose our direction and we're here because this place for me, is one with the best memories. Or it had been before this happened.

But I had a feeling the day might go something like this when I got up and saw it was pissing down with rain. Raining hard enough to make staying indoors and watching Jeremy Kyle or even Bargain Search an attractive proposition. So how did I end up on a bleak hillside half-expecting to spend a cramped, cold night in the Green Dragon? Mainly, that was down to Clive. 'What ole BJ needs is a breath of country air,' he'd said to Diesel, as we finished a plastic bottle of strong cider in my room last evening. Clive more than anyone knows how closeted I've been this last week (because he's my neighbour, not because he's closeted himself).

We'd take a trip into the country, never mind Faruk's brother saying there were one or two minor adjustments to be made before we could take the car out. Everyone wanted a day in the country. Faruk and Clive had been talking about going somewhere new in the Green Dragon ever since it had became uncomfortably recognisable in town, following an embarrassing incident when the car broke down by some trendy cafe bars, where the city's poseurs were sitting outside, preparing themselves for a night's clubbing.

I had been lucky enough to be recovering from the flu just then, but from what I hear, there had been some posing in the

Green Dragon too. Diesel, Faruk and Clive – shades on, windows down, music pumping – had been cruising around, trying hard to impress the girls at some kerb-side tables, when the Dragon chose to have its latest breakdown. It hadn't seemed too serious at first – all that was lost was a little cool as Diesel and Clive pushed it along the street before Faruk let out the clutch. The real injury came when a year 9 chode on a BMX decided it would be extremely funny to tip his McDonald's super-sized cola through Faruk's open window, managing to soak Faruk and Diesel and even to wet Clive in the back too, before he rode off, laughing like an evil puppet on a seaside pier.

Watched closely by the crowd at the kerb-side tables, who all stood up at once to get a better view, the car lurched forward as Faruk attempted to give chase, but something had happened to the gearbox and he was unable to get the stick out of first. So now they chased the kid on the bike at no more than five miles an hour, with the kid having to hang back and pedal really slowly, still cackling manically while he stuck up his middle finger and shouted obscenities. Diesel reckons it took about half an hour for the car to kangaroo to the end of the street, where the kid got bored and pedalled off and where the three Horsemen could no longer hear the people standing outside the cafe laughing themselves stupid and applauding wildly.

Diesel had called back, 'Thank you, we're here all week.' But it was no good, about a year's worth of street cred had been squandered that night. So it was more than a selfless concern for my respiratory system which had prompted the idea of a jaunt up country. It wasn't safe for that stupid car to be seen within three miles of the city centre, very probably a lot further.

However, Clive had been dead right, I needed to get out. I needed to escape from the foetid atmosphere of my bedroom, where the air was even more noxious than usual. It has sometimes crossed my mind to keep a caged canary, for the same reason miners did, down the pits. You'd know that the gaseous mix of stale breath, seminal fluid and curried farts had reached dangerous levels when the canary fell off its perch, or turned green. I had spent way too much time in such conditions and I was ready for a lungful of God's clean air. I felt like I had been banged up in that room for five years, not five days.

But even five days is a fuck of a long time to be stuck in one place, and having kindly taken an interest in me so far, you're probably wondering whether I spent this time profitably, or just wanking? Good question. Well, I'd spent the first post-fever days in bed, not feeling much, except for myself, of course. Then I had started reading some books that Nana had left for me before she and GD returned to Narnia, her treatment over for the moment at least.

It was worth having some down time from the Xbox to know that I was making progress with my grand design to impress Rosalind Chandler, if that was still an attainable objective, of course. I read more than I have ever read before, which wasn't hard and I read books which I would never have thought of reading myself, which I imagined would be hard, but wasn't. I'm not saying I actually finished them, but I read enough to keep up my end if I ever had to talk about them. That said, I still found time to become a highly competent would-be contestant of Countdown, could estimate within £5,000 what a two bedroom maisonette in South Norwood would fetch at auction three years ago and became word pretty much perfect in Season Eight of The Simpsons.

Also, like an eighteenth century king holding his levee (I'm expecting a B in History), I entertained visitors to my boudoir. In this way, I'd been able to catch up on what had been occurring while I was away, if not with the fairies, then with the frightening phantasms of my fevered imagination. (Fevered dreams are the worst – they're uncannily realistic and often repetitive too. I'm haunted by the thought of repeating my experiences with the toothless, sex-crazed crones of my nightmares – who have all, terrifyingly, popped their grey heads around my bedroom door to ask how am I doing. Not being nearly so old as I had made them out to be, Mum's friends Aggie, Iris and even Doris have all been able to make it up the stairs easily enough, to express an unsettling depth of concern about my welfare).

But I hadn't been completely cut off. Not all of my visitors wanted to spit out their teeth and drain me of my essential fluids. Some, like Clive, just dropped by to let me know what had been happening. And what had been happening, he said, had mostly been happening to Diesel. Clive and Faruk knew something was wrong the minute they clocked him coming out of Next with Lauren, wearing a buttoned up beige cardigan and a pair of chinos and the sort of expression that might be worn by people about to be hung, drawn and quartered in front of an enthusiastic crowd. Thinking of the public good, they had secretly followed the pair, filming them on Clive's iPhone, which he now pulled out of his pocket and played back for me.

It is depressing viewing, though Diesel's range of expression is actually quite impressive. Jim Carrey would struggle to match Diesel's fast-changing repertoire of anger, frustration, flickers of hope and desolate resignation. These are all caught by Clive as he and Faruk lurk behind pillars, duck into doorways and crouch behind parked cars. Between them, they have accumulated a damning mass of evidence pointing to the disturbing and unavoidable conclusion that Diesel and Lauren Sykes are now, despite Diesel's protestations to the contrary, fully paid-up members of the couples club.

We watch the small screen, shaking our heads, as Diesel follows Lauren into Claire's Accessories, where he stands for five minutes by the door, contemplating suicide, it looks like. Then there are some shorter clips of Diesel and Lauren visiting New Look, Burton's, Body Shop and River Island, outside which Lauren fishes into a bag and holds another cardigan, grey this time, up against Diesel's chest. He says something to her, and as a really long shot you might guess that he was making an expression of his gratitude, but personally, I think he'd wear the same expression to tell the hangman that the noose was just a little too tight.

Then they pass Burger King, where a lively argument breaks out. Diesel is pointing to something in the restaurant, the backlit image of a Double Whopper with Cheese, it could be, but Lauren is shaking her head and poking Diesel in his generous stomach. But this time Diesel isn't letting the matter drop, and we can see him standing his ground, hands on hips, almost certainly offering Lauren his opinions of women who won't let their men have a hamburger and fries with, perhaps, a large chocolate shake. It's a pity Clive couldn't get close enough to capture sound, but the dumbshow tells the whole sorry story.

After a while, Diesel has had his say. There's a pause, while he flashes a quick smile, clearly satisfied with the irrefutable logic of his argument. Then Lauren herself says something. She appears to makes one simple, concise statement, quite loudly, to judge from the reactions of other shoppers, and then she swivels on her pink high heels and flounces off.

Diesel stays where he is for a moment, unsure of his next move. He peers in the window of Burger King, looks around to see who is watching. Then he looks at Lauren's retreating figure, disappearing down the aisle of the shopping mall. He takes one last loving glance through the window, where a man eating a large hamburger eyes him with deep suspicion, and then turns, sighs, it looks like, and trots off after Lauren. It's a dreadful sight, something a man shouldn't be asked to witness.

But even this isn't as nauseous as the scene which follows, which features Diesel and Lauren, differences clearly settled in Lauren's favour, feeding the ducks in the park. Diesel passes Lauren a piece of bread, Lauren throws it to the ducks the way girls throw things, which is badly, and they both laugh, before wrapping themselves in a big hug and then we see Diesel giving

Lauren a truly sick-making kiss. There's no excuse for this. He doesn't even have his hand on her arse. It is sick, and not in a good way.

Having suffered this horrendous slice of bliss-porn, I shouldn't really have been surprised when I found myself squashed in the back seat with Diesel and Lauren, headed for a day out in the country with my three best mates and a gabby cow who will probably spoil it for all of us. Nobody is actually saying 'who invited her?' though it's the question on everyone's mind, despite the fact that we all know the answer – Lauren will have invited Lauren. Diesel knew this was a lads' day out and that he'd be contravening a whole section of statutes and rules as clearly set out in our much-planned Rulebook For Being A Proper Bloke. He'll have let her come along only under the severest duress. But so far it's been almost, but not quite, worth it, just for the laugh we got when Diesel and Lauren turned up wearing identical hooded jackets – not hoodies, but the sort of waterproof jackets middle-aged ramblers buy from outdoors shops. 'What?' he'd said, when we couldn't keep a straight face between us.

I hadn't actually met Lauren until that moment, though I'd have recognized her arse anywhere. It's impossible to see two water melons side-by-side on a supermarket shelf without thinking of Lauren in her green leggings. Diesel has lived in awe of Lauren's arse for years. It's an arse which has filled many a conversational gap in the Casablanca, though such conversations have tended to be one-sided. You either adore Lauren's arse, like Diesel does, or are slightly frightened of it, like we are. Diesel has even talked about wanting to sculpt it and has considered the merits of various materials, from plaster of paris to Italian marble. Faruk says that somewhere on the internet will be a forum for big bottom fans, run by someone with spelling just like Diesel's.

So yes, I knew her by arse and also by reputation – she was known as Lauren the Gob, which I had dozily thought was because of her large mouth, a feature I've pondered on more than once in connection with my own problem. That was when that old joke sprang to mind, the one about the woman who refuses the bloke's offered cock, saying she'll smoke it later. But Clive and Faruk came to see me while I was recovering and told me that she was Lauren the Gob for a very good and much more obvious reason. They'd found this out from firsthand experience, when Diesel had brought her to the Casablanca, presumably so he could break the ice between Lauren and his mates. It goes like this:

Clive and Faruk haven't been expecting female company and don't know how to deal with the contingency. Clive stands up to shake her hand while Faruk mumbles something about her being most welcome in his humble establishment, which just confirms why we never get anywhere with girls, though Clive, of course, has another reason. Diesel sits down and tries to stir up some lively chatter but Faruk and Clive don't know how to include a girl in their usual banter and so many subjects now seem off-limits, notably, Who Would You Shag In Year 12? My Very Best Wank and one that Diesel usually loves, Who's Got the Biggest Arse At St Saviour's Not Including Any Nuns? Diesel quickly exhausts what he's got to say about the weather, Sheffield United FC, whether you could teach a parrot to convincingly imitate Joe Pasquale and how nutritional and low-cal the kebabs are here and then shuts up, leaving Lauren to have her say.

It's quite a long say, too. She asks which do they like best, *The X Factor* or *Britain's Got Talent*? And as they don't answer immediately, she goes on to enumerate the differences between the two shows and the reasons why she thinks that, on balance, *Britain's Got Talent* is the superior show. 'I watch them both just for Simon Cowell,' Lauren says, and when she's finished listing the qualities of Simon Cowell, which are mainly that 'he's gorgeous' in so many ways, she launches straight into the interesting differences between Cheryl Cole and Amanda Holden, two names which might ordinarily have cropped up in our own conversations, though for completely different reasons.

Then she talks about how much her friend's mum is paying to have liposuction, how smoking curbs your appetite but is never cool unless you're like in a movie or something and then asks if they've been watching the women's tennis. (They have, but again, probably for different reasons). She talks a lot about hair, her own, her friends' hair, our hair and the five different salons she's tried on this road alone. She's thinking of becoming a hairdresser, perhaps having her own salon one day, which might one day offer a range of therapeutic and beauty treatments too, which she details and explains, slowly and exhaustively.

Eventually, Clive says, she seems to realise that she might be monopolising the conversation, just a bit, and she asks what they are going to do with their lives. Diesel must have already told her about how he wants his own record shop, something dealing in dance and hip hop vinyl rarities, which won't be affected by the download market, though it's hard to imagine her listening to all that. Clive is about to tell her about his plans to study interior design and perhaps get a slot on a TV show, where he will kick some Bowen ass and show Nick Knowles a thing or two and Faruk is all ready to outline his plans to be a TV chef, graphic designer, private investigator, paparazzo, police helicopter pilot, barrister, forensic pathologist, Formula One mechanic, travel rep, rock photographer or a DJ (all he has to do now is decide which).

But Lauren sees Faruk's music mag lying open on the table and instead of asking him if he wants to be a gangsta rapper like Snoop, whose picture fills half a page, she sees the small Army recruitment ad and thinks he's been looking at that. 'That's a good idea,' she says. 'A uniform would really suit you,' and then, glancing at Diesel, who is eating two kebabs, with chips, adds dryly, 'It wouldn't fit him.'

Then she tries to include Clive in the conversation. 'I suppose you'd be more at home in the navy?'

So it's not just Faruk and Clive and me and Diesel who are marooned on a remote hillside in Derbyshire as the rain starts to come down, it's Lauren too, who is sitting in the back seat, keeping herself to herself as she has done throughout the day and which is as unexpected as it is somehow unsettling. Faruk and I are having words about it, under the bonnet. 'They've had a barney, that's favourite,' he says, unscrewing something which then slips from his grasp, rattles its way through the engine and drops into long grass beneath the car, never to be seen again. 'Or she's on the rag,' I say, offering my bottomless understanding of the female condition. Clive wonders if Diesel's not letting her have any cock, a possibility we dismiss with derision, considering that it's only very recently that he's found the instructions for it.

The man himself comes over, looking well pissed off. 'Have you called your brother, Faruk?'

'He won't pick up,' Faruk says, which may or may not be true. He did look like he was calling someone at one point.

'Try him again.'

'I have,' Faruk says. 'Twice.' Which isn't true.

'Fuck me,' Diesel said. 'I don't want to be stuck out here with you, them sheep and a cow who's got the strop on.'

'Yeah, what we gonna do then?' says Clive. 'We can't sleep in the car.'

'Impossible,' I say, which it would be, stuck in the back with a couple of sumos like Diesel and Lauren.

'Don't your grandparents live round here?' says Faruk, deviously shifting the focus in my direction.

'Yes, they do, just over the ridge, but...'

I have a nasty feeling about this.

'Is it far?'

'Not really, but...'

The last thing I want to do is arrive at Narnia with these nerks, when Nana is ill and needs as much peace as she can possibly get.

'Well for fuck's sake, let's start walking,' Diesel says, as the rain starts to shovel down.

'I'm down with that,' Clive says. 'Get somewhere dry.'

'No,' I say, and immediately feel outside the group. They're looking at me like the sheep are looking at them. 'We can't.'

'What the fuck?' Diesel says.

And I'm just about to tell them why it wouldn't be a good idea for a bunch of cold, wet, hungry, noisy and generally insensitive youths (plus Lauren, who may well have recovered the power of infinite speech by then), to impose themselves on a frail, dying woman for however long it takes to get us sorted – when a familiar blue camper van crests over the ridge and appears to get air for just a second before it thumps back down upon the tarmac. The silhouette inside is recognizably GD's and though I don't think he's seen me and won't have set eyes on the Green Dragon before, he's slowing right down, pulling over on the grass bank beside us and already is asking Faruk if he can give us any help. What a treacle my grandfather is.

CHAPTER 10

Our House

To my huge relief, Nana's on an upswing. That's what it looks like, because she gets up from her chair to greet us, spritely enough. Perhaps the last treatment has done her some good. She seems overwhelmed by our unexpected visit, but it's in a good way. I don't like the colour of her face, which I think is called sallow and her eyes seem to have sunk a little more into her head and when she gives me a hug I can feel her bones. But the smile, the smile I've known all my life and which is the very soul of Nana, that hasn't changed one little bit. She asks if I'm recovered (I am, of course I am, how can she ask about how other people are?). She asks too whether Mum has thought any more about her flower shop (she does nothing else) and how is Dad (he's as well as he has time to be, I think). Then she greets my friends like they're an extended part of the family. She's met them all before at least once, all except for Lauren, of course.

She tells GD to take our wet things – two soaked hoodies and a sweatshirt – and dry them on the Aga in the kitchen and to put the kettle on while he's there. 'Make a pot of good, hot coffee,' she says. 'And Arty, bring out my sticky toffee cake.' She tells everyone to find a space, sit down, make themselves at home, but Faruk, Clive, Lauren and Diesel, they're still standing over by the door, just blown away by the coolness of my grandparents' place. We could see the little stone cottage as we rounded the last corner, a half mile up the road, light behind the thin red curtains and a lantern over the door sending out a warm glow of welcome across the valley.

Inside, it's cosier than a hobbit hole, with stone flags and a Welsh dresser full of Nana's home-thrown pots in the kitchen, while stepping down into the living room is like stepping back in time. Two small rooms have been knocked into one, which is still quite small. The whitewashed walls look like they were rendered by a really useless plasterer, the mortar following the bumps and indents of the limestone beneath. Pictures, big and small, cover the walls, one or two framed. There are prints I recognize from art class, such as Arthur Rackham's illustrations for *Alice in Wonderland*, a psychedelic-style tour poster (advertising the Grateful Dead, of course), which is scribbled on and might even be signed. On a handbill for a poetry reading at the Royal Albert Hall, among some names even I can recognize, is Nana's, or Ruth Nash, as she was, back in the sixties.

The room is furnished with a comfortable-looking sofa covered in a home-made patchwork blanket (where Nana is now settling with Clive and Lauren), then there's Nana's own rocking chair, which I've already staked out and an old pine table with chairs in the corner (made by GD in his workshop behind the house). Next to the open fireplace is a stack of smaller tables supporting what looks like an old but high-end stereo system, with a turntable and an amplifier and speakers, which really have to be heard to be believed, especially if all you ever listen to is headphones or the speakers on your PC. No CD player, no MP3 input. No TV, for that matter.

But that doesn't seem to worry some: Diesel and Faruk are getting comfortable on a couple of huge red cushions in front of GD's enormous, carpet-stacked row of vinyl records and Faruk's already starting to tell Diesel what's good, in his opinion, and what's just 'old hippy stuff'. In another corner is a compact open pine staircase, which turns back on itself (also beautifully made by GD), and under this are shelves filled with hundreds of books and a folded-up daybed. The room is lit by a pink bulb inside a huge paper globe decorated with turquoise Chinese dragons, which is suspended from the heavy oak roof beams and a couple of wax-caked candles in bottles.

Nana asks Faruk about the breakdown and gets a lot of guff

about leaky cylinders, sludgy fuel lines and a dodgy coil. She nods and tells GD to pop next door to see Tim, a neighbour who knows all about cars and who will probably be able to take a look at ours in the morning. He won't want paying, Nana says in answer to Faruk's unasked question, 'He likes to do things for me.'

By the time we've phoned our parents and told them where we are, GD has brought in just what we need. We drink big mugs of GD's coffee, which is scalding and sweet, and eat sensational mouthfuls of a toffee cake, which Nana swears she didn't bake herself, though it's one I've never had before (and never have found since, despite a thorough search of supermarket shelves). GD sits on the window seat, commenting on the selections Diesel pulls from his extensive stack of records. Faruk is in some other place, just him and the music he's put on the stereo.

Having told GD to think about what they are going to give us for our dinner, Nana picks up an old photograph album and starts to leaf through it, pointing out this or that to Clive and Lauren. I get up from Nana's chair to look over her shoulder at page after page of stuck-down colour prints, some with captions in Nana's neat handwriting, and as I hear her frail voice apologising to her guests that what they see was all a long time ago, when times were very different, I'm able to patch up my own crumbling memories of the time I spent in this house as a temporary but well-contented resident of Narnia.

Lauren still hasn't said a word. What Nana is saying as she shows her the photographs must all be strange to her – actually, famous poets dropping by with bottles of wine and professors of literature running riot, bollock-naked in the garden sounds odd to me, too – but I can see she's smiling and trying to understand. In fact, like the others, she may be starting to see Nana as I do, as a cool and motherly source of inspiration and advice – and love, too, of course. Nana turns the leaves, sometimes chuckling at some old memory or at a photo of GD with long black hair and a cowboy hat. Then she shows her guests page after page of pictures of her travels in India – Nana spent three years there, working for an Indian charity.

There are pictures of wild-looking men and women, mostly taken in this room. Clive sits on the other side of Nana, taken as much by the fashions as by anything else. In the really ancient shots, long haired men wear colourful cheesecloth shirts, patched jeans, velvet jackets embroidered with flowers and granddad T-shirts, brightly tie-dyed. There are Zapata moustaches, chains and amulets, CCuban heels and broad and big-buckled leather belts. The men sit on cushions or drape themselves over armchairs, playing guitars, laughing and gurning at someone's camera. The young women wear long, flowery dresses, headbands and chokers, bare feet and, from what I can see, no bras. No one takes photographs of sad or dull occasions but to look at these is to think that life chez Arthur and Ruth Johnson was one big and friendly party.

GD picks up a tortoiseshell kitten which tries to scratch him as he glances at what Nana is doing. 'Those were the days, my friend,' he says in a singsong voice.

Nana looks up from her photo album.

'You can still talk bollocks, husband of mine,' she says. 'These are the days too. Look at these kids, living through the biggest technological revolution since the steam engine and, Arty, being young enough to see how it all plays out. These could be the best of days, the very best of days, if everyone gets it right.' She pauses, like speaking is sometimes an effort for her. 'But yes, these here were ours. And we had a load of fun, didn't we?'

'We did that,' GD says, bending to kiss Nana on her forehead before helping Faruk and Diesel to choose another record to slip on his old turntable. 'Here we are, then, Grateful Dead, *Europe '72.*'

I catch Nana rolling her eyes. 'Not again,' she says. 'If we must have the Dead, how about *American Beauty*?'

'It's always been a bone of contention this,' GD says. 'I love the live stuff, the long improvised jams, but Ruth has yet to see the light. Stubbornly sticks to the studio albums, don't you, mule? We nearly divorced over that, once. I'd have had grounds, too.'

'Rubbish, Arthur. Don't listen to him, kids.'

GD disappears into the kitchen, from where appetizing smells start to filter. There's a lot of clattering, the sound of something falling and skittering across the floor and GD singing about being 'trailed by twenty men'. But the bowls of pasta dowsed with a sweet chilli sauce – which we eat on our knees – are exactly what we need after a long and frustrating day out, trying hard to have fun. After the meal, which Nana barely touches, GD stands in front of the hearth as if he's warming his bum, though being summer, there's no fire there just now. He puffs out an impressive stomach and says, 'Did I ever tell you people about how I joined the Dead after they played Hollywood?'

'You joined the Grateful Dead?' Faruk says.

'You were in Hollywood?' says Diesel.

Granddad unwraps a boiled sweet and pops it into his mouth.

'Oh, aye, yes indeed,' he says. 'Hollywood Music Festival, Newcastle-under-Lyme, 1970. The first time the Grateful Dead played on these shores. I joined the band as a roadie for a spell, after I rescued them when their tour bus broke down outside Stoke-on-Trent. I was reminded of that when I saw you lot broken down today, though Brian here would need a little more hair to pass as Jerry Garcia. I picked them up with their guitars and everything and got them to the festival with only minutes to spare.'

'Amazing,' Faruk says.

'It certainly is,' Nana says.

'It was raining then too, and that was before I'd had the roof on the van fixed, so they did get quite wet. Not that it dampened their spirits, not the Dead. In fact, they were so grateful that Bob

Hunter wrote a song about that van, and called it *Box of Rain*. And Jerry took me on as driver-cum-roadie and once I'd introduced him to Newcastle Brown ale (I always carry an emergency crate in the van) we became firm friends. He never forgot me, either, you know. Always a card at Christmas.'

'Incredible,' Faruk says.

'Isn't it?' Nana says.

'When the band wasn't playing, Jerry and I used to jump in the van and go off in search of a pint of real ale, or a decent drop as we called it then. Jerry became a hard-core fan of British beer. It's a little-known fact that *Dark Star* was actually inspired by Jerry's love of Newcastle Brown. You check out the label on the bottle – two dark stars. And the idea for *Uncle John's Band* came from a story I told him about my Uncle Jack, who was banned from every pub in Chesterfield.'

'Arty,' Nana sighs, but it's no good, GD's on a roll.

'Soon, Jerry and I had converted the rest of the band. They loved it. Couldn't get enough of the stuff. We went everywhere, in search of the perfect pint. Some nights, you'd find three great lorries full of amps and tour gear parked in front of a little country pub in the wilds, and you'd walk in and there would be San Francisco's finest, Jerry, Phil, Ron, Mickey and Bob getting outside a few pints of Sam Smith's or Timothy Taylor, and me and Bill enjoying a game of darts. Fantastic days.'

'Fantastic is the word,' Nana says.

'Then, one day, we got pulled over by the police and searched, following a tip off, probably made by a rival band. The New Riders of the Purple Sage or the Quicksilver Messenger Service, I expect it was. Anyway, the cops pulled everything apart looking for drugs and couldn't believe there was nothing on board. Even Owsley were clean. Not so surprising, really, because Jerry and me had been obliged to ditch several kilos of top grade Mexican grass in the Manchester Ship Canal, to make room for another six crates of Boddingtons.'

Faruk, who has been following every word, starts to laugh. The penny rolls, clatters and finally drops for Diesel too and everyone's laughing, though as for me, I'm wondering about the signatures on the poster and an almost indecipherable scribble which might just read, 'Your round next time, love and peace, Jerry.'

We have been so engrossed that we haven't noticed that Nana and Lauren had gone into the kitchen and when they come out, it looks like they've been talking. Lauren looks a little more cheerful, anyway. Nana looks exhausted, and GD decides it's time he and Nana retired. A little later, Lauren and Diesel, who have been assigned the spare bedroom, go upstairs. I see that Lauren's talking to him for the first time that day, but softly, so she doesn't disturb Nana. Clive takes the sofa and the patchwork blanket. Faruk, after one last look through the records, unfolds the camp bed. I'm not tired, so I volunteer to sleep in Nana's rocking chair, where I sit and rock and think about Nana, and what GD will do when she's gone and how unfair it is that she has to go like this, so long before her time.

I think happier thoughts too, of the warm welcome we've received, of the amazing toffee cake, and of how I want to tell Ros all about this place when I'm back at school next week – if I can engineer a meeting and if she will speak to me, of course. But drowsy, warm and happy, I am confident too and think that she will. I'm wondering if I can stay up and perhaps see the dawn in a few hours time, like we used to when I was here before. I'm not aware of having fallen asleep but when I feel GD's big hand on my shoulder, gently shaking me awake, there's the faintest sliver of light bordering the edges of the curtains. He puts his finger to his lips and beckons me to follow him. We step over Faruk in the low day bed and quietly open the door, which someone has forgotten to lock. It's cool and fresh outside, with just enough light for us to make our way along the narrow lane that leads to the hillside, where a faint glow behind the distant castle is announcing the coming of the dawn. I look at my watch as GD strides ahead. It's 4.44 in the morning.

'Have you told your father?' GD asks, as we enter the ring of standing stones. In the centre, one of these ancient slabs looks like it has been extracted from the earth and laid upon two others to form a seat. We make use of it.

'Not yet,' I say.

'You'll know when,' GD says. 'It'll be a shock at first. But once he knows, he'll be all the better for it, I'm sure he will. We were mistaken in taking him, I think. We weren't right for him, though we tried to be, we really did.'

'He does love you,' I say. 'In his own way.'

'I know,' GD says. Rabbits are starting from their holes and scuttling across the close-cropped grass. 'And he loves Ruth, too, in his own way. But all this talk of hospitals and hospices. He just doesn't know her, Brian. Not like we do.'

I find it hard to talk about Nana's condition. It seems like a betrayal, but I do. Surely Dad is right about wanting Nana to have proper medical care? 'You wouldn't keep her here, though,' I say. 'Not if she was in pain?'

'I'll keep her here with me for as long as she wants to stay,' GD says, stubbornly, it sounds like. 'No matter what anyone else says.'

'But if you can't?' I say. 'If she's too ill?'

GD sits quietly for a moment. 'We'll cross that bridge if and when we have to.' Then, after we have sat in silence for a few minutes, he says, 'Now, what do you think of this place?'

There's no need for an answer. It's gobsmacking. There's a watery sunlight thinning the sky, silvering the clouds and throwing a pattern of faint shadows into our stone circle. Below, I can see green fields and granite walls dipping towards a winding road and further down, the tree-lined river bottom. Across the water there are forested slopes and farmhouses and pastures dotted with cattle and sheep, then the suggestions of distant hills and valleys behind these, and then more, fading eventually to blue smudges on the far horizon. And just beyond us, on the edge of the great ridge along which we've been walking, is Nana's Rock, where I sat with GD not so long ago – but probably wouldn't have, if I'd seen how precariously we were perched. From here we can see how the single mass of granite reaches out above the valley, high above the bracken and boulders below.

'I'm glad you like it,' GD says. 'Philly loves this place. In fact, she's decided on it.'

'What do you mean?'

GD turns to look at me, sizing me up, I think. As if he's making sure I'm ready to hear something that he needs to tell me.

'I mean that right here is where we will say goodbye to your grandmother. When the time comes.'

'I don't understand.'

'You will, but all in good time,' GD says.

I want to know more and I don't. This all sounds too ominous. And yet it can't be, not if GD is saying it. But GD just looks out over the valley and adds nothing. We sit there in companionable silence, while the place fills with bright morning light and – to borrow a phrase I remember Nana reading to me once – whatever mystery was upon the land in that between-time has withdrawn into the woods.

GD unwraps another sweet, pops it into his mouth and sucks noisily. I know him well enough to know that he'll be turning something over in his mind and that I'll hear all about it as soon as he has it right. Sometimes this process can take a couple of boiled sweets.

'If I could leave you with one thought,' GD says, finally, 'it's this.'

I'm suddenly panicked at the thought of GD leaving too. Then I wonder what he will do when Nana is gone. And then I reproach myself for even thinking of Nana being gone. These are all things which just cannot be.

'There is always an alternative way, Brian,' my grandfather says. 'Question everything. Don't think what people tell you to think, don't live your life just to please others.'

If I ask what he means one more time he'll think I'm a retard. And anyway, I always seem that much more intelligent when I keep my mouth shut.

'Back in the day, my day,' GD says, 'a lot of us questioned what had previously been set in stone. Why was sex for after marriage? Why did your class or your race determine your future? Why should America be at war with a country we had barely heard of? People wrote about these things and others sang about them. We made our feelings known in every way we could. There were demonstrations, sit-ins, all kinds of protests. Some people were just along for the ride but most of us, I like to think, were deadly serious. We didn't watch the world pass us by on a screen, we did something. And in the end, we changed that world, just a little.'

Changed the world? Some days, it's all I can do to change my socks.

'Of course it was easier for us then,' GD adds.

'How?'

'We had nothing to keep us at home. No addictive video games, no internet, nothing on telly. You met people when you went out, not when you went online. We had more money than previous generations but we were stony broke beside yours. There wasn't yet the rampaging consumerism which keeps people dull-witted and takes their eyes off the balls they should be on.'

'I didn't know you were such a radical,' I say.

'I'm not. I'm just a carpenter who works with wood and wants to live in a world without knots. Or a few less of them, anyway. What you do about your world is up to you,' he says, shaking a stone from his boot. 'You are the future. Join it and subvert it or reject it and fight it. Not a revolution, those things are doomed to bloodshed and failure. But think for yourself. And don't add fuel to this consumerist nightmare – question whether you really need that new thing they're asking you to buy. Recycle. Make do. A smaller economy needn't be a bad thing. Vote for anyone who tells the truth and wants to do good, regardless of party. Start your own party, or work from within. Love one another. But do something soon, before it's too late.'

'It's not as bad as all that, is it?' I say, which sounds dumb, but I don't quite know how to react to this new side of GD I'm discovering.

He turns and looks at me, like he's judging just how much I really know about life and the world. If he has much else to say, he swallows it. 'We'll see,' he says. He stands up, dusts himself off and takes one more sweeping look at the majestic view.

'Come on, Brian, let's make tracks,' he says, the early morning sun lighting a smile. 'There's something else I wanted to speak to you about.'

'I'm listening,' I say.

'Good, says GD, as we stumble over stone and heather towards the village and the cottage on the hill. 'Because I've been wanting to tell you the real story behind the now-legendary Macclesfield pub crawl that Jerry and me went on, back in '72.'

Much later that morning, after Nana's neighbour has fixed our car, we think about going home. It's Sunday, so there's nothing much to rush back for, but GD has told me that at times like these, Nana will find energy she doesn't really have and that she may pay for her exertion later. In the front room, Faruk and GD are talking records – Faruk is being encouraged to borrow whatever he likes. Clive is telling Nana all about what he has been doing to the Dyson house and how he might borrow some of her ideas. I'm sure Roger will like hippie retro, once he becomes accustomed to it. Diesel and Lauren have gone for a walk at Nana's suggestion. Having got up so early, I've been dozing in Nana's rocking chair.

We are drinking tea and eating warm cheese scones when Diesel comes puffing up the garden path and bursts into the room. He stands there in his silly jacket and wide eyes, with his mouth moving and nothing coming out. GD sees something is wrong and lays a hand on his shoulder. He says, 'Are we okay?' Lauren stays at the bottom of the garden path, with her hands plunged into the pockets of her jacket, her face partially hidden by her hood. Back in the room, Diesel looks about wildly, like he has something to communicate, but can't decide who to tell first or whether it should be communicated anyway: it's impossible to tell; I've never seen him like this. 'It's Lauren,' is all he's able to offer by way of an explanation.

'What's up?' Faruk says.

'What's she done?' Clive demands.

Diesel's face is paler than I've seen it before, his eyes strangely vacant. He looks like he's had some sort of a shock, a bad one too, I'd guess. Nana watches him impassively.

'It's Lauren,' he says again.

We're all looking at him and then glancing through the windows at Lauren and wondering why she's not come in with Diesel.

Then we find out.

'She's pregnant,' he says, and sinks deep into the sofa next to Nana, burying his face into her body while Nana herself waves to Lauren, telling her to come on in.

CHAPTER 11

Oliver's Army

The menu at St Saviour's school canteen has been changed, yet again. This time last year Monsieur LeClerc's reign of terror finally came to an end. It had lasted just over eighteen months but it had seemed an awful lot longer. Previously, we'd all had a normal, healthy fear of green vegetables. By the time Monsieur LeClerc had donned his chef's hat and got cooking, our fear had been ramped up to an acute horror of anything even suggestive of a leaf. There were vegetables on our plates we had never heard of, much less actually seen.

Then there was the meat. Its provenance was never made clear enough for me or for many others. We devised elaborate schemes to avoid actually eating any of those strange, stringy bits of tissue, which we thought were frogs, of course, but could as easily have been calf's brains, or (a thought which had reduced the pony club girls to tears), horse meat. We didn't trust Monsieur LeClerc. It wasn't as if he was a real chef anyway. Monsieur LeClerc had been a supply teacher, until his contract ended, a time which had coincided with TV chef Jamie Oliver's campaign to Get Kids Eating Stuff They Don't Like At School Lunch. I may have got the title wrong.

The school governors had seen the way things were going and had taken note of government directives and decided to change the school menu. Out would go the pleasantly palatable diet of before – crinkle-cut oven chips, instant mashed potatoes, carefully processed tinned peas, delicious oven-baked beans in tomato sauce and more body-building protein in the form of giant fish fingers, cryogenically frozen beefburgers and partly pork sausages – and in would come fresh, nutritionally approved and, we were repeatedly assured, wonderfully tasty food.

Jamie Oliver has said that eating habits affect mood, behaviour, health, growth and even our ability to concentrate. And I must say, he was bang on with all of that. Monsieur LeClerc, whom we had grown to know and mistrust as a teacher of French, had barely pulled on his checkered trousers and a new Raymond Blanc accent (Monsieur LeClerc may have a French name, but he grew up in Huddersfield) before our mood began to change. Just as Jamie had said it would. First it was alarm (where the fuck have the Turkey Twiddlers gone?) then it was fright (what is this thing on my plate?) and then complete and utter despondency when we realised that despite the April 1st launch date, it wasn't an elaborate joke and we'd be getting variations on this awful muck for the foreseeable.

Jamie was right on the other points too. Diet did indeed affect our behaviour, to the extent that two boys were arrested for stealing Ginsters pasties from the local Spar, while any kid foolish enough to openly display a pork pie in the playground risked being savagely mauled. To be honest, I don't know if the new food affected our growth. There wasn't time to find out before everything changed again. But it did affect our ability to concentrate. It stands to reason. I mean, how can you possibly concentrate on the reproductive system of a dissected rabbit when there's a good chance you'll be finding it on your plate in an hour's time?

Emergency committees swung into action. Diesel's mum, who you probably saw on *Newsround*, was a shining example to us all. Each break time she would be down at the corner of the playground where a hole had mysteriously appeared in the wire netting, offering to run errands to the local chippie for the very reasonable fee of £1 per trip. It was agreed by all that a fried Mars bar had never tasted quite so good. The school black market boomed. Chocolate bars doubled in price, Jelly Tots realised 80p per pack while a retro Curly Wurly fetched a record-breaking £1.85 at auction (the one held in the boys' bogs at morning break).

Anything with Mr Kipling's name on it was worth its weight in Gold bars, by McVitie's. It's a pity you couldn't buy shares, as a canny investor would have made his fortune.

There had been various attempts to make us attend the canteen and actually eat some of what Monsieur LeClerc cooked up, but it was hopeless. Food disappeared from plates in the time it took a sweaty palm to pass over it. It was then spirited out of the hall like escape-tunnel sand in trouser turn-ups. And turn up it would at some later date, discovered mushed into someone's games bag, dropped in the foyer aquarium (where even the guppys and angelfish had refused it) or rotting pungently behind a warm radiator. Even the teachers were at it. Always encouraged to sit and eat their meals with their students, an arrangement as popular with them as it was with us, they were supposed to set an example and show us that sampling the new menu would not bring on immediate stomach cramps or a slow and agonising death.

For a while they were our food tasters. We closely watched their every mouthful, waiting for signs of pain and distress and preserving what distance we could, for fear of projectile vomiting. To begin with, they were quite game about it, I have to give them that. Some finished whole platefuls, or very nearly and Mr Hartlebury, who taught physical education and so was entitled to an abnormal appetite, was rumoured to once have asked for more, but this turned out to be an urban myth. In the end they could no more keep it up than we could keep it down. Empty places appeared at the heads of tables. Officially they had been called away on urgent business, had gone home sick or had extra marking to do in the staff room. Then some year 12s on a chippy run had seen them through the window of the Nag's Head, clustered around a table loaded with pints of beer and huge plates of lasagne and chips and shepherd's pie with baked beans.

Eventually, like a town suffering a long siege, with the

difference that the besiegers became fewer and fewer until only a trickle of die-hards, masochists and the terminally weird appeared at Monsieur LeClerc's counter, something had to give. In fact it was M. LeClerc himself, who was encouraged to tender his resignation after it was discovered that he was no more qualified to prepare food than some year nine chode doing food tech. And so, rather than have an empty canteen and no cash in the coffers, the chips and the beans and the fish fingers and those greasy little pizzas we all loved were back on our plates. The only concession to change was the continued absence of Turkey Twiddlers as a staple of our balanced diet. On the first day of the new old regime, the place was heaving – filled to capacity, I mean.

And it's still fairly full today, with a long queue behind me and five or six diners in front of me as I await my turn at Sylvie and Pamela's food-filled counter. They've done us proud. An appetising smell of fried food is filtering down the line and the array of pastries, sausages and mountains of chips is a reassuring sight to a hungry school kid who probably hasn't eaten a single thing since morning break. I have my eyes on a steak pie, which I'll have with gravy, a decent portion of chips and some mushy peas, or baked beans. No, mushy peas and baked beans. There's some sort of jam tart with custard which will sort me out for afters. I just wish these chodes in front of me would hurry up and make their choices – any hungrier than this and I'd qualify for foreign aid. I look down the line, to see what the hold-up is.

Ahead of me is Titch Taylor, opting for curry sauce on his quiche, I see, Andy Towse, having a bit of everything as usual, Chris Eshelby, who's going for sausages, beefburger and the bolognaise sauce, brave lad, and then, holding everything up at the cash register is someone partially hidden by the portly form of Mr Brentnall, who has stopped to talk to another teacher. Finally, he moves off, bearing what looks like a model of the Swiss Alps sculpted from mashed potato and mushy peas. And that's when I see her, at the till, talking to the new catering assistant like there's all the time in the world and no long queue behind her, impatiently waiting to be served.

At last, Rosalind Chandler pays her money and lifts up her tray. On her plate is a mixed salad and coleslaw and rather than opting for a Sunny D, or a Diet Coke from the machine, there's just a simple glass of water. Well, it's just another interesting facet of her altogether wonderful personality. She drifts down the queue, seems not to notice me as she passes, leaving the gorgeous scent of some exotic perfume trailing in her wake. I'm so distracted that I don't notice Sylvie talking to me or Darren Alexander prodding me in the ribs from behind. 'Go on, you prick,' he says. 'Your fucking turn!' Sylvie's tongs grip a huge sausage which droops heavily over my plate.

'Double sausage, large chips and what else today?' she asks. I might have settled on a fat steak pie for today's feasting, but double sausage and large chips is my usual canvas, on which I add creative detail, like a serving of mushy peas, spaghetti hoops in tomato sauce or maybe, if I'm feeling adventurous, one of Sylvie's mystery pasties.

'No, no,' I say in horror, waving away her tongs and her sausage. 'Just a salad and a glass of milk.' I can hear myself saying this but I can't believe it's me. I wonder if Darren has been practising ventriloquism. I seem to have no control over what I'm saying. 'And a little potato salad on the side,' the voice adds.

I pay at the till and stand there, probably looking like a chode, as I scan the fast-filling canteen. Ros has found herself a seat at a nearby table that's almost empty. There are a couple of speccy nerds at one end talking about gigabytes and terabytes as I edge behind them with my tray, and just Ros, sitting at the table end. I rest my tray next to one of the geeks, leaving a gap of one empty chair between me and Ros. I don't want to look like I'm pushing myself on her, though that is of course something I'd very much like to do. She looks amazing today, having really gone to town on her gothy make up and her shock of black hair is adorned with all kinds of especially interesting plastic knick-knacks. She's wearing some thin black blouse with the suggestion of a dark bra beneath and some kind of knitted black shawl over the top. She's sporting a *diamanté* brooch fashioned in the shape of a skull, I notice. No one else dresses like Ros, she is a complete individual. As usual, she has her headphones in, but responds with a nod when I say, 'Hi.'

'God, I'm so hungry,' I say, partly to myself but also loud enough for Ros to maybe hear and respond to, if she wants. 'I could eat a horse.'

'I'm a vegetarian,' she says, fiddling with her iPod, turning it up or down, I don't know which. 'So horses aren't exactly on my menu.'

'Right,' I say. 'Me too. It's just an expression.'

She takes an earphone from her gorgeous ear. 'You're a vegetarian?' she says.

'A vegan, actually,' I say. I'm not totally sure what a vegan is, in fact there was a period I thought a vegan was what Mr Spock was, on Star Trek, but I've said it because it sounds a bit more impressive, a little more hard-core than vegetarian.

'How long have you been a vegan?' she asks, as I take a sip of my milk. This is the first time Rosalind has talked to me and I treasure every word, committing to sacred memory the way her mouth opens and words come out. I try hard to abort some heathen thoughts occasioned by a glimpse of half-eaten coleslaw on her tongue.

'Oh, long enough,' I say, airily. 'I think it's important to make a stand on certain things, don't you?'

'Uhh,' she says. 'I'm not, like, all political and stuff. Whales should be big enough to save themselves, you know what I'm saying?'

'I'm not a full time vegan,' I start to say, but then she looks at me oddly.

'Aren't you the boy who, like, saved my life? That was so cool.'

It's odd, but whenever I had imagined her speaking – she never does in the classes we share – I thought it would be in standard Helena Bonham-Carter Edwardian English. No hint of American at all. It's cool, though. She probably has American relatives. She looks at me and seems to be thinking of something. Her future with me, I hope. 'Oh no, wait a minute, you didn't save my life. You got my stomach pumped. That wasn't cool.'

I must look as uncomfortable as I feel because after a period of reflection, or maybe she's just waiting for the track playing on her iPod to end, she says, 'It was cool in a way, though.' (She loves the word cool, which I think is really, well, *cool*.) 'It was, like, an experience, right? Did you know that no one else in our year has been stomach-pumped? Not a single person?'

I know for a fact that is not true but I let it go. She won't want to hear about the time Nick Garnett and Andrew Fitzpatrick emptied the booze cabinet at The Party to End All Parties or when Don Fell and Caroline Eyre drank what they thought was a bottle of vodka they'd found among the cleaning products under the kitchen sink. Probably not, anyway.

'I think that makes me kind of special, right?'

I take only a moment to consider this.

'Yeah, right, it does,' I say. Because stomach pumped or not, she is special.

'It's funny how you have to be stomach pumped before you meet other people, isn't it?' she says. 'I met some amazing doctors and some really nice nurses and like, wow, I've just met you!'

'Phenomenal,' I say.

'You know what we should do,' she says, her head moving closer to mine in a gesture of shared confidentiality, I think. 'We should…'

And I will never know whether Rosalind was about to

suggest that we should slip off somewhere quiet and get to know each other better, meet after school to discuss her Kerouac and Kafka or just start a support group for people who have met after one or both parties has been stomach pumped. Because right then is when Faruk and Clive choose to crash-land their trays at this table, like there aren't any others in this massive hall that is actually full of them. They're followed by Andy Towse and Chris Grayson, who edit *Smeg!!* the underground, online school paper, and talk about sex all the time.

I was about to compare their intrusion with Ozzy Osbourne appearing at the Queen's garden party, but I think something like that actually happened and it went rather well. In this respect, Clive and Faruk and anyone else are less welcome. I now see they are incredibly noisy – they clatter their cutlery and talk with their mouths full, they are inane – what they talk about is complete rubbish – and they are amazingly coarse. How can they talk about Lauren Sykes, let alone Lauren Sykes's enormous arse, and be totally oblivious to the staringly obvious fact that this table has been graced with the presence of someone very special, a princess among plebeians?

'Pass the f-f-f-salt,' Faruk says.

'I'll have the f-f-f-pepper, please,' Clive joins in.

'I've had a f-f-f-terrible morning,' Faruk says.

Apparently, they have invented some new and sophisticated word game.

'I've had Mrs Bennett, who is f-f-f-strict.' Clive.

'But she's got a f-f-f-nice arse.' Faruk.

'And I suppose you'd like to f-f-f.' Clive.

'Fill in my UCAS form with her, yes,' Faruk says, and stuffs his mouth with greasy pizza and chips.

Clive is the first to notice. He's struggling to cut one of Sylvie's giant sausages, which can sometimes be like lengths of durable rubber hose, when he sees my plate.

'What's the score, BJ?' he says, loudly. 'What's that?'

'What's what?' I say, though right now I'd much sooner suspend our friendship, for the duration of lunch at least.

'That stuff on your plate,' Clive says.

'If that's some sort of meat, I should take it back. It's gone green,' Faruk says.

'Gangrene, you mean,' Clive says.

'It's salad,' I say and affect an interest in what Diesel and Lauren are doing, sitting by themselves at a corner table. In fact, they are doing nothing, just sitting there, looking glum, neither of them talking, Diesel appearing not to be eating his food, which is a first.

'He's eating salad,' Clive says, showing off his acute powers of observation.

'BJ eating salad,' Faruk says, shaking his head.

'You on a diet, then?' Clive says. 'Or what?'

'And if he is, why's that?' Faruk wants to know.

'He's not on the pull, is he?' Clive suggests.

'I saw him watching Jenna Berry run the 400 metres in her tight little shorts.'

'No!'

'Jenny Berry? With the tits like freckles, BJ?'

'Fuck me,' Clive says. 'Even I wouldn't shag her.'

'Probably not,' Faruk says.

'Must be the time of year, rising sap etcetera,' Clive says. 'We blokes'll shag anything then, right?'

'The balls get heavy,' Faruk allows. 'They seek release.'

'But Jenna Berry, fuck me,' Clive says. 'I'd sooner fuck Brendan Berry.' He laughs, uncertainly.

All this is delivered between imprecise mouthfuls of food, some of which end up around, rather than inside mouths or on the table, dangerously close to Ros's plate. Ros appears to have missed everything and to be giving her total attention to whatever she has playing on her iPod. I want to go, but I also am wondering if Faruk and Clive, who both eat like street-cleaning machines, might actually finish up and go off to carve cocks on the bog doors, or whatever is this week's chosen amusement. Be nice to have one last word with Ros, I'm thinking, if only to assure her that these two idiots aren't actually my friends. Seconds later, I decide I should have gone while the going was good.

'Fucking salad, though,' Clive's saying. 'You gone veggie or something?'

I see Ros' eyelids flicker. 'Actually, I am a vegetarian.'

'You, a veggie?' Clive says.

'I'm a vegan,' I say, hoping they don't know what a vegan is.

'Isn't that a veggie sausage?' Faruk says. 'Linda McCartney?'

They don't, thank God.

'Since when?' Clive demands.

'Since that dodgy quarter pounder in town last week?' Faruk says. 'I vommed that up, too.'

'Never thought I'd see BJ without his big sausage,' Clive says.

'BJ's big sausage,' Faruk says loudly, as they've sussed that Ros is listening faster than I have.

'The things he's done with his big, porky sausage.'

'He's fed it slowly into his mouth,' Clive offers.

'He's wrapped his lips around it and given it a good old suck,' Faruk says.

'And he's swallowed it. And I'll give him this, he's never spat it out.'

They fall about with laughter and Chris Grayson and Andy Towse join in.

I'll leave you to imagine my inner turmoil at this moment. I'm trying to keep half an eye on Ros, to register how much she's hearing of this, while trying at the same time to pay her no attention at all, in case Dumb and Dumber here finally realise that it's not Jenna Berry who's the object of my affections. Then Clive makes a misjudged remark about Faruk's sister, Deniz, but the ketchuppy sausage-end Faruk flicks in immediate retribution falls short of its grinning target and drops onto Ros's plate, where it sits among the last of her lettuce leaves.

'Whoops!' Faruk says.

'Kindergarten's out early, I see.'

Standing behind Ros is her keeper, Teresa Davenport. Can't Ros do anything without this girl abruptly appearing to whisk her off to some sado-Nazi lesbian encounter group? Which is the sort of thing I can see Teresa Davenport would think was fun. What is her problem? And why does Ros always seem to go along with her? Today is the first time since Prom night that I've seen her separated from her Siamese twin. Poor Ros – it must be like having a human version of an electronic tag. But Ros had already decided to leave before it all becomes a sort of sausagey Agincourt and has gathered together her iPod and shouldered her bag. Before she heads off with Irma Grese in the direction of the doors and TD's lesbian group, she takes out her earphones and says to me, 'See you around, Bernie.'

'It's Brian...' I say, but Ros and her parole officer are already being borne away by a low-flying cloud of year 10 sports chodes, heading for the games field. I'm only vaguely aware of Faruk looking at Clive and then at me. I'm still looking at the doors Ros has just passed through.

'Bernie?' he says.

'What?' That sounds like me.

'See you around?' Clive says.

'BJ?' says Faruk.

'Oi, Johnson!' Clive says.

'What?'

'Oh fuck me,' Faruk says to Clive. 'You thinking what I'm thinking?'

'Very unlikely,' Clive says. 'But I am thinking BJ's gone terminal for Ros Chandler.'

'Fuck me,' Faruk says, as he watches her disappear through the swinging doors. 'Rosalind Chandler? Are you sure?'

'Trust me.' Clive says, but Faruk's still looking like he's been given a puzzle with square holes and a full set of round pegs.

'But why?' he says, which is when I begin to think that Faruk might not be in possession of his full quota of marbles. It's funny that I didn't notice it before.

CHAPTER 12

Mama Told Me Not To Come

'What you want, my son, is a big party.'

It's not my father talking, though, it's Roger Dyson, fresh from the shower. He's been working out in the yard, shifting rusty metal, chucking oily components in the compactor. He'd have had to shower even if Clive hadn't made a strict rule about it and even if the house wasn't looking less like the residence of a scrap metal dealer by the day and more like the winning entrant in a homes and gardens competition. Well, obviously not the garden bit; Roger's still resembles an ancient battlefield, despite the first signs of a tidier mind at work here and there. The dogs, who should be straining on chains in the yard ready to tear the bollocks off anybody with big enough ones to brave a visit, are sitting either side of the hearth, looking like a pair of fireside ornaments – albeit with that pissed-off look they have when they've just been shampooed. Roger was still finishing up in the shower when I arrived with Clive, but he's told me to make myself at home in the sitting room.

Which is harder than it sounds. The place is spotless, the cushions plumped, Laura Ashley curtains tied back with little red ropes and vases of carefully-arranged flowers placed on every surface. I notice that the photograph of Nick Griffin in the Cath Kidston frame has been changed for one of Nick Clegg. I walked home from school with Clive, invited to his for a session on his Playstation. (Roger's bought him *Call of Duty 7*, but unless my luck or Clive himself has changed, we'll be setting up home together in *The Sims* again tonight.) Now, though, Clive has gone off to see if any of 'the fucking fabric samples' he's been sent 'will do for the fucking bedrooms.'

That was when Roger had appeared in the doorway, wearing

a very short towel and his tattoos.

'That's right, a fucking party,' he repeats. 'Think about it, Bri. You invite all that muff in your little black book, then you pump the boy up with alcopops or whatever he's drinking now.'

'He likes "Sex on the Beach".'

Roger takes a moment, then understands.

'Then you get him dancing, the birds wetting themselves for him, and Bob's your mother's brother. Have a bedroom reserved specially for him. We'll set the mood beforehand: soft light, a packet of Durex ribbed on the bedside, maybe a tube of KY in case she's a little tight. I tell you, Brian, it can't fail.'

I'm not so sure. I've never been to a party where everything has gone right. Or one where anything has gone right, now that I think about it.

'And you invite that Rosie What's-her-face and you take her aside and you tell her all about your shared interest. What was it again?'

'Books.'

'Right, you tell her all about the latest Chris Ryan and then you cop a quick feel of the goods and it's all systems go for launch.' Roger grabs himself through the towel and gives an extravagant thrust in my direction. 'So what do you say?'

Okay, so he's crude, rude and probably thinks *The Guardian* is a film starring Arnold Schwarzenegger. I mean, knowing the names of a few dead artists doesn't constitute intelligence, does it? But now he's put it like that, now we have Rosalind in the picture, his idea doesn't sound so bad. I'll have to tell Ros that the invitation doesn't include one other, though. Especially if that other is Teresa Davenport. And talking to her, one to one, at a party won't attract the attention I'd get if I talked to her at school. A party would be noisy, of course, and we'd probably have to take a walk outside to hear ourselves discuss books or whatever. Maybe in the direction of the park and the band stand, who knows? This idea is sounding better by the minute. On a more practical note, though, we'd have to clear a lot of the furniture out of this room to make space for the dancing, a point I now raise with Roger.

It's a point which elicits an unexpected reaction.

'Have the party here?' he says, like he's choking on something sharp. 'You're having a fucking laugh, aren't you, Brian? Of course you are. Do you know how much that fucking wallpaper cost? Or those fucking curtains? And I'm not having some cunt empty his dinner onto this fucking carpet, no fucking way. Fuck me, what would Clive say?'

There's a colourful movement in the doorway.

'About what?' Clive's changed out of his school uniform into his silk kimono, which he says makes him look like an off-duty Samurai. It really doesn't.

'Brian here wants to throw a party,' half-naked Roger says.

'I'm down with that,' his geisha son says.

'He wants to have it here,' Roger says.

'I don't think so!' Clive snorts.

'I thought no fucking way, too,' Roger says.

'Where else can we have a party?' I say. 'Hang on, this wasn't even my idea.'

'What about your place?' Roger says. 'If you can get your old man out of his watchtower for the evening.'

'Not a good idea,' I say. 'Not after the last one.'

'The Party To End All Parties,' Clive reminds his father.

There is complete silence for a moment.

'Oh yeah, I'd forgotten about that,' Roger says. 'I've still got the fucking newspaper clippings.'

'We can't do that again,' I say. 'It's unthinkable.'

'I suppose so,' Roger says. Clive nods.

'Somewhere else, then?' Clive says.

We agree to hold a party somewhere else.

The Party To End All Parties. This is how we talk of it now, because it very nearly was. A lot of kids in our year who were scheduled to have parties, didn't, because their parents had seen what had happened at this party (aka, The Mother of All Parties) and had cancelled them out of hand. And I'm not talking just about our year at our school. It was a complete knee-jerk reaction. No one bothered to find out exactly what had happened and how it had all been the result of one silly mistake which anyone might have made – particularly me.

My parents still talk about it as if it happened last Friday night, not almost a whole year ago. I've only to put a foot out of line, e.g. leaving unwashed plates in my room for, like, a few weeks, and out it all comes again, the fag ends and the roaches trodden into the brand-new carpet, the pink vomit floating in the fishpond, the soiled underwear in the microwave and the fire in the garden shed. Then the broken upstairs window, the trampled flowerbeds (which still gets Dad's back up), and the bright orange, buck-toothed rabbit which was spray-painted on the dining room wall are all brought up one more time. It's pathetic. And anyway, this is all stuff which happened before the party had properly kicked off.

I could understand their attitude much better if the thing had happened at our house. But it didn't, it happened at a house on the far side of the estate. If you have a good memory, you'll probably remember some of the details. What had attracted the attention of the national newspapers was partly to do with the massive SOS banner, which Wendell Marney had nicked from a Sons of Sodom gig and had somehow managed to hang across the roof, by way of the dormer window.

It was supposed to attract the attention of the hip and the happening of the neighbourhood, who would see it and identify with it and come on by. And he was right, it did get the place noticed – first by the Neighbourhood Watch, who made dozens of phone calls to tell each other not to panic, and then, interestingly, by the pilot of a Boeing 737 bound for Nicosia, whose report of a huge distress signal on a suburban home where suspicious black figures lurked in the grounds and a fire raged behind the house brought a totally disproportionate response from other agencies.

The police helicopter, which clattered overhead, its search-light playing on the gnomes sat fishing in the back garden, confirmed the sighting of an SOS signal and the presence of black-clad, possibly para-military figures in the garden (most of us wore black and Doc Marts were pretty much obligatory that month). Not long after the tins of paint and chemicals stored in the garden shed had ignited with a fantastic explosion, some serious paint-ballers arrived, or that's what we took them for at first.

They were wearing helmets and carrying some fuck-off paint-ball guns. The paint-ballers turned out to be an anti-terror squad from either the police, the SAS, Special Branch, MI5 or the council. They crouched behind cars and fiddled with body armour and pointed things but as soon as it was realised that someone had fucked up big time, they were bundled into a van and spirited away, leaving the local plod and various emergency services to sort the mess. Who paid for the operation was never established, despite questions in the House.

The Daily Mail reported it all and accompanied its spread with pictures taken from another helicopter. They took the 'failure of modern parenting methods' line while the Sunday People concentrated its investigative efforts upon the mysterious, naked girl who was witnessed vaulting across a succession of garden fences before disappearing into the morning mist.

I can kind of understand the perverted gratification some people derived from all of this. Seeing the house on TV, the burned-out revellers still staggering home when other kids were queuing for the school bus, the shell-shocked faces of Mr and Mrs Colby, the owners of the house, as they returned home from a boating holiday in Abersoch to find a TV crew, two pink sheep and much of their furniture on their front lawn. The two ambulances bearing customers for the overworked stomach pump and a fire crew, which was too late to extinguish the blaze in the garden shed, had already departed. From some perspectives, it was a sensational event, and we might have enjoyed it as much as the other partygoers, had we (that's the Four Horsemen) not been held mostly responsible for this horror.

I won't bother you with the grisly aftermath, suffice to say that if Mr Colby hadn't been a Mason, and if Dad hadn't been able to pull some strings, and if an insurance company chairman hadn't also been a Mason with wayward kids of his own, then we would probably have been charged with crimes not yet on the statute books, transported to some long-forgotten tropical penal colony and left there to rot. It would have been hard to see the punishment as more than we deserved, too.

There are photographs. You can find them on Flickr or the Facebook pages of most of the guests, both the invited and uninvited, if you happen to know them. I have a page of them up right now:

Img 1: Darren Alexander grins at camera as he pours Coco Pops into the goldfish bowl.

Img 2: Andy Towse and one unknown other moon from the front windows.

Img 3: Someone's cock, peeing in the toilet.

Img 4: Two unidentified cocks, peeing in the kitchen sink. Washing-up in sink.

Img 5: Dave Brownhill wearing a pair of blue satin ladies' briefs.

Img 6: Shelly Lark, Janet Carstairs and Jenny Wright, all topless.

Img 7: Shelly Lark on sofa, with half-naked man on top, possibly having sex.

Img 8: A dog being sick.

Img 9: Dave Fletcher, Martin Heard and Alice Jameson smiling, with green (caged) parrot.

Img 10, 11, 12: Various unknown faces, arms flailing as they try to capture (uncaged) parrot sitting on curtain pole.

Img 13 Parrot caught in flash as it escapes into the night sky.

Img 14: Dave Fletcher being sick, mostly in toilet.

Img 15: Shelly Lark kneeling in front of, to judge from indie-style jeans around Converse trainers, Derek Bacon.

Img 16: Shelly Lark being sick in fishpond.

Img 17: Unidentified male rifling bedroom underwear drawer.

Img 18: Martin Lloyd, wearing a black bra with matching knickers (on head).

Img 19: Someone's hands skinning up a monster spliff.

Img 20: Two policemen and one policewoman surrounded in the living room by four naked men.

Img 21: Dave Fletcher wearing a policeman's helmet.

Img 22: Dave Fletcher in back of police car.

Img 23: Blurry crowd in the hall. Someone who might be Ros, sitting all by herself on the stairs.

And so on. There are thousands of them. There is footage on YouTube, too. The audio quality is so poor that the music is just a deafening roar of undifferentiated sound but these phone-shot sequences would be more than enough to convict a number of faces I know – but can't name here – of criminal damage, petty larceny, animal cruelty and stupidity in the first degree. Then there are the physical artefacts which are now in the keeping of various party veterans and which are prized as bizarre souvenirs, to be brought out and discussed at length down years to come, until they have taken on the mystery of Mayan glyphs or Egyptian scarabs.

Martin Wright keeps the charred trainer which was unearthed among the ashes of the shed and is the foundation of a rumour that someone was unaccounted for when the party ended. Jen Edwards is thought to have the super-sized dildo which formed the basis of many of the impromptu party games. Tanya Jordan has a pair of police handcuffs which supposedly date from the party.

Then there is Frank the tortoise, which we keep in our garden and which I said I bought from someone in a cafe because now that its shell has been carefully painted with the words Tortoises Do It Eventually on one side by someone with patience and humour, and then daubed with MY PRIVATE sHELL on the other, by someone else, I have been unable to bring myself to take it back. And so it lurks under the lilac bush, too embarrassed to come out.

So, you must be wondering, how does such a thing happen? How can we learn from your mistakes so that our parties will run smoothly and be looked back on in years to come as sources of nothing but fond memories?

Another good question. I can't remember exactly whose idea it was to have the thing, but as soon as The Horsemen got wind that my dad was taking Mum away for a long weekend at Headingly (Dad going for the cricket and Mum going because Dad wanted to), there was never any question about the venue. It would be great to have a little do, just the four of us and one or two friends, female if possible.

But we could see immediately that would be a criminal waste of opportunity. We'd invite one or two more, just so the thing rocked a bit. Not too much, as I didn't want to annoy the neighbours and everything would have to be spick and span, as Mum says, by the time the parents returned. So there would be just us, a few girls and one or two sensible, yet fun friends. Deciding who to invite and who not to was just about impossible. Suppose the party went really well and everyone talked it up at school? Anyone we didn't invite would never talk to us again.

That was how the invite list got a bit longer. A lot longer, in fact. Then Diesel suggested that it might be a good idea to invite a few people who were actually old enough to get served in the offie, so they could buy the booze. So we added one or two safe people from the year above. Booze sorted; what else? We wouldn't want any drugs of course, but it would be terminally uncool if there wasn't a token amount of weed, so Manic Mick was invited, him being St Saviour's tried and tested traveller in pharmaceuticals. But that would be it, no one else, just us and this hand-picked crew.

I would be in charge of the invitations, which I'd email to the lucky people on our exclusive list. No problemo. But then, looking through my contacts, I realised that I only actually had the email addresses of four people on the list and two of them lived on our street anyway. I admit I went into panic mode for five frantic minutes – it was Wednesday evening and the party was scheduled for Friday night. So I was more than a little relieved to remember that all I had to do was post the invite on Facebook and all my friends would see it and no one else. Brilliant. And those who weren't one of my 39 Facebook friends, would be given the nod by mutual acquaintances.

Of course, I now see how it's possible for some of those friends to extend the invite list simply by forwarding the details to their own list of friends and acquaintances and also how the less scrupulous might elaborate on the party plans, so that anyone reading them would feel they had to go to that party or die trying. It now appears that some people arrived fully expecting a free bar, live music and strippers. But back in my bedroom on that Wednesday night, I bigged up my party as BJ's Big Bash, promised an evening of fun and frolics, entered the address and time it would kick off and hit 'Send' in the full expectation that my invitations would be seen only by the eyes of those I wanted to come.

The party was supposed to start at 8pm, though we didn't expect anyone to turn up quite so unfashionably early. The cooler kids would want to come when they were sure that things were under way. As we sat on the sofa in the living room, washed, waxed and waiting, with the dining table laden with all the booze and plates of nibbles we could afford and listening to Diesel's party mix on Dad's music centre (my stereo having inexplicably caught fire earlier that evening), we reckoned that 9–9.30 was a much more realistic time to expect company. By 10.00 we were having doubts about our popularity. No one? Were they all now in the Queen's Head, that notorious den of under-age drinkers but would be piling in at closing time? Or was it more fucked up than that – was there some other party, which had been deemed cooler than ours? And which we hadn't been invited to?

Where the fuck was everyone, we asked? Had I sent out the invites, Diesel wanted to know? Faruk said I had, because he'd heard people talking about the party at school that very day. So was it something one of us had said? Was it somehow possible that one or all of us had somehow managed to offend the whole school? It was possible, we conceded, but not that likely. We paced, we ate, we drank plastic cups of cider, which was all we had, until people started arriving clutching bottles of something better. And then it got worse.

We heard a car pull up, doors slam and footsteps on the path and all rushed to the door to greet our first guests with the customary, 'All right, you wankers!' which we delivered loudly and in perfect unison, but into the faces of Mum and Dad, who had come back home after the England v Pakistan game had been cancelled because of an unspecified security threat. I don't think they understood what we had shouted, I think they just thought we were pleased to see them. They were too tired anyway and Dad was still obviously miffed that he'd not been able to see Andrew Strauss in action. They dropped their bags in the hall and made for the living room.

'What's all this?' Dad says, looking at the three big bottles of White Lightning on the table and the little bowls of Twiglets and Doritos. 'Not having a party, are we?'

'Oh, Charles,' Mum says. 'The boys need to blow off a little steam now and then. All that studying for their end of year exams can't be good for them. So let's not get this out of proportion. It's just apple cider and there's only the four of them. Heavens, any other child left alone for a weekend would probably have thrown a real party and invited the world and his wife.'

Dad considers this for a moment, and brightens. He's got off lightly, he's thinking, but he doesn't know how lightly (and nor do we, at that moment).

'I suppose you're right, dear,' Dad says, as he claims his usual chair by the fireplace. 'I don't often say this, Brian, but I think we're lucky to have you. We've brought you up well, Violet and me. Vi, get these young men a glass of that cider. And you can pour me one too. No reason to spoil their evening, is there?'

Diesel, Clive and Faruk sit on the sofa sipping their ciders and accepting nibbles when Mum offers them. Dad tells them about the last England tour of Australia, game by game, ball by ball, and all about the origins of the Ashes. I sit in the armchair next to Dad, wondering what exactly would happen if I've got the time of the party wrong and everyone arrives all at once, at 11.00? I can only wait and see. Meantime, I'm wondering why I sometimes hear a helicopter clattering above.

On the sofa, Diesel is making it clear he wants to go, shifting uncomfortably in his seat, yawning and checking his watch. Faruk and Clive look equally awkward, but no one has an exit line handy and it seems rude to interrupt my dad, who has gone on to describe the conditions at the Oval when England were victorious in 2009. And so we sit there while the night wears on, until at last Dad says it's time for him to 'hit the hay,' but that it's quite all right if we boys want to stay up another half hour or so. He wishes us goodnight and goes upstairs. Quite an evening, you'll agree.

It wasn't until the next day that I find out what has happened, when a reporter from *The Sun* calls up to 'get my side of the story first'. Before I have properly woken up and understand why a national newspaper might be calling me, of all people, she's asking me about a riotous party and a fire and about police helicopters and an anti-terror squad. I really don't have an idea what she's on about and I'm just about to tell her she'd dialled the wrong number when she asks me, straight out, why I had given 111 Laurel Gardens as the address, rather than Number 11?

CHAPTER 13

Lust For Life

Mr Dawson, who takes me for English, says, very loudly, and clearly, 'Time's up, put your pens down.'

Not that I had been holding one. I finished my English exam at least twenty minutes ago. It was much easier than I had expected and maybe Mr Dawson is right after all and I do have some competence in this area (just don't ask about maths, sciences, practical subjects or anything involving common sense). Across the crowded hall, one or two chodes are still trying to scribble a few more mark-salvaging words before Mr Dawson and Miss Smith collect in their papers.

At lunch break, Mr Dawson catches me outside the library, where I've gone in the hope of finding Ros. Mr Dawson is the last of the old-school teachers. I don't mean that he only teaches at old schools like ours, or that he's an old school teacher, which he is, in fact, I just mean that he has that tweedy, leather-elbowed look which has you imagining him smoking his pipe and listening to classical music in the evenings, not gaming and clubbing like some of the younger ones claim to do. He may not know what an app is or even that he's the subject of a surprisingly good-natured group on Facebook (Rowley Dawson Rules KO) but he's a good teacher, he loves his subject and he takes a real interest in as many of his kids as his dodgy memory will handle.

I tell him I thought the exam went quite well. Mr Dawson nods, pops his empty pipe into his mouth and says I should practise my writing, make it a habit. Who knows, he says, perhaps you might do something with it in later life? He advises me to write for pleasure, to write stories or articles for *Smile!* the official school paper (you can see how the samizdat *Smeg!!* was born), and to keep a diary, or a journal and to be sure and take it with me wherever I go. He seems to have forgotten that he suggested this writing malarkey to me last year. He probably says something similarly encouraging to anyone who shows a flicker of interest in his chosen subject. And I don't tell him that I have indeed been writing a journal, this one.

Which is good writing practise, I suppose, but the last thing I'd want to do is upload or publish it. I'll maybe show it the Horsemen one day when we're older, and we'll have a few beers and a laugh about the old days. Clive saw a page which I'd carelessly left up on my computer screen one night (not, thankfully, one that mentioned him or our suspicions about him) and he reckoned I should take it further, too. Clive, our resident specialist in English, says there's nothing like writing for improving your command of the English constabulary.

Mr Dawson is impressed to see the titles of the overdue books I'm returning to the library. Top of the pile is Great Expectations, which was recommended by Nana and – once I'd got used to sentences which could fill a flyer – was actually okay. Then, in case Ros is still on the "K"s, I have some poetry by Keats along with a double "K" whammy, Kim by Rudyard Kipling. I'd meant to read these too but couldn't get around to them, what with having so much exam work and Clive having lent me Call of Duty 7.

Mr Dawson says I really should think hard about doing something in the field of writing, consider becoming a serious journalist, perhaps, and putting the world to rights in print. He sucks on his pipe, producing a spittly whistle in the mouthpiece, as he stares out of the window, lost in thought. 'You might even write a novel,' he says, indicating the books in my hands. 'But always remember, Brian, that in order to write well, it is imperative that you read well, too.' He peers over his glasses, expecting a reply, and I promise him that I really will think about it.

And I do, for all of two minutes, as I give in my books, renew the Keats, scan the library and see that though Teresa Davenport is there, cramming for her next exam, the swot, there's no sign of Ros. I've not seen her for days now and I'm a little concerned. Writing, Rowley says. That's what I'm thinking as I cough up a 20p fine. Does he know how much time and effort it sometimes takes me to write a postcard, let alone a novel?

I pull a few books off the K shelves, some K Fiction, some K Drama and, it seems, some K philosophy, though I'm holding *Fear and Trembling* by someone called Søren Kierkegaard only because I've mistaken it as a sequel to the totally exceptional *Fear and Loathing in Las Vegas*, by Hunter S. Thompson. So there I am in the library reading, but not reading, a bunch of books and plays by Charles Kingsley, Thomas Kyd and Dean R. Koontz and wondering just when I'm going to be able to put my sketchy knowledge of authors whose names begin with K to its intended use.

I think about this for a while, imagining Ros's surprised and interested expression when I tell her that I read the same stuff she does. Then I get that feeling you have when you're being watched. It's Teresa Davenport, who seems more interested in my choices than I am. 'I didn't know you read so widely,' she whispers across the table. 'Kierkegaard to Koontz is quite a leap.'

Five minutes later, we're occupying a couple of seriously uncomfortable chairs in the Sixth form common room, separated by a small table. We lean across it, trying to communicate over the jungle rhythms pumping out of communal speakers. The music's turned up so loud I can't hear what Teresa's saying, though I'm nodding and making what I think are appropriate faces as she speaks. It's not often I have a one-on-one with a woman, though, and I'm making the best of it.

As a matter of interest, she's really not that bad looking, now that I'm up close and personal, and she smells quite nice too. She's wearing an open necked shirt with a pendant on a slim gold chain, which draws my attention downwards, where I can just see the lace edging of a deep pink bra. She's wearing faded jeans again, which hug her trim figure and accentuate her small, boyish bum, which is probably enveloped in a pair of satin knickers of a matching colour, I guess. It's funny how I hadn't really noticed her before. Never noticed she was sort of fanciable, anyway. All I had noticed, in fact, was her fiery protectiveness of her best friend and my ideal, the mysterious, the beautiful and the worryingly well-read Rosalind Chandler.

'So that's the way it is,' Teresa is saying as the bell rings and half the common room drifts out and I can finally hear what she's saying. 'It's because of this that I have to look out for her.'

I nod, but I'm wishing I had the nerve to ask her to repeat everything she's just said, because I'm pretty sure that most of it was about Ros. But at least it appears that I'm not in her guardian's bad books any more. Maybe she sees me as someone interesting now, a vegan who reads Kierkegaard, rather than a weirdo who just likes getting other people's stomachs pumped. And, come on, winning her approval can only boost my chances with Ros.

She sits back and looks at me like it's for the first time. 'You know,' she says, 'I didn't have you down as the school intellectual. Not that you look immensely thick or anything, but you know, the people you hang out with? But, hey, if you're reading Kierkegaard, I must have got you wrong. I have to say, I'm impressed.'

I smile shyly, modestly.

'What is it you like about him anyway?' Hmm. I wasn't expecting this.

'Who?' I say.

'Søren Kierkegaard.'

Which puts me on the spot, as I haven't even opened the book. But I'm not going to admit this and lose the points I may already have racked up with my newly acquired go-between.

'Søren, yes,' I say, weighing my answer. 'Good old Søren K.' I wish I had Mr Dawson's pipe to snatch from my mouth as finally, after much ceiling gazing and nodding thoughtfully, I say, 'It's like you either get him – or you don't.'

'Wow,' she says. 'His existentialism, you mean?'

'Exactly,' I say. She nods, like she's totally interested.

'Or his humanism?' she adds, annoyingly.

Again, I'd take a good draw from Rowley's pipe if I had it here. That would add gravitas. As it is, I wait a moment before I make a measured reply. 'That too, to an extent,' I venture.

'Interesting,' Teresa says. 'And what about those tendencies we now interpret at post-modern?'

I smile, as if acknowledging a well-known problem in the study of Kierkegaard.

'I think we have to take them for what they are,' I say. She nods again, like I'm really impressing her. I think I might be enjoying this. As she leans forward to hear what I'm saying, I get to see more of her deep pink bra and I'm hoping this conversation can go on a little bit longer.

'And what about Keats?' she says. Another loaded question, if she did but know it.

But I think I'm getting the hang on this now, so I reply almost straight away. 'What about Keats?'

I say, employing my wry smile. 'What is there left to say about him? Hasn't it all been said before? I think we just have to enjoy him…'

'For what he is?' Teresa chips in, eagerly.

'Exactly,' I say. At which point, I would have upturned my pipe and emptied it noisily into a glass ashtray.

Amazingly, Teresa Davenport appears to be enjoying this as much as I am. It looks like she's having fun. She seems to like my company.

'What's your all-time favourite poem by John Keats?' she asks.

I consider her question. 'It's hard to say,' I tell her and this is very true. 'He wrote so many blinders.'

I'm not sure that 'blinders' is an appropriate expression in this context, but she seems pleased with my answer. In fact, she laughs with pleasure. I am a hit.

I really want to steer the conversation towards *Great Expectations*, something I've actually read, but there seems to be no need, as Teresa is telling me it's so nice to talk with someone as widely read and obviously intelligent as myself. She's smiling like I have genuinely entertained her, if you can call a serious discussion about philosophy and literature entertainment. She gets me to write my phone number on the back of her hand. Then she writes hers on mine.

'Ros's friends need to stay in touch,' she says. 'Call me if you see her doing any of those things I mentioned.' I have no idea what she is talking about. She gets up to go. 'Next time I want you to tell me about what we can take from the philosophy of Dean R. Koontz.'

I'll be sure to do that, I say, as she swings open the doors. 'And you'll remember what I said about Ros, won't you?'

'Of course I will,' I assure her, wishing I knew what on earth it was. 'You can count on me.'

I've not seen Ros lately and none of us has seen much of Diesel, either. Obviously, we've scoped him at school, but he always seems to be with Lauren and as we don't always feel like discussing the *The X Factor* and *Britain's Got Talent*, or what Faruk will do in the army, we let them get on with whatever they're doing, which doesn't look like a lot of fun anyway. Lauren is always talking and Diesel is always looking like he's about to kill himself.

Just the other day, we saw him coming out of Mothercare with Lauren. He looked like he might be about to throw himself under a supertram at any moment. We can see that our friend needs help, needs the benefit of advice based upon our impressive total of 42 years of solid experience. Besides, we urgently need to ask him if we can hold a party at his.

There's still another week of exams, but this Saturday, Diesel's mum says he's at the shop as usual, so Clive and I decide to intercept him after work, before Lauren can get her claws into him. Faruk is paying one of his irregular visits to his mosque. Diesel worked in the record shop on the eve of his first exam, when if anyone needed to be locked in his bedroom cramming, it was Diesel. He's naturally very bright, but 'almost completely lacking in interest and application' according to the last report card we saw. Unless it's at the record shop, where he seems to really make a difference. It doesn't take us long to see that the shop has changed.

Since his visit to Narnia, Diesel's widened his musical interests, which has led to some interesting changes at the Caterpillar, where Magic Mick is pleased to give his enthusiastic Saturday lad a free hand. Diesel's rearranged everything, we see. It's no longer necessary to go in the back room to find the old or rare vinyl, because it's been filed in with everything else, so that Mark is now with Mick Ronson, Wu-tang Clan share a crib with Wishbone Ash, while Grandmaster Flash is with someone called Grand Funk Railroad and GD's favourites, the Grateful Dead. Magic Mick says it works surprisingly well. People come in for MC Hammer and leave with MC5 as well. Selling a supposedly defunct format at a time when downloading is putting other shops out of business, Alice and the Caterpillar isn't doing so badly, Mick says.

Mick asks me about his friend and my grandfather, GD. I'm not sure what to say to him but he tells me he knows all about Ruth's illness and that he's been doing what he can. I ask him what he means. 'Your grandmother wants a good death,' Mick says. 'And GD will do anything to see she gets one. Ruth wants to die at home with your grandfather and we all hope that's what will happen.' He turns away, to file some vinyl discs in the shelves behind him. 'But GD'll have his hands full then and he's going to need all the help we can give him with the arrangements.'

'What arrangements?'

'Her funeral,' Magic Mick says, turning to us again. His cheeks are wet but his voice is firm. 'GD's told me exactly what Ruth wants and how it should all go down. What I'm asking is this: can I count on you? And your friends?'

'Of course,' I say, and the others nod – they all like Nana. But I'm not sure what sort of help we could provide at a funeral. I hope we don't have to be pallbearers – it's hard not to imagine the most awful of accidents. I hate talking about it. The thought of Nana's death is always with me. I try and get on with life as best as I can but whatever I do, it's always there, lurking in a corner, ready to ambush me when I'm least prepared for it. Now Mick asks me to jot my number on the inside of his outsize Rizla packet and says he'll be in touch when the time comes.

I don't want to think about this business of the funeral, not until I have to, anyway. I distract myself with another trawl through the re-ordered record bins while Diesel helps Mick to shut up the shop. Soon, the three of us are slouching past the Wheatsheaf, where Diesel stops and says that the best place to talk on a hot day like this would be in a pub garden, with four ice-cold pints of Kronenbourg.

'We won't get served in there,' Clive says. I think it's the pair of ceramic lions guarding the Victorian pub's marbled entrance that's putting him off. That and the enormous, pony-tailed wrestler who's mopping the bar top as he watches three probably underage youths loitering in his car park.

'Course we will,' Diesel says, uncertainly.

Clive and I walk straight through the pub and out into the pub garden at the rear, choosing a table where we can see and hear Diesel at the bar. Diesel looks very small in front of this goliath of the beer trade. I hadn't realised his voice was so high either until I hear him squeak, 'Can I have three pints of lager, please?' Perhaps he's wearing tight underpants.

The landlord, on the other hand, has his bass turned all the way up, with enough volume to reach drinkers down the end of the garden.

'Of course you can, sunshine,' he says. After pausing for dramatic effect, possibly, he booms out, 'ID?'

People at nearby tables stop talking and listen. I can see Diesel shifting uncomfortably in his trainers.

'Did I say lager?' he says at last, slapping his head. 'I meant lager shandy. Three pints please.'

'ID?' the landlord says, again.

Diesel makes a big pantomime out of checking his pockets, slapping his sides, and probably rolling his eyes. 'I'd forget my head,' he's saying. 'Must have left it at home.'

The girls at the next table, who can only be months older than us, have started sniggering.

'Oh, dear,' the landlord says, loudly. 'We've forgotten our ID, have we? What are we going to do now?' I think he's playing to the crowd, who are now openly laughing.

Diesel must have heard it, because very clearly and rather crossly, he says, 'I'll have three pints of your finest lager shandy – and as soon as you like, please.' Which seems to interest the crowd. But it's gone so quiet now that everyone in the garden can hear him add, in a much quieter voice, 'Without the lager, please.'

'What is the point,' Diesel is saying, as we extract the pink and yellow cocktail umbrellas and bright red plastic straws with which the landlord has rather humorously decorated our glasses of lemonade. 'What is the point, I'm saying, of exams, when I'll be going straight out to work anyway? No uni-pigging-versity for me, now.'

'You weren't going anyway,' Clive reminds him.

'I'll be at Magic Mick's until I die, now,' Diesel is saying. 'Or at least until he does.'

'But why?'

'Oh, bloody hell, Clive, try and keep up,' Diesel says. 'Because Lauren's going to have the kid, isn't she? And there's nothing I can do to stop her.'

'Fuck me,' Clive says.

'No, fuck *me*,' Diesel says. 'She won't even talk about losing it. Last week when I had that black eye?'

'Yes?'

'I didn't walk into a cupboard door.'

We act surprised. 'So what happened?' Clive asks.

'I gave her a leaflet about terminating pregnancies,' Diesel says.

'Fuck,' Clive says.

'So what are you going to do?' I ask.

'What can I do? You tell me?' Diesel says. 'I'm fucked.'

'Fuck,' we say.

I can imagine what he's seeing: the future with all the best years edited out. He can't go off travelling with a kid, won't be joining us on any road trip. He won't even be able to go to pubs and clubs unless he can find a babysitter. And he probably won't be able to afford it anyway. It'll be nights in with the telly while we're off at festivals or going to gigs. And, of course, he's going to miss out entirely on The Shagging Years.

I don't want to say what I'm going to say, as I quite like Lauren. She's gabby but she's got a good heart. I've seen her helping new kids on their first day at school and I've not heard her backstabbing her mates like most of the girls do. But she should have been on the pill, shouldn't she? She can't just rob our mate of the best years of his life, all because of a five-minute fumble in the park. So I'm probably only voicing what Clive is thinking too, when I say, 'So why don't you tell her to do one?'

'It's not just me, is it?' Diesel says. 'There's Mum, who's over the moon about it, can't wait to be a grandmother at thirty nine. And her parents, who aren't exactly thrilled with the news but who I think will fucking kill me if I don't go through with it.'

'With what?' Clive says.

'Marriage. Kids. Work. Home. The whole train set.'

'As if,' Clive says.

'Well, couldn't you do one?' I say. 'Just go somewhere they don't know you and start over again?'

'I haven't started here yet,' Diesel says. 'Where would I go? What would I do?'

'What about going to stay with your Uncle Lol?' Clive suggests.

'He's in Leicester,' Diesel says.

'Leicester's not so bad,' I say.

'The prison is,' Diesel says.

We sit in silence while we ponder the enormity of Diesel's fate. We've had pregnancies at school before, but it's always been the ones you'd expect it to happen to. Weird when they turn up at school with their carrycots to show them off. They don't look so happy when I see them in town, pushing strollers and watching their mates getting ready to go out. I saw some girls pointing out Lauren's swollen belly in the common room and I so nearly said something. I wish I had; it shouldn't happen to someone as well meaning as Lauren. It shouldn't happen to Diesel, either.

'There must be something you can do, mate,' Clive says.

'This is your life,' I tell him. 'And sometimes you just have to do the wrong thing. Say, "Sorry, Mum, no big wedding, no grandchild with your name". And then you'll just have to man-up to her lot. You have to leave her, Diesel.'

'I can't,' he says. Disconsolately is the word I want here.

'Why not?' Clive and I say, together.

Diesel's staring into the future like he's watching the carpenters building his gallows.

'I love her, don't I?' he says.

'Oh, fuck,' we chorus.

We don't ask him about having a party at his.

CHAPTER 14

Hey Girl, Don't Bother Me

Mum has been talking to Russell Crowe again. I've caught her at it before, when Dad was at work and I should have been at school, but wasn't. If she thinks we're out, she doesn't bother to close the door to her sewing room, where she spends an increasing amount of her spare time. The sewing room is really the box room, the sort of room which will either be filled with junk or get turned into someone's office or games station. Dad's office is his shed. His personal space is the garden, which no one uses much as it seems almost too manicured and perfect to spoil by actually walking on. Plus, it's overshadowed, literally, by the fence which Dad added the high trellis to recently, to block out any sign of the small mountain of metal which is growing daily in Roger Dyson's garden-cum-scrapyard.

In her sewing room, Mum's got an antique sewing table and a newish sewing machine, an old wardrobe, an upholstered chair with broken springs, a stack of cardboard boxes mostly containing bits of material, and, I discovered, a five year diary, which she keeps in the drawer of the table and whose flimsy lock I've often been tempted to pick so I could find out what goes on in her mind. (It's funny how your parents remain mysteries to you). I'm thinking, does she still love Dad? Did she ever love Dad? Where does she find her pleasure these days? Does she still have hopes for the future, or is this it? I'm thinking of what she might write in that diary when I have finally told Dad that GD and Nana are not his parents and how this will affect her, because GD is certain that it will. But I'm forgetting the other thing she keeps in her room, which stands in the corner by her desk and is called Russell Crowe.

Russell Crowe arrived when Dad's department store was

having a facelift and a lot of old junk found its way onto the skips around the back. Russell had gone from being a mannequin dressed in the latest fashions and carefully posed in one of the plate-glass windows, to a naked dummy sharing a skip with a gang of condemned standard lamps, a broken down sofa and some old office chairs. Mum was doing a lot of sewing at that time, running up summer dresses she never wore and making me shirts which I never wore. She'd mentioned her need for a dressmaker's dummy and Dad must have thought it would save a few quid if he took the mannequin from the skip and made her a present of it.

She called it Russell and carried it up to her sewing room. I thought Dad had done a decent thing at the time. I didn't know it was no earthly good to her, not as a dressmaker's dummy, anyway. But Russell did turn out to have other uses. The next clothes she made were fitted around Russell's frame in much the same way she would have used a dressmaker's dummy. The difference was that once fitted, they stayed where they were. I soon caught on that she was making clothes only for the mannequin, whom I would see in her sewing room fitted out with a new suit of clothes every few weeks. He became as well dressed as Mum's sewing skills allowed. She bought a number of wigs from the fancy dress shop and styled them to suit his look.

One day he would be sporting a two-piece suit, worn with one of Dad's old shirts and a new tie, which I suspect Mum had bought for "him", as she referred to the doll, and a brown mullet. The next time he would be wearing a floral print shirt, made from the old living room curtains and a blond pageboy hairstyle. Eventually, he had a suit of clothes and wigs and even facial hair for every occasion and Russell was as likely to be stood at her side as she read her True Crime magazines at her desk, dressed in a smart but casual ensemble of V-necked jumper, white tee shirt and charcoal slacks as he was in a formal dinner jacket and black tie. Soon, Russell's wardrobe was filling the wooden version by the door. Mum laughed off any questions about Russell, saying he was helping her improve her understanding of clothes design and didn't we all need a hobby?

Recently, though, she's stopped all pretence of making clothes. Russell's clothes now come from Oxfam and Help the Aged. She spends whole days trailing around the charity shops and it's hard to know what to say when she drags me in one of these places, holds up a purple polo shirt and asks me much too loudly whether I think it will suit Russell Crowe? The whole episode has been weird and until recently, I've not known what was at the bottom of it.

Then I heard her talking to someone upstairs on the day I came back early from school, having blagged a study afternoon. At first I thought she was on the phone, but the sewing room hasn't got an extension and Mum hasn't got a mobile. It sounded like she was having an enjoyable chat with someone, though. She sounded much brighter, livelier than she usually is with Dad. Curious, I went halfway up the stairs to eavesdrop.

'One day,' she was saying, 'I'll have that shop, I really will, and it'll sell the nicest flowers in town. I can arrange them beautifully, you know, much better than they do at Flower Power, though I do say so myself. We'll start small, just a corner shop somewhere, but we'll grow, you know, just like the flowers. And we'll blossom, Russell. Violet's will be the place to go for cut flowers and potted perennials for all occasions. And you, Russell, when you're not making your films, you'll help out in the shop, won't you? And we'll live above the shop in a lovely flat, just you and me and the dogs and the waterbed.'

There's been other stuff, involving the waterbed, which I won't detail here because I'm too busy trying to delete it from my own memory. But at the bottom of all this is the inescapable conclusion that Mum is not only dissatisfied, but she's lonely too – lonely in the midst of her own family. When I heard that, I slipped back down the stairs and let myself quietly out the back door. It's been a sad revelation and one that I know I won't be able to do anything about. I can't talk to Dad and tell him. He wouldn't have a clue what to do either, and I don't know how he would receive the news that he has rivals for her affections, even if they are an international film star and a plastic mannequin, both called Russell Crowe.

I am amazed that I made such an impression on Teresa Davenport. The other day, in the common room, she was hanging on my every word, lapping it all up. Clearly, I'm more of a ladies' man than my past history has led me to believe. It's true that I haven't been spectacularly successful with women up to this point, but bearing in mind what a hit I was with Teresa, I'm persuaded that when it comes to girls, I've just made some wrong choices.

For instance, there was this girl I kept seeing outside the YMCA, who once smiled at me and whom I became kind of fixated on for a few weeks, engineering occasions where I'd accidentally-on-purpose bump into her again just to get that same smile. She was totally gorgeous, with long black hair and big, hazel eyes. I guessed she was shy, too, because she never said anything to me. She just smiled and nodded, but even that was enough to send me home deliriously happy.

I decided that I was in love with her. I picked a name for her, deciding she very probably was called Cordelia (we'd been doing King Lear in Lit). I imagined she was from a modest family, who probably lived in a neatly painted cottage on the edge of town, where her father probably worked as a landscape gardener, while Cordelia's mother probably spent her days tending her herb and vegetable garden and selling the produce at a roadside stall. Cordelia herself would be a student at the local FE college, studying art and design. I got to know where she liked to hang out, which cafes she used, which parks she walked in.

I wouldn't say I stalked her exactly, but if you had taken a picture of her at this time, you might well have spied me somewhere in the background, still working up sufficient courage to go over and say hello to her. Eventually, my longing for her overpowered my cowardice and, seeing her leaving Expresso's one afternoon, I caught her eye, forced a smile and actually spoke to her. I can't remember the exact words I used, my heart was pumping so fast and my face was so red I must have looked like a tomato on a stick. But I think I said something like, 'Forgive me for interrupting your day, but I just had to tell you that I think you are the most beautiful girl I have ever seen and I was wondering if you would like to come with me to see Iron Man at the Odeon tonight?'

For a moment I was terrified that she wouldn't reply, just brush past me, outraged that I should have had the temerity even to speak to her. But no, she came closer and she did speak. I'll never know exactly what she said because it was all in a foreign language, one I couldn't even identify, much less understand. But whatever it was, there was a lot of it and it was all spoken very quickly. Then my stupid expression must have told her that I wasn't actually an advanced language student and that I wasn't making any sense at all of what she was saying. So she slowed right down and in a halting, broken English, she enunciated very carefully, 'I do not know what it is you talk to me. I know that I see you much a lot, all the days. I am going home to my country today. Goodbye and, oh, yes, how is it that you say? I hope that your spots will clear up.'

But that was then and this is now. My talk with Teresa has done wonders for my confidence and when I see Rosalind sitting on the grass by herself, on a mound, which overlooks the sports field, I'm sure that my moment has come. The mound is called 'The Grassy Knoll' now, after the school bookie's favourite in last year's 400 metres was knobbled by a catapult shot thought to have been fired from this spot. Today, the school's Olympically-inspired athletes are warming up on the track, shaking themselves down as they stretch their limbs and jog on the spot.

Behind them, on the far side of the track, a lone runner moves steadily around the circuit. They all look so dedicated and active, they make me tired just watching them. It's Wimbledon fortnight too, so chodes who couldn't ordinarily have aspired to be ball boys are suddenly gripped with ambition and spend their lunchtimes pulling muscles on the tennis courts, while their friends enjoy a laugh at their expense and a crafty fag in the bushes.

Various people are lolling on The Grassy Knoll, soaking up the late June sunshine with buttons undone and, in one or two cases, bras showing. A few are doing some last minute cramming before the afternoon's exam, but most are just lying there, pole-axed by the heat. The sun only has to show its face and all the non-uniformed sixth form is in light summer dresses – that's the girls, mostly – or tee shirts and cargo shorts. Everyone looks summery and everyone has lightened up in both colour and mood. Everyone except Ros, it appears. She sits on her own in a clearing on the Knoll, knees drawn up to her chest and a distant stare on her face.

In contrast with those around her, she's dressed all in black, some antique, Victorian-looking dress, which comes right down to her hook-and-eye boots. Her hair is tied up with what looks to me like a bit of a netting, or a veil, maybe, and she's got black crosses, which my years of watching Antiques Roadshow with Mum tell me are made from jet, hanging from her ears. Her lips are the usual blood red and she's gone to town with the mascara again. To say she stands out from the crowd hardly does justice to the chasm which yawns between her and her nearest sitters on the Knoll, two year-ten blondes who are practising a synchronised R&B routine which is clearly taxing their combined brain power. 'Not like that, Chablis,' one of them is shrieking. 'It's right arm over left, hands together and push, 'ave you gorrit now?'

Ros is different, and how. The others have cleared this space around her, like they think themselves unworthy of her company or they're intimidated by her originality. That's the price you pay for beauty and intelligence, I guess. But it's all good as far as I'm concerned. With the end of term approaching, I may never get a chance as promising as this again. So I wander up to her in what I think is called a nonchalant fashion, hands in pockets, taking a grand survey of the sports field, the running track and all those chodes actually using trainers for training and track suits for the track. Then it's like my gaze takes her in only accidentally – like I hadn't known she was there at all.

'Oh, hi, it's you,' I say. 'Cool day, isn't it? Not cool, like cold, because it's really warm, in fact I'm a bit sweaty, but…'

While she's digesting this, I sit down beside her and draw up my knees. She's still staring out towards the track somewhere and I'm not entirely sure she's heard me. If Ros has one fault, and it's a really little one, a peccadillo, it's that I never see her without her headphones in. I'd be interested to know what she's listening to. Probably something ice-cool and super-intelligent. I raise my voice, anyway.

'I've been wanting to talk to you,' I tell her, fixing my attention on the lone runner coming off the track and doubling over with exhaustion. 'It's amazing – I've discovered you and I share the same taste in literature. Almost exactly the same in fact. Crazy, isn't it? You read Kafka and Kerouac, right? Well, so do I! What are the chances? I read Ken Kesey, too, and Dean R. Koontz.'

There's still no reaction. I wish she would take out her earphones, just this once. I have to talk louder still. 'I'm reading Kierkegaard,' I tell her, and everyone else on the mound.

I begin to recite everything I can remember from the Wikipedia entry for the ultra-boring but clearly girl-impressing Søren Kierkegaard, dressing it up so it appears that these are original observations of my own. I throw in a few jokes too. I stand up and try to amuse her with my ready wit. An old song title and another philosopher's name produces 'Hegel, don't bother me,' which I think is exceptionally funny and laugh myself hoarse, wiping my eyes, only to see that she hasn't batted a single purple eyelid. 'It's funny, isn't it,' I try, desperately.

'No.' That's the voiced opinion of several of the recumbent bodies around me.

'I've been reading Keats too,' I tell her, just as loudly.

'Poof,' says one of my other listeners.

'What about you? What are you reading now?'

I turn and look at her and am surprised to see she's not actually wearing her headphones today. I needn't have shouted. 'Ros?' I say, and am puzzled that there's not a flicker of a reaction. Strange, I think. I try 'Rosalind?' with the same result. I consider the possibility that she has recently been struck deaf, perhaps in that lightning storm we had the other night. Hard to tell whether her clothes are singed or not. The other possibility is that she is ignoring me, cutting me dead, as they say in some of the older books I've dipped into recently. This is a terrible thought and I rack my brain for how I might have offended her. Did she think I was taking the piss when I said I was a vegan? Was it the behaviour of my so-called friends, Clive and Faruk at the dinner table, was it that ketchuppy sausage landing on her plate? I feel the need to speak plainly.

'Look,' I say. 'I don't know what it is that I'm supposed to have done, but I just want you to understand that I'm very sorry, okay?'

I realise that I'm as close to Ros as I will probably ever get and that it's now or never.

'I don't know what is going on here,' I say. 'But you might as well know that I respect you, Rosalind.' I don't notice that the hubbub of conversation has suddenly died. 'In fact, I think you are the most wonderful girl in the school.' I'm not really registering the barely-suppressed giggling and one or two ironical Aaahs. I blunder on. 'I admire you for the depth of your reading, your brilliant mind, the way you dress, the way you walk and probably the way you talk, too. Whether or not you want me,

Rosalind, I'm telling you here and now that I LOVE YOU.'

And now I can hear the noise around me, the almighty cheer, the clapping, the wolf-whistles and the coarse and suggestive comments from Dave Fletcher and his dumb mates. I stand there, awaiting Rosalind's response. It's like waiting to hear my fate.

I stand there what seems like an hour, but is probably ten seconds. The noise has subsided, like everyone else is awaiting her answer too. But amazingly, Rosalind Chandler is oblivious not only to my presence but to that of everyone else on The Grassy Knoll, to everyone else in the world, for all I know. She just sits there, with her knees pulled up a little tighter, maybe, and stares towards the track, where the lone runner is nowhere to be seen, not, that is, until she appears directly in front of me, a red faced, freely perspiring and very angry Teresa Davenport, who is saying, 'How could you do this, after everything I told you about Ros? How could you?' And she's helping Ros to her feet and Ros is still saying nothing as Teresa, dressed fetchingly, I'm ashamed to notice, in a sweat-dampened track top and tight blue shorts, helps Ros down from The Knoll and towards the Brian Johnson-free zone of the school itself.

You can imagine how I am feeling. Actually, no, you really can't.

Teresa Davenport stops play – again. I think about her close relationship with Ros as I follow the pair back to school, bathed in humiliation. What is it with her? Why is it TD who gets to spend so much time with Ros and not me? It's not natural, I think, then the thought flashes through my mind that maybe I have a rival. Maybe Ros is mistaking Teresa's attentions as friendship when Teresa has something very much more personal in mind. Teresa doesn't look like a lesbian, at least not like the ones I've Googled, but who knows? Maybe you get pretty ones too?

The end of term exams are over.

Most of mine seemed to go okay, but I've said that before,

when I produced results which had my Dad ranting and raving and tearing out his remaining hair. The terrible thing is, you never know, with exams. Chance and fate always seem to be involved somehow. But they are over at last and though we still have to go into school, part of the time, anyway, it's all much more relaxed. People are bunking off on the flimsiest pretexts and there's no real teaching going on, not for us, at least. Everyone's thoughts are turned towards what they'll do with the imminent summer holidays, like which festivals they're getting tickets for, where they're going on holiday and what summer jobs they'll be taking to fund their various recreational and shopping habits.

Dad is planning to take Mum off for a few days in Edgebaston, but there's to be no party at mine. Not after The Party to End All Parties. In fact it doesn't look like we'll be having a party anywhere. Diesel's is right out, now that he's steaming towards a wife and 2.4 children, poor bugger. Faruk's family's flat is always so crowded with friends and relatives that a party would get lost amongst them all. And Roger won't hear of it, despite it being his idea and him being so desperate for Clive to 'dip his wick', which he is so certain will immediately cure his son of any untoward tendencies.

Roger won't have it at his because he and Clive have finally got the bungalow's interior just the way they want it. It is spectacular, I have to say, with linen blinds and potted palms offering a sultry, tropical vibe in Roger's bedroom and a new ethnic thing going on in Clive's. The scrap business has obviously been doing well, as Roger has upgraded the floor coverings in several rooms and Clive's latest choice of designer knick-knacks looks on the expensive side. But it's not, I can understand, a place where either of them would want a lot of chodes in dirty boots dancing on the Persian rugs and doing the other party stuff in the boutique bedrooms and smart bathroom.

So instead of a party, we're going to have a weekend away,

somewhere there's something going on. And because Roger is a mate, sort of, and because he looks like he just might be a dangerous mate, we'll have to try and get Clive laid. After we've got ourselves laid, ideally. I'm not sure which is the more unlikely eventuality, but all sounds good right now. Cornwall could be a rocking venue: there's ravers and surf girls at Newquay, or posh kids with money down at Rock. We thought about Brighton, but getting Clive laid in the nation's gay capital might be making work for ourselves. The point is that we'll go somewhere, have a brilliant time and I'll be able to avoid thinking about Nana for a while, and also about how I have, apparently, completely distressed Rosalind, the one and only love of my life.

On days like this I think my top-end mobile phone has been worth every pound of the money Mum paid for it. It's got the usual roster of features I'll never use, plus a touch-screen, multi-mega pixel camera and an unusually detailed call log, which for today lists the following activity:

Friday. Outgoing calls

8.25 am. Violet Johnson: I call Mum from my bed, tell her I'm not feeling well and ask her to phone me in sick at school. I also tell her I'm quite hungry and could do a bacon sandwich, if there is one in the offing and hang up before Mum can reply.

8.45 am. St Saviour's School: I ring in sick, citing suspected appendicitis. Miss Eliot in the office says she'd tell my form teacher, Mr Lodge and hopes I'll get better soon.

8.25 am. Diesel: I call the Big D to ask if he's doing anything Saturday. Tell him Faruk is otherwise engaged. Diesel says he'll come over mine early on Saturday and we'll have some fun.

Incoming calls

8.27 am. Violet Johnson: Mum calls to tell me that if I am going to skive school I can do the phoning in for myself. She also enquires what my last servant died of.

9.05 am. Bernard Lodge: My form teacher calls to tell me that according to his records, I had my appendix removed last summer holidays. He remembers it well, he says, as my recovery extended three days into the new term. He wishes me a miraculous recovery and says that he is very much looking forward to seeing me tomorrow.

11.17 am. Faruk: FA reminds me that he won't be around on Saturday as he's been roped into a five-a-side with his mates from the mosque.

11.49 am. Diesel: Says he can't make Saturday after all as he's already booked for another shopping expedition with Lauren. Wants to know if I knew the price of cots and strollers these days?

And then:

Voicemail from: Teresa Davenport

Hello, Brian? Listen, Ros is not so good, She's in her room, refusing to see anyone. Don't worry, it's not your fault. Not all of it. But we need to do something. (Pause.) Look, you may act like a cretin sometimes, but I know you care about her, like I do. So call me. We need to talk.

Saturday. Outgoing texts, late pm:

To: Teresa Davenport.

Sorry, only picked up your message today. Phone lost in sofa. How is Ros? Would have called or come over but it all kicked off at Clive's. Will explain when I see you. Talk very soon.

CHAPTER 15

Please Mr Postman

There was a time, Clive says, when Roger Dyson, or Nutter Dyson, as he answered to then, would spend his Saturday afternoons with his friends, Frank Mad Dog Pemble, Hammer Harry Piercey and Les Stanley McGregor, in and around the leafy suburb of Peckham, South London. This, I'm told, is necessary background if I'm to understand what caused the disturbance at 13, Laurel Gardens earlier this afternoon. The one which resulted in two lost teeth, one fractured pelvis and a broken nose; the destruction of various pieces of quite expensive designer furniture, and one of Roger's Rottweilers shitting itself in fright all over the Persian rug.

In South London, Roger was a keen supporter of Millwall F.C. and liked to take his three pals down The Shed, where they would meet other like-minded pals, and, on a good day, watch his favourite team trounce the visiting side. Many of Roger's friends weren't actually Millwall supporters. They didn't much like football, even. They wore the Millwall shirts and scarves the way an army wears a uniform, to differentiate between friend and foe in the confusion of battle.

Because what Roger's friends liked more than anything, was a good scrap. A big set-to, with iron bars, broken bottles and knuckle-dusters was their idea of healthy, vigorous exercise. In the periods just before and after the match itself, pockets of enemy fans might be lured into secluded dead-end streets and taught that trespassing on Millwall turf was a dangerous idea. Not that Roger and his mates actually wanted to deter the other supporters from coming. Without them, Saturdays would have been very much duller.

But after a few years of this, Roger's mates started to grow up, have kids, get jobs – good jobs, some of them. You couldn't spend your weekdays as a City trader and your Saturdays trying to beat the living shit out of Chelsea supporters. Their numbers dropped off and simultaneously, the whole ethos of the game changed. The clubs themselves changed. There was seating in the stands, where a safe family atmosphere was promoted and good old boys with lumps of wood were looked upon as dinosaurs rather than heroes. And now, when Roger and his much diminished crew did find a rumble, they were often outnumbered and, Roger told his son, 'given a proper kicking'.

The time had come to move on. Roger tried to wind things down; better to watch the footie and go for a pint. But other firms still came mob-handed, looking to settle old scores and take scalps like Roger's. And the police still regarded him as a menace and circulated his details to pubs and football clubs, and to border agencies whenever there was a fixture on the Continent. And on top of that, Erica Dyson, Clive's mum, was giving him a right old earful every time he got into trouble. Things were getting too warm for Nutter. The opportunity to move up North and take on his Great Auntie Ethel's bungalow could hardly have come at a better time.

The lads were sorry to see him go, of course, and he had a memorable send off in a pub down the Old Kent Road, with a lock-in and a finger buffet. Everyone 'got ratted' and the whole affair ended with a huge bar fight for old times' sake – and with Roger extending an open invitation to any Southern jesses who wanted to experience the man's life of the North, first hand. It was a little joke which had gone down very well but one which had been loaded with unforeseen consequences.

I knew nothing about all this. I didn't know that Roger had been a notorious football hooligan, or that he had three friends who would, after these intervening years, look exactly like the three suspicious characters who tossed a tin of Tennent's over our front garden hedge at 2.20 this afternoon. From my bedroom window I'd seen a big shaven-headed bloke wearing a camel Crombie, a small, fat man in denim jacket, denim jeans and brown Doc Marten's and a middling-sized man with a scarred cheek who wore thick-framed glasses and an ill-fitting suit and looked like Michael Caine with a bad haircut. These were the descriptions I was going to supply to the police, should anyone's house get turned over that afternoon.

But I'm getting ahead of myself. Earlier that day, according to Clive, he and Roger had donned matching blue fleeces and had gone to an antiques fair to put in a spot of practise for a projected appearance on TV's mid-day antiques game, *Bargain Search*. The fleeces were worn partly to get into character and partly to get over the shock of having to appear in such unfashionable items of apparel on TV. Because by this time, Clive had extended his father's interest in life's finer things to his wardrobe and Roger was rarely seen without his Armani jeans and his Prada light-weight nylon jacket, funded, like the interior makeover, by the deceased ancient relative who hadn't set eyes on him since he was a 'darling little boy' in shorts. Roger had had a fit when Clive told him that he'd signed them both up as contestants on *Bargain Search*. 'I'm not wearing a fucking fleece,' he'd told his son. 'End of.'

But Clive had been very persuasive. Clive said he'd be bound to land a bird if they saw him on the show. He didn't say that being on telly might sell his dad too. By Clive's reckoning, there must be thousands of single women sitting on their sofas in the middle of the day just waiting for someone like Roger to give them a purpose in life (like doing the cooking and cleaning and providing a gossipy female friend for Clive himself). But the application had been made months ago and though they both were looking forward to it as a bit of a laugh, Clive had since been visited by an idea for sorting out his dad which was much more certain of success.

This morning, Clive tells me, after a successful visit to the antiques fair, where Roger had bought a Victorian swordstick and Clive had bagged a Lalique bowl, they had returned home to find a large envelope bearing an illegible foreign postmark waiting on the doorstep. Still wearing their matching blue fleeces, they had thrown themselves down on their bright new Conran sofa, torn open the packet and begun to devour the pages of the July issue of Asian Bride magazine.

It was several weeks since he had first mooted the idea to his father.

'Do wot?' Roger had said. 'A fooking mail order bride?'

By then, Roger had got a handle on the Northern tongue. You had to, if you used the boozers he did. Fooking, not fackin', bath as in Kath (not sarth, like in Sarth London). Grass rhymed with ass, but arse was the same north and south of the Watford Gap. Not that nuances of the English language were uppermost in his mind just then.

'What are you suggesting? That I get one off Amazon or leave a bid on eBay? Or maybe wait 'til the new Argos catalogue comes out and choose one from there? Fuck me, Clive, have you thought this through? Who are these people you've been writing to without my say so? I don't even know what these birds are like.'

Clive noticed that at no point did he reject the idea out of hand and proceeded to explain to his father the benefits, as he saw them, of using the simple expedient of ordering his next wife online or through a catalogue. 'I'm not sure about this, Cly,' Roger had said at first. 'Is it like ordering other mail order goods? I mean, can I send her back if she doesn't fit? If she isn't fit for purpose, I mean?' Roger had a thousand and one questions. How would he know she'd make a good wife? How would he know if she was good in bed? Could he try her on approval? Would she speak English? Would she know how to cook a decent meat and potato pie? Would she be able to drive, at least as far as his local boozer? Would she appreciate all that he, as a connoisseur of fine living, had to offer?

Clive outlined the system, explaining that by the time he met her, he'd already know his intended well enough through letters and emails. He reminded Roger that none of his pub pick-ups had lasted more than a few weeks and usually were one-night stands. He pointed out that neither Roger nor himself had time to do the cooking and the cleaning any more – what with a busy scrap business to run and high-standard décor to maintain – and that if this were a restaurant, health inspectors would close down the kitchen and several streets around it as a public health hazard. The kitchen wasn't Clive's thing at all.

And these being Asian girls, they'd be all right about doing a bit of work around the house, unlike British birds, who preferred to divide their time between nail bars and the ones in pubs. And Asian birds were lookers, as far as Clive could tell. It wasn't long before Roger was persuaded and had started exchanging letters and photographs with a tall, slim and very striking Malaysian girl, called Pao-Pei.

Clive and Roger had spent the early part of this afternoon talking about Pao-Pei, whose name Roger still struggled with, and how she would fit into their lives. 'Pom Pei will love it here,' Roger assured Clive, mooning over her slender neck, her very un-British white teeth and her eyes, which seemed to look deeply into his. 'She won't have to eat all that foreign muck for one thing. And she'll be able to watch proper TV, without subtitles.'

'Course, she'll love it here,' Clive said. 'Look at all the shops Sheffield's got.'

'It says here she likes football too,' Roger said. 'She's a hard-working, twenty-two-year-old student of home economics whose interests include cooking, housekeeping and – fuck me – soccer! And with looks like that, son, pardon me, but she's got to like a bit of how's-your-father too. Doesn't get any better than that, believe me.'

Clive read out her details for himself. 'Pao-Pei is looking for a kind English husband who will help her perfect her English, broaden her understanding of Western culture and widen her sphere of interests.'

'Widen her what?' Roger said.

'Her sphere of interests,' Clive said.

'I think I have something which will widen that,' Roger said.

He wrote to Asian Brides, who forwarded his introductory letter, together with a photograph of Roger Dyson looking every inch the prosperous English gentleman, to their client in a village by the sea in Malaysia. When at last they received a reply, Roger and Clive were most impressed with the standard of Pao-Pei's written English. It was better than theirs. She said how delighted she was with Roger's letter and that she thought he was a very handsome man. She was fascinated to hear about Roger's exotic life in that far-away land and said how much she would like very much to see it for herself.

She told him something about her own home life, about her parents and her sisters and her brothers and how keen they were that she followed her dream and found herself a new and satisfying life in the West. Roger wrote back and then, discovering that she had a computer, they exchanged increasingly amorous emails and Pao-Pei sent photographs of herself wearing sarongs in several vivid colours. Roger hinted delicately that she might like to send him a photograph of her without the sarongs, but clearly Pao-Pei was a highly decorous girl as in her next mail, she made no mention of his suggestion, but she did ask him when they could be together. As soon as she liked, Roger thought and proposed to her there and then.

After paying a generous fee to Asian Brides, he set to with a will, dealing with all the red tape which had to be sorted out before he could send Pao-Pei a one-way air ticket and finally meet his bride-to-be in person. Clive was almost as excited as his father. It was just like Faruk's arranged marriage, he told his friend, though Faruk didn't really see it that way. While he

waited for permissions to be granted, Roger spent his days
making sure everything in the house was ready for her reception.

He did everything that Clive said had to be done: he cleared
out a drawer for her smalls, installed a new wardrobe for her
things, bought scented soaps, candles for the bathroom and an
air-freshener for the toilet. And then, much to the consternation
of my own father ('He's up to something, Violet'), Roger set about
clearing his garden, shifting the huge heaps of metal and
compacting the scraps, fencing off untidy areas and then, under
Clive's direction, rescuing and restoring the greenery. When at
last they had done, the bungalow featured a pleasant little garden
with flowerbeds, a shrubbery and a winding gravel path which
led the eye to a freshly-painted bungalow with roses around the
front door. If it also had its own scrap yard around the side, then
it was, as Mum observed, the tidiest, and perhaps even the
prettiest scrap yard in South Yorkshire.

And now Roger had only days to go until the day he would
drive down to London Heathrow and meet the gorgeous Pao-Pei
off her plane. He made lots of last minute preparations,
arranging to have flowers delivered to the house on the day of
her arrival, bought a new bottle of mouthwash and some
flavoured condoms and crossed off the days on the calendar. The
mood in the house was infectious: Clive was as feverish as his
father. He couldn't wait to meet Poon-Tang, as his dad was
already calling her, and take her out shopping in Sheffield.

If I'd known Clive had visitors I wouldn't have dropped round,
but Clive had insisted I come in all the same. Now I'm sitting in
the corner, my right hand recovering its shape after the mangling
Frank gave it when Roger made the introductions. No one looks
comfortable. Frank has done his best, draping his Crombie on a
chair and then dropping himself onto the new sofa and then his
big boots onto the new coffee table. He sits there waiting for
someone to say something. No one has taken a blind bit of notice

of Clive's own notice, which hangs by the back door: Whether you live in palace or mews/ it's always polite/to take off your shoes.

Behind Frank, Harry and Les look still less at ease, sitting rigidly erect on a pair of straight-backed, reproduction Rennie Mackintosh chairs. Harry sits with his pork-pie hat on his knees, while Les is taking quick glances at everything, like a chicken pecking for corn. They're just a little intimidated by the colours, the fussy newness of everything, by the wotsit? The design. Roger stands by the window, screening a group of fragile figurines and looking little more at home than his unexpected guests. He must be seeing his gaff through their eyes and wondering what they're thinking. When they used to roll up at his old drum on Peckham High Street, as Roger told Clive, it was the sort of place you could happily flop down wherever you liked, bang on the telly, crack open the beers, pass out the fags and put your feet up. And it's Frank's feet, or rather Frank's boots, still resting on the coffee table, which are the focus of all attention now. Even Les and Harry can't take their eyes off them. Finally, Frank catches on, removes the boots, coughs loudly and crosses his legs.

There's the first of many pauses.

Then Frank coughs again and says, gazing about at the pristine room of many colours and unexpected items. 'We was at Hillsborough but this eagle-eyed twat—'

'On the fucking turnstiles,' Harry says.

'Recognizes us from our mugshots.'

'And has the old Bill escort us off the premises.'

'No fucking football for us today.'

'So being as we was up your way,' Frank says. 'We thought we'd take you up on your invitation, like.'

Les breaks his silence with an economic, 'Yeah.'

Frank's taken a good, hard look at the strange way Nutter's chosen to sort out his place up North. But it's not the room but

Roger himself that Frank's looking at now.

'Nice fleece,' Frank says, then turns to see Clive coming in with the beers. 'Fuck me, does everyone wear them up here?'

Clive offers around a tray of small, lager-filled glasses. They have never had beer from anything but pint pots and bottles before and each man takes the little glass gingerly, as if he's not sure what it is. They drink, however and Les shows that although he might be quiet, thoughtful, if you like, he's also the sophisticated one. He grips his glass and cocks his little finger.

There is another pause. Frank tries to throw off first impressions and be as genial as surroundings permit. He coughs again. 'So, Nutter, my old old mucker, how's life treating you up here in the sticks?'

Roger says he's doing okay, business going well and everything on the up. He's not going to tell them that he hasn't felt so happy in years and the reason for this is that he's shortly to marry a woman more beautiful than any they will have ever seen in Peckham, or Peckham, New Cross and Lewisham put together, for that matter. He knows instinctively that having them turn up at the Registry Office might not be a good thing.

'We had some times, didn't we?' Frank says, thereby opening a fertile field of reminiscence as he and Harry try to outdo themselves by recalling ever more violent incidents in their not-too-distant pasts. Like the time Harry and Les picked up a security guard and tried to use his head as a battering ram against an off-license window.

'He was a Northerner too,' Harry says. 'Ain't that right, Leslie?'

'He was thick-headed, all right,' Les agrees.

'There we were, banging his head against this plate-glass window and all he can say is—'

'Gee' o'er, lads, tha's giving me a headache.'

There's some more chat along these lines and Frank fills Roger in on what's happened to which of their old mates, who's got

ROSS GILFILLAN

hitched, who's still in hospital and who's in which prison. Then they all look into their empty glasses until Clive takes the hint and carries them off for refills. The men watch him leave.

'Dainty on his feet, innee?' Les says.

Harry gives him a look. They've all had their suspicions about Clive since he took his embroidery along to a gentleman's boxing evening in Catford, but he's Nutter's boy and Nutter is, or at least, was, Nutter. You don't go casting asparagus, as Clive would have said, at members of their firm, past or present. Or their offspring. They have a code of honour, these men. Roger has begun to relax. He talks about my dad and the trouble he's had running a business when he's had a barrage of complaints via the Council, all emanating from the house over that big fence out there.

Now it's my turn to feel uncomfortable. The lads immediately offer their services. They'll fix him good, they say. Trash his garden, torch his car. Post something nasty through his letterbox. Threaten the cunt. But Roger says, no, that's not the way you do things in places like Laurel Gardens. What you do, Roger says, is you ignore such provocations.

'Ignore them?' Frank says, clearly amazed.

'That's right,' Roger says. 'You rise above them.'

'Fuck me, I see. It's different up here, innit?'

For his part, Frank seems prepared to ignore Clive's dainty walk as he returns with another tray of little glasses and perhaps to overlook the way Roger's gaff has been decorated, entirely by Clive, he's certain of it. And also to overlook the way his old mate dresses himself these days. Though, fuck me, I can hear him thinking, it's all going to make for some funny stories down the Dog and Duck when they're all safely back down South. But what he can't ignore is whatever bulky item he's sat down upon, and which he's been aware of ever since but has been too uncomfortable in other ways to do anything about. Now he reaches under his big arse and pulls something from under it. It's a

185

magazine, or something. It's porn, a jazz mag, he reckons. Looks like Asian Babes. No, wait a minute, he thinks, as he holds it up to get a better look and the thing becomes a magnet for the gazes of everyone present, it's only a fackin' catalogue for mail order brides!

But he doesn't say that, just flicks through pages and pages of smiling female faces, while everyone else is silent and then he finally pronounces, in an almost amiable way, 'You're a bit of a dark horse, Nutter. I didn't know you liked a taste of the tar brush.'

But no matter how Frank has tried to treat it lightly, Harry and Les snigger behind him like a pair of Muttleys behind Dick Dastardly. Roger himself is wearing a look like Frank has probably never seen before, because the magazine has naturally fallen open on Pao-Pei's page and her silk-covered breasts are beneath Frank's fat thumb. Frank sees he has made some sort of a mistake, a little *faux pas*, and tries to back-pedal.

'Not that there's anything wrong with that, mate, not in this day and age. And to be honest, now, who could blame anyone for fancying a piece of that, eh? I mean, Harry, you'd poke that, wouldn't you?'

'She'd look all right with a bit of British beef inside her,' Harry concedes.

Les's turkey neck is craning for a better view. 'I'd not kick her out of bed, either,' he says. 'Not until I'd given her a proper porking, anyway.'

Roger is doing his best to keep a lid on it, but Clive recognizes the danger signs. If he looks carefully, he can see that his dad's eyeballs appear to be rolling independently of each other. Only a little, but he's sure he's seen it. It's not good. But Frank and Harry haven't noticed. Harry's now on about a piece of scientific evidence a friend of his read about on the internet, saying that coloured people were 85 percent less intelligent than white people. All of them, even their doctors, he's saying.

'That's right,' Les says. 'I heard that.'

Frank's unsure about the figure and says so, though he thinks the general idea is right enough. But, he says, having another glance at Pao-Pei's smiling face, that needn't stop you wetting your willy where you want to, need it? Especially if you wore a nice, thick condom.

Which is where Clive thinks it might all kick off. But it doesn't, as at that moment, the door chime plays I Will Survive and Clive goes out to let in Faruk, with two of his mates from the mosque. 'Fuck me, blinding game,' Faruk's saying. 'Four nil. Four nil, Clivey! I'm fucking fucked! Got anything to drink? Is BJ here? I thought we could all go down the Casablanca. You up for that?'

But Clive isn't saying anything as he leads the three newcomers into the living room, where jaws do a little dropping at the sight of the two Asians and Faruk.

'Tell them we don't want any,' Harry says. 'Whatever they're selling.'

'Christ,' Frank says. 'Can't an Englishman have a little privacy in his own castle?'

'This is Faruk,' Roger says. 'A mucker of my boy's.'

'I don't give a toss about him,' Frank says. 'It's the monkeys with him.'

'They're my friends from the mosque,' Faruk says. 'Khalid and Sadik. What's your problem?' Having a low fear threshold has often been a problem for Faruk.

'Oi, Roger, Clive's mate or not, this bloke's out of order,' Frank says.

There's a moment when it seems to me that positions are being reconsidered. Then—

'They're all fucking Muslims!' Harry says, remembering what a 'mosque' is, at last.

'No, no,' Roger says. 'That's Faruk. He's not a Muslim.'

'Um,' Clive says. 'I think he is, Dad.'

Roger takes a minute. 'But he's white.'

'He's Turkish.'

Another minute. Roger's face performs some awkward contortions.

'Well fucking hell, so what?' he says, when he's straightened things in his mind, apparently. 'He's still Faruk.'

Which, of course, doesn't play well with Roger's mates.

'He's a Muslim but he's white,' Harry says.

'Which makes him not just a Muslim, but a traitor,' Les says, fingering something in his pocket.

'I don't think it does,' Roger Dyson says, uncertainly.

'Tell that to some squaddie who had his legs blown off,' Frank growls.

'What's a poof like him know about real men, anyway?' Harry says.

I have an awkward feeling that I ought be standing up for Clive at this point.

'You call my son a poof and you'll answer to me, you cunt,' Roger tells Harry.

Is it now, Clive's thinking, will it all kick off now?

'He's just saying, Nutter,' Franks says. 'That's all.'

'I'm not having it, Frank,' Roger says. 'You come around here, insulting my boy and his friends…'

'But come on, Nutter, they're fucking Pakis,' Frank says, reasonably.

'And Muslims,' Les mutters from behind.

'What need teaching a fucking lesson,' Harry says, 'if you ask me.'

It's now, Clive's thinking.

And he's right.

Frank, Harry and Les are on their feet. Les has something in his hand. It's a Stanley knife, probably made in Sheffield. I'm pumping adrenaline, heart hammering. Roger clocks the knife but keeps his hands in his pockets. Faruk and his mates stand their ground, the silly sods. Clive is with them, but must be wishing he wasn't.

'I want an apology, Nutter,' Frank is saying.

'An apology? For what?'

'For putting three Englishmen in the same room as these fucking Muslims and Pakis. For this poncy house. For leaving Peckham. For fucking changing, Nutter. I want an apology for all of that. And especially' — he points a broken-nailed forefinger at Clive, who is flicking back his floppy hair – he does it unconsciously in times of crisis — 'I want an apology for him.'

One final, brittle pause. And then:

'This is all the apology you're getting today, Frank.'

Nutter swings a brick fist squarely at Frank's jaw. Something flashes – who would have thought there was a knuckleduster in his Hugo Boss chinos – and there's a sickening cracking of bone or tooth. Frank spins about and lurches backwards, smacking into Harry and Les and all three land neatly on the sofa, looking briefly like visitors just arrived for tea before scrambling to their feet, Frank with a nasty, bloody mouth, Les nursing his craft knife and Harry wielding one of Roger's bone china vases.

'Not here, Frank,' Roger's saying, casting a rueful glance about him. 'We'll finish this outside.' But though Faruk's flung open the French windows, Frank, Harry and Les are going nowhere – until Frank takes a fatal step forward – which is when Clive stuns everyone by making the first move. He picks up something from a side table and throws it – it's his prized Lalique glass bowl. It misses whoever he might have been aiming at but smashes expensively against a wall.

But his father's face lights up. 'Nice one, my son!' he growls. Taking advantage of the moment, he helps himself to a big handful of Harry's denim jacket and – shaking him like he's plumping a big blue cushion – he sends him crashing heavily into Frank. It's cushions that Clive's brandishing now as he swipes repeatedly at Les's surprised face. Whatever Les was expecting, it clearly isn't a pair of burgundy scatter cushions, which distract him just long enough for Roger's Burberry boot to connect forcefully with his balls. I can feel his pain as he drops his knife and doubles up on the floor.

Whether the cavalry is needed or not, this is when it turns up, in the forms of Jalil and Zahid, the remaining members of Faruk's five-a-side team, who have apparently stopped off to buy packets of crisps and big bottles of Coke. They're still wearing their football boots for some reason. These two are much bigger and older than Faruk and the others and visibly fitter than anyone present. Jalil is known as The Taj, 'because he's built like the fucking Taj Mahal'. They've sized up the situation in a flash and while Zahid plays cat and denim mouse with Harry, the enormous Jalil pursues Frank around the sofa, totally oblivious to Roger, who's chasing them both, screaming, 'Not in your football boots, for fuck's sake! Not on this fucking floor!'

The French windows being open, everything spills into Clive's garden. I follow, but not being a fighting man, there's nothing much I can do but spectate. It's total chaos – Neighbourhood Watch, if they're watching, must be having heart attacks – and it's noisy, too; 13, Laurel Gardens is sounding like Wembley after a disputed goal by Germany. I wonder if Dad has heard the shouting and is now peering from his lookout on the stairs landing. If he is, he'll see several blokes in football strips dodging and weaving about with no actual football in sight. He'll see Roger chasing after someone who's holding a camel coat but doesn't appear to have the ball either. And it'll look like this game of invisible football is getting out of hand, because now a couple of the players are swapping punches, and there's no sign of the ref.

And then they're all at it and I wouldn't like to be the little bloke in the broken glasses or the fat one in the denim with the crushed pork pie hat. I'm dodging here and there, undecided whether I'm looking for an easy piece of the action, so I can claim to have got stuck in, or for a safe way through the melee to the garden gate – which I see swinging open now to admit a familiar figure. Predictably, it's my dad – afternoon in deckchair with Alan Titchmarsh on *Desert Island Discs* ruined, he's storming up the garden path to complain about the racket from over the fence. As soon as he sees Roger, his hand shoots up like a referee with a yellow card. He was very probably about to say, 'Hoi, you! Dyson! Just what is the meaning of this?'

But at the moment his hand shoots up, Frank is in the wrong place as he swerves to dodge Roger's boot. He catches Dad's fist full in the face and topples over like a sack of spuds. Dad springs back as if he's been attacked himself, then Roger's all over Frank before he can recover himself and together with Rashid and Jalil, he teaches Frank that trespassing on Dyson turf can be a very dangerous business. It's not at all nice.

They think it's all over: Rashid catches Harry a neat swipe to the shins, wonderful footwork, I think, and Zahid disarms Les of a lump of scrap iron, while Sadik put him out of play with a studded football boot to the kneecap: teamwork. Harry tries to scale the fence between our house and theirs but it's too high for the little man and he's dragged down by Faruk and Clive. Roger and Frank are rolling about on the lawn. Frank looks like he's missing a tooth or two and I can see that Roger's designer chinos are absolutely ruined. Five minutes later, Faruk's two defenders, Khalid and Sadik, are sitting on Harry, who is still managing to splutter obscenities with a mouth full of earth and grass. But with Les being minded by Clive, who has unsheathed Roger's new swordstick, we think it's all over. Then someone notices that Frank has disappeared.

Roger and Faruk don't have to search long because Frank's South London whine is quite recognisable, especially when it's in the grip of mortal fear – and the grinding mechanism of Roger's compactor. In the new fenced-off scrap yard, Frank's chosen the wrong place to hide from The Taj, who now has one huge hand grasping Frank's tattooed throat while the other appears to be stretching out for the start button. I have that sick-in-the-stomach feeling you get when you think you're about to witness something really awful. 'For fuck's sake,' Frank is bleating, looking in my direction. 'Get this maniac off me!'

The Taj, too, looks our way but it seems like all he wants from us is a thumbs-down to turn Frank into a messy bale of bits. Instead, I am relieved to see, he just gives Frank a resounding slap on his bald head and releases him into the care of the rest of Faruk's five-a side team, who are ready to escort Frank Pemble from premises for the second time that day.

All is confusion. The last time I saw it, the front room of Clive's place looked like it'd been hit by a rocket. Out here, I can see odd shoes and torn off pockets and somewhere in the grass there must be two incisors rightly belonging to Frank Pemble. The participants of the Battle of Laurel Gardens look equally fucked. Dad is staggering up the garden path, supported by Roger, of all people, who is clapping him on the back and saying, loudly, 'Well played, nice one, mate,' as he guides him into the house. I stand in a flowerbed amazed, not least by my dad apparently talking amicably with Roger Dyson. The five-a-siders and Faruk are already swapping stories about their parts in the action and Clive is wandering about the garden with a worried face, tutting at trampled flowerbeds and looking like he's going to have to use up the last of his courage to enter the house. A few minutes later, I see Peckham's finest staggering off in the direction of the Midland station, turning towards us every so often to let us know what'll happen if we ever find ourselves anywhere near South London.

'So that' — I wind up my story to Teresa — 'is why I couldn't get back to you right away.'

'Is this true?' Teresa asks. I must have a liar's face, or something.

'Of course it's true. Do you want to see my bruises?' I may

have exaggerated my part in all this.

'And you want to be a writer?' she says.

'As a matter of fact, I do,' I say modestly, proud that my story-telling potential is being recognised.

'Well, you're going to have to work at it,' she says.

We're sitting by the fountains in the Peace Gardens, off the City Centre, watching kids and drunken teenagers run through the eighty-nine jets of spray and around the cascading water features. The air is cool and wet and the July sun is dipping slowly from its apex in a cloudless sky. Teresa is wearing a light cotton shirt, which is partly see-through when she's against the light, and her frizzy brown hair is, I don't know, shiny and nice. She's wearing a cotton skirt and looks very cool and relaxed, sitting there with me, brown legs drawn up beneath her, sucking on a blade of grass. Only her expression betrays her concerns for her friend.

'So how is she, really?' I want to know.

'That's the thing, Brian, that's what I've been trying to tell you. She's fine now. In fact she's up. Laughing and buzzing like she's on something. No, don't worry, she's not. Nothing apart from her prescribed medication, anyway.'

'I'm sorry?' I say. 'Have I missed something? Rosalind has a condition?'

For which I am rewarded with the kind of tired smile usually reserved for idiots and little children.

'You missed everything I told you, didn't you?'

'It was so noisy. And I had something else on my mind,' I say. I think it was the colour of Teresa's knickers, but I'm way too smart to say that now.

'Well, it's not good, Brian. They're not sure, but it looks like Ros may be bi-polar or something. Massive mood swings. One day she's okay, chatty, optimistic about the future even. The next she's somewhere else entirely, off in some private place of her own where no one can get through to her. She knows what's happening and that's why she has the headphones in all day. Better to have people think you're into your music than you're lost in some black place you can't see your way out of.'

'I had no idea.'

'Why should you? You've hardly even talked to her. Ros has been some kind of dream figure for you and I tell you this, Brian, whatever idea of Ros you've dreamed up, there is no way she's going to be able to live up to your expectations.'

'I'm not so sure,' I say. Because at this moment I couldn't be sure of my home address. This is too much too soon. Ros has a condition. I could handle that, learn to become whatever support I'm capable of being. But Teresa being so certain I'm on the wrong track is hard to handle. 'Isn't there something I can do?'

'I don't know, Brian. It rather depends on Ros and how she feels about you. Which, given your recent record, isn't guaranteed to be positively. But hey, don't look so glum. I've met bigger idiots than you. Just make sure that your watchwords when dealing with Ros are subtlety and tact, okay?'

'Okay.'

'And if she does like you and wants to go out with you, then you won't just have a girlfriend, Brian, you'll have a big responsibility. Do you think you're ready for that?'

I have to think about that.

'I don't know,' I say, when I have. 'Not for sure, anyway. I don't think I know myself that well yet. But I know I'd do everything I could to be a help to her.'

'You're sounding almost mature, BJ. I can call you BJ, can't I?'

'It's what my best friends call me.'

'So listen up, BJ, for I have a cunning plan. One which will give you your best chance to find out once and for all if Ros is for you and you are for Ros. Come closer and I'll tell you what it is.'

And there in the concrete gardens with the fountains playing and the children laughing, I feel Teresa's hot breath in my ear as she tells me about a place where Ros feels more at home and more at ease with herself than anywhere else. And if me and my friends can possibly scrape up the cash, we might all go to this place together. After our exams, it will be a well-earned break for us all. If Rosalind Chandler is ever going to be receptive to a declaration of undying love from yours truly, then this, Teresa assures me, will be that time.

CHAPTER 16

Changes

Earlier this week I had been gobsmacked by a dramatic lift in the spirits of the family Johnson, a freakish development I first became aware of when I arrived home knackered, after a very long afternoon spent with Diesel, traipsing around Mothercare, of all places. He'd shown me everything expectant parents had to have. We assessed the merits of various cots, mattresses, bedding, baby baths, changing mats, baby monitors, sterilising kits, strollers and travel cots. And then all the stuff Lauren herself will need: maternity leggings even more capacious than her present ones, (very) big knickers, nipple cream and breast pads, support cushions and hospital bags. I wasn't sure why he was showing me the instruments of his own torture and have been concerned that it might have been some kind of cry for help.

But anyway, arriving home after this, I hear laughter coming from the living room. Unusual enough, but odder still is that it's Dad's. I sometimes hear a burst of the more maniacal kind from my mother, when she's doing the ironing and watching reruns of *One Foot in The Grave* on telly, but Dad's laugh usually has something of the ironical about it. Not today though, as he's laughing like a drain, if you've ever heard one of those being vastly amused. But a bigger surprise is waiting me as I pop my head around the door – to say hello, I'm back, once again I've braved the mean streets without being either attacked and molested or abducted – to see Roger, sprawled in Dad's armchair, with a tin of Dad's Christmas beer in his hands. No one looks up as Roger approaches the punch line of his joke.

'But this bird, she says, "No, thanks – I'll smoke it later"!'

Roger's howling like an escaped lunatic on a full moon while Dad's chuckling like a major arterial waterway in the town drainage system. Mum, well, I haven't seen anything like it: she's got tears streaming down her face. I never noticed before, but she looks sort of pretty when she's happy.

'No, I've another one,' Roger is saying, but then he sees me and grins. 'I just came round to thank your dad for getting stuck in like he did yesterday,' he says. 'You should be proud of him, Brian. Regular hero, he was!'

I know I want to be a writer but I'm still learning and right now there is no way on earth that I could begin to describe Dad's expression. Proud comes into it somewhere, though. Pleased, well pleased, somewhere else. He sits there, puffed up, trying and failing to be modest and just like Violet, hanging on his new friend's every word. And now Roger's up off the chair and, putting down his tin of beer, is showing just how Dad strode boldly up the garden path and right into the melee. 'He didn't give a toss about his own personal safety,' Roger's saying. 'He was driven by a fearless sense of what's right, your dad was.'

More likely intense annoyance at missing Alan Titchmarsh on *Desert Island Discs*, I think.

'And here comes your dad' — Roger's showing me — 'like a Roman gladiator into the arena.' He strides around the room like a gladiator about to despatch lions and tigers at the same time and stops. 'Oi, Violet, can you see me as Russell Crowe in that *Gladiator*? I looked just like him, when I had hair! So here comes your old man, Vi, looking for the action. And he knows what he's doing, does old Charlie here. Goes straight for the head man, the ringleader, Frank Pemble. "Mad Dog", they call him down at Peckham nick, he's got a record as long as Bohemian Rhapsody. And what does Charlie here do?'

We wait for Roger to show us. He swings his huge fist at an imaginary opponent.

'He floors him with one punch. One punch! Fuck me, Violet, excuse my French, but Mike Tyson had better not show up at Laurel Gardens!'

Dad's watching Mum as she laps up everything his new friend has to say. Whatever he's seeing seems to please him. And while they're all laughing like various items on a plumber's shopping list, I close the door and retire to my bedroom to put this new twist of fate into some sort of perspective. Roger, here? Drinking Dad's beer? Dad bigged up as a hero? Dad and Roger, friends? I pinch myself and try to remember my every movement of the night before, just in case I can recall some skank slipping something hallucinogenic into my Smirnoff Ice.

'You can misjudge people, Brian,' Dad says.

I nod my head. I had been reading about the Hanratty case in Mum's *Ghastly Murders* magazine. Mum has a fascination with the dark and the dangerous. She likes the real crime mags, she's *Crimewatch*'s Number One fan and there's not much she doesn't know about the Brinks Mat bullion raid. James Hanratty was misjudged all right – he was hanged for a murder he probably didn't do.

We're sitting at the kitchen table, just Dad and me. Talking, man to man. Mum is in her sewing room, with the door closed, but every so often, we stop talking to listen. She's laughing, up there, talking to herself, or Russell, rather, and laughing.

'She's not mad, you know,' Dad's saying.

'I know that, Dad.'

Dad sighs and then he looks me over, like he's deciding whether to tell me something or not.

'It's just that your mum and me, we've had our problems. The fact is, Brian, that I've come to realise that I've not been all she might have wanted in a husband.'

I say nothing. To be talking for any length of time to my dad at all is weird enough, but to be talking about his marriage is not just weird, it's a bit of a nightmare, actually. Dad looks about him, at the neat kitchen with its little feminine touches, which include a posy of flowers on the sill of the window which gives onto his own strictly-ordered garden.

'I've given her no fun, Brian. Weekends at Headingly. What did she want with them? There's been no joy in this house, save for what you've brought into the place. Roger next door's given her more fun this last few days than I've given her in years. I've reduced her life to one of dull routine. She cleans the house, I do the gardening. Never any surprises for us, same old thing, day in, day out. And do you know why?'

'No,' I say.

'Because it's safer that way, Brian. If I can remove all possible threat, if I can timetable my day and bring order to nature, even, then I have created a semblance, or an illusion, if you like, of order. And with order comes reassurance, Brian. I know I have misjudged Roger Dyson. Now I've seen his house I can see the scale of that misjudgement. He's not a bad chap at all, you know, and a good father too. But I'm not the hero he's saying I am, Brian. You know that. I was frightened of him. Not of Roger, the man, but of the chaos he was creating, which seemed to be creeping ever closer, ready to engulf us all. Does that sound ridiculous?'

'Well...'

'Of course it does. And it's taken an outburst of violence right here in Laurel Gardens for me to realise it. We're having this talk because there are going to be changes around here, changes that are long overdue. There will be big changes for us all, Brian, but I know now that you are ready for these changes. In fact, I know that we all are.'

'What sort of changes?' This is unsettling, but somehow thrilling, too. My dad has never talked like this before. It's like talking to a different man. He's not stuttering, either.

'I can't tell you yet. We shouldn't have secrets, but this will be the last one this family has, Brian. And it won't be long before you understand all. Secrets are terrible things. Secrets have made me what I am, Brian, what I was, perhaps.'

'I don't understand,' I say.

He's looking at me now like he's just decided that I've grown up.

'Perhaps it's time you did understand,' he says. He frowns, bites his lip. Then he says, 'What do you know about my childhood, Brian?'

'Your childhood?' I say, as if I'm surprised he hadn't gone straight from nappies and romper suits to cardigans and cavalry twill slacks. 'Well, obviously, you lived with GD and Nana…'

'Brian,' he interrupts. 'Do you know what is the first birthday I can remember celebrating at that house?'

I have no idea. I think I can remember my own third, though. Something about Marmite soldiers and a pink cake.

'The first birthday I can remember is my seventh. I got a little bicycle, with stabiliser wheels.'

'That sounds nice,' I say.

'What's not so nice, Brian, is that I can remember nothing of my life before that point. Not a thing. I must have gone to a nursery and started school at four or five, surely? But do I remember anything at all of those years? I have to tell you, Brian, that I do not. And I have no idea why. And because I have no idea why this can possibly be, I've entertained the darkest, most horrible thoughts.'

'About this…amnesia?' I say. I want to tell him what I know, this is the moment. But he's still talking.

'I've tried to imagine what might have happened to me as a child. A shock, surely, some terrible trauma? I still don't know. I have obsessed about this enormous hole in my life. What exactly caused it? I've always needed to know and over the years I've considered every possibility. Even the most dreadful.'

There's a tone in his voice I don't like. He's about to tell me something I don't want to know.

'Brian, I started to harbour certain feelings, suspicions if you like, about GD and Nana. I had read about such things, adults and children. Did they do something to me?'

His face is a picture of anguish and I feel for his suffering, I really do. This is a side to my dad I never knew was there. But I'm appalled at what he has been able to think GD and Nana might have been capable of. And so I'm unable to cushion the shock of what I have to tell him with, what's it called? A preamble. It just comes out.

'GD and Nana are not your parents,' I tell him. Just like that.

At first it's like he's not heard me, so I have to repeat myself.

He shakes his head, looks at me like he's just discovered that I am mad.

'It's true,' I tell him. 'Just listen to what I have to say.'

Dad folds his arms, but his eyes, which at first are squinty and mistrusting, slowly widen as I give him back, piece by piece, the missing bits of his life. Or as much as GD knew about his life before his parents were killed in the car crash. I tremble as I speak, wondering what kind of a shock my words are giving him. Maybe GD was wrong and this isn't the right thing to do at all. I've never had to break news of this magnitude to anyone before. I don't know what to expect. Anger? A big scene? What?

After I have told him everything I know, I can barely look up from where my eyes have been focussed on a housefly, which is rubbing its legs together as it squats on one of Mum's homemade scones. But when I do, I see that Dad is strangely tranquil. He's sitting back in his chair and two big and glistening tears are inching down his pale cheeks. He is strangely calm. I am worried that somehow I have done the wrong thing, perhaps an awful thing. I sit where I am and watch him as he gazes up at the ceiling or perhaps somewhere beyond. But then, when eventually he looks at me, I see that he is smiling. Actually smiling. He doesn't say anything, in fact I think he is unable to say anything. He holds my gaze for what seems like an eternity. And then, at last, he puts a hand on mine and squeezes it, hard.

'Thank you, Brian,' he says. 'Thank you so much.'

Whatever I had expected, it wasn't this.

CHAPTER 17

Love Me To Death

The repetitive chuga-lug-lug of the train has had a soporific effect upon its passengers. That and the Madeira wine generously provided by the gold-monocled gentleman wearing the frock coat and the top hat, who produced bottle and glasses from a capacious carpet bag. People are dozing fitfully, as the train rattles over the lines and branches of trees brush at the glass. One young lady resisting the general torpor has taken off her bonnet to lean from the window and see if our destination is yet in sight, but steam from the engine and what might be sea mist obscures her view.

My companions, perhaps sensing proximity to our desti-nation, are rousing themselves. They rub sleep from their eyes and look about them, at women with high buns and dangling curls, at whiskery men and at the gentleman sitting across from our party, the one who was very short with his wife when she was trying to arrange her hooped skirt in such a way that she might be comfortable in her seat. The ladies, it has to be said, have acquitted themselves well for their excursion.

Aboard this train are acres of crinoline, satins and silks, some ladies with feathers in their bonnets and others wearing gauzy veils and carrying little parasols. Careful thought and hours of labour must have attended the production of such finery and for their part, these ladies have lined the pockets of their dress-makers. And now everyone is awake and there is a bustle of excited chatter as the train rounds a bend and begins to slow up and through the mist, perched high upon the cliff, we can discern the silhouetted ruins of the ancient abbey at Whitby.

With difficulty, we disembark, struggling with valises and portmanteaus, for there is not a porter to be seen. My party has less to carry than most, but our evening attire has to be carried somehow and there are the other necessities thought to be indispensable for the spending of two days on the Yorkshire coast: warm undershirts and stout boots for walking. I shall, perchance, return to this experimental journal when I am settled in our lodgings, but there again, once I am returned home it can await my leisure. Before I put down my pen and join my companions upon the platform, I must make note of the strangest group of gentlemen I ever did see, who are wearing long coats made of leather and pendant jewellery about their necks, who stand with ladies whose faces are as pastey-white as their painted lips are ruby-red, the whole ensemble making a remarkable sight as they stand awaiting passengers from the train, under a banner whose strange message reads, Welcome to Whitby Goth Weekend.

The Gardenia Guesthouse, no dogs, no single women, no smoking, no sea view and nowhere near the station, is rumoured to have had a lengthier list of proscriptions before the laws promoting equal opportunities started to bare their teeth. The wheelchair ramp was a begrudged expense, the elderly chambermaid tells us. But, amazingly, The Gardenia Welcomes Goths, as a notice tacked to the hotel's old signboard proclaims. Why the proprietors of this selective establishment, which only recently turned away a blind man because he had a dog, should welcome the most outlandishly, garishly eccentric subdivision of British youth culture is hard to fathom. Unless it's for their chalk-white skin. And why the goths should want to stay there is just as puzzling.

But the more I learn about goths the more I understand that these are people who can never be sure of their reception anywhere and if a place says, unequivocally, we welcome you, then goths will come in cash register-filling numbers. And judging from the number of funereally-attired customers in the bar and passing me on the stairs, I guess the Gardenia does well out of its goths. As a matter of interest, it seems that Whitby was chosen for the once or twice yearly goth weekends because it was already accustomed to receiving Dracula addicts and Christopher Lee lookalikes. Hey, the townspeople must have thought, what's a few more more pale-faced punters?

Lauren and Diesel have the bigger room, the one which would have a sea view, were it not for the projecting gable of the house next door. Faruk, Clive and I share two beds in a cramped adjoining room with a slice of harbour visible between the walls of two more guesthouses. Clive is getting a bed to himself. We start to unpack, keeping quiet in case we can hear what Lauren is saying to Diesel in the room next to ours. She was unusually quiet on the train, a state which I've come to interpret as ominous and has in the past presaged an important announcement, but I could be reading too much into this. All we can hear now is mumbling, Lauren's low, continuous mumble, then Diesel's high, short protestations. In our room, there is a dressing table-cum-writing desk where I'm continuing this journal, which I hope will be sufficiently interesting and well enough written, to show to Rowley Dawson next term.

Faruk and Clive have begun to get into their hired costumes: this evening, the Four Horsemen of the Apocalypse will be weekend goths. The cost of our travel and some of the expensively-hired gear is the generous gift of one Roger Dyson, who has done this because I have assured him that the Whitby Weekend will be a great place to get Clive off with someone and also because it's his way of thanking my dad and Faruk for their parts in the Battle of Laurel Gardens and, above all else, because he is stupendously elated about the imminent arrival of his Poon-Tang, at London Heathrow, next week.

But, I hear you ask, why are we here? Why is Clive helping to fix Faruk's cravat? Why is Clive himself dressed up as a Victorian dandy, in his black velvet jacket and matching waistcoat? Why will I shortly be transforming my own appearance, until I look like an extra in a cheap horror flick?

You should be asking Teresa Davenport. Whitby's Goth Weekend is her 'cunning plan' for finding out just what Ros's feelings for me are. Not that I've told the Horsemen that. Maybe she's thinking that if I actually get off with Ros and prove to be someone who can help and support Ros (as well as fuck her brains out, I'm thinking) then it'll be a huge weight of responsibility off her shoulders. I don't know. I just know that Teresa's dad has given them a lift all the way to Whitby and that we're to meet them in the graveyard of St Mary's Church, at 8pm this evening.

We walk down towards the harbour, where there's a spot of unexpected bother with the local plod who are bored enough to give me a body search. I'm not worried, though, and I'm in too much of a holiday mood to be angry. All I'm thinking, as they start to pat me down, is that even the policemen look old-fashioned, somehow, here in Whitby. It all gets a bit more personal after that and I don't think I'll bother you with the details. However, I'm certainly not going to let it ruin my holiday.

As we cross the swing bridge, I can understand why Ros has come here every year since she was fourteen. I can see why Teresa says it's the one place where Ros feels at home and at ease with herself. Because all along these ancient narrow streets, with their little fudge shops and windows displaying items crafted from Whitby jet, are hundreds of people just like Rosalind Chandler and already I've mistaken three young women for Ros herself.

Middle-aged tourists make way for wild-haired men in scarlet-lined cloaks or take photographs of pretty girls in lace sleeves, leather bodices and Victorian hook and eye boots, just like Ros's; it's all very strange. You might imagine that the whole town has been visited by a vast intergalactic space ship, whose advanced stealth technology has let it pass undetected by the early warning golf balls at nearby Fylingdales and release its cargo of infiltrators in a secluded place outside the town.

Five hundred million light years is a fair old distance and when you're planning an expedition on this scale, you can come a cropper on the details. It's easy to cock up your calculations for the Estimated Year of Arrival when the I.T. bots haven't bothered upgrading your operating system and your Starcruiser is still using the Klargian equivalent of Windows Vista. And because of this, the hundreds of aliens making their way into the town from every direction are attracting more attention than they might have liked, being dressed entirely in the fashions of another age.

But the numbers of Victorian goths are balanced by late-twentieth century ones. As well as common-or-garden goths with jet-black hair, black clothes and white faces, there are vamps in sex-shop chic and men dressed even more outlandishly, as alien freaks, plague-ridden monks and assorted other monsters. One who's covered his face and head with pins looks like the victim of an over-enthusiastic acupuncturist. We all think it's bonkers, but in the best of all possible ways and are finding everything quite wonderful as Faruk points out the silver streaks in so many hair-dos, the girls aiming at the Morticia Addams effect, the guys a Count Dracula, Prince of Darkness look or, in the case of one or two older and dumpier goths, Grandpa Munster.

I'm amazed at how many older goths are there, some of the rake-thin ones with droopy grey moustaches looking like under-takers out on the razzle. Everyone else is startling, sexy, fright-ening or funny. Not that we must appear any less bizarre ourselves. Clive looks like an older Mark Lester as Oliver Twist, the professional mourner at children's funerals, Faruk could be Mr Darcy's kid brother in the next remake of *Pride and Prejudice*, while I'm here as just one more bog-standard vampire: old-time dinner suit (Dad's), floor-length curtain (Mum made my cloak) and artificially-ashen countenance. Mind you, Clive's done a lovely job with my mascara. Also looking like characters from

Oliver are Diesel and Lauren, bringing up the rear as we start to climb the two hundred steps up to the church. An American tourist has already excitedly identified them as the fat Beadle and his wife.

We reach the top of the steep steps. Behind us, the red tiled roofs of Whitby cascade towards the harbour, while before us is St Mary's Church and the most evocative graveyard I have ever seen. Perhaps it's not the graveyard itself, but the people who are in it. Not those in the graves themselves, but the ones standing or sitting five and six feet above them. Period-dressed youngish people pose by stones, taking each other's pictures or eat picnics off tabletop tombs with lighted candelabra and cans of Stella or, more authentically, bottles of port and Curacao. Some of these stare out to sea, presumably watching for the ship that must eventually blow ashore, with the earth-filled coffin of Dracula aboard.

The candles aren't necessary, as it'll be light for ages yet. The view is spectacular. I fill my lungs with sea air and look about for Ros and Teresa, who should be here somewhere but if Teresa has got herself done up anything like Ros, then it might take a while to find them among all the undead gathered here this evening. But as Diesel and Lauren struggle up the last few steps, I see someone running through the crowd and looking very familiar, despite an unfamiliar black knee-length skirt with fishnet stockings, a clinging black satin top and a black beret. What Teresa's come as I can't decide but I have to say, she's looking decidedly horny. But then I realise that she's not running in our direction because she's pleased to see us – she's upset, panicking.

'It's Ros,' she says, breathlessly. She's run up all two hundred steps, from the look of her cheeks. She supports herself on my shoulder as she says, 'She's gone!'

'What do you mean, gone?' I say.

'She walked out of the hotel on her own.'

'That's nothing to worry about,' Lauren says. 'Is it?'

'She'll be down the Pavilion watching Desolate Dogs tuning up.' Diesel suggests. 'Best bit of their act.'

Teresa ignores everyone else and turns to me. 'She's not herself, Brian. I know the signs. She'd never have gone out without me. Her moods can be dangerous. We have to find her, quickly.' And now I'm as anxious as Teresa. As for the others, Ros mightn't be a mate but she's from our school. We all have to find her. Teresa tells me that as they approached Whitby, Ros's mood, instead of becoming lighter and easier, had darkened. When she talked at all, it was about 'the big change that was coming' and she was saying all kinds of weird stuff, like she was 'through with it all' and was 'going to move on'. As they walked up the steps to the hotel entrance, where a couple of goths were helping another to free his long coat tails from the revolving door, Teresa thought she heard Ros actually say that it was time to end it all.

She was going to ask her exactly what she meant just as soon as her mood had lifted. After they had registered, Ros was supposed to join Teresa on the terrace for tea and something to eat, but had stayed in her room. Teresa had last seen her examining the clothes she was to wear, with the strangest look in her eyes. The others have grasped the idea that Ros is in trouble, that she's vulnerable and may somehow be putting herself in danger. We hit the streets of Whitby and split up, promising to call or text as soon as she's found. Teresa and I start asking anyone who looks sufficiently alert to have noticed a lone girl in distress. But asking if anyone has seen a person in a dark cloak with jet-black hair and a pale face results in a lot of confusion.

We try all the well-known goth hangouts, the pubs and hotels and places where people can take in the view and meditate upon soulful things, or just think about suicide. At one such place we find a girl who sits alone on a bench, engrossed in The Works of Emily Dickinson and I try her, because she looks like a kindred spirit. 'Waste not a look upon my head,' the girl replies, which isn't strictly helpful. 'For I am not sleeping, I am dead.'

'Fuckwit,' Teresa says as we run down into town, through pockets of ambling goths and evening walkers, re-cross the bridge and try likely places on the West Cliff. Clive is sent to look in The Dracula Experience, a favourite haunt of Ros's, but it's hard for him to distinguish between what is a ghoulish exhibit and what's only a goth standing very still.

Then, catching our breath beneath the arching whalebones high upon the West Cliff, where we can see the harbour and the still-busy streets below quite clearly, Faruk points to a black speck moving along one of the distant arms on the granite harbour walls, which stretch out into the sea, ready to gather troubled craft into the safe waters of the River Eske. 'You said she was cloaked, didn't you?' he asks Teresa.

But Teresa is already feeding a coin into a mounted telescope and tilting it on its gimble as she focuses on the figure on the harbour wall. 'It's her,' she says.

'Are you sure?' I say.

'It has to be,' she snaps and sets the pace as Clive, Faruk and me tumble down steep pavements and then race each other along the bank of the river, to where we can see the monumental stonework of the harbour. Diesel and Lauren remain behind, in case we're wrong and she turns up there. And so Diesel is able to watch through the telescope as Teresa and the Horsemen mount the harbour wall and run towards the distant cloaked figure, which stands now with back towards us, looking out to sea and reminding me of some DVD that I watched with Mum, years ago.

By the time we are anywhere near, I am choking for breath but determined to keep up with Teresa. I don't want to be seen as someone who has let Ros down in any way. Faruk and Clive have fallen a little way behind, but they're still close enough to get the same jolt I do when the hooded figure swings towards us – and we're staring into the bone-white visage of Death himself.

I look into the eyes of Death and Death looks unblinkingly into my eyes and Death speaks first. 'Stee-fuckin'-rewth, mate.'

His bony hand clutch at his presumably stilled heart. 'You could scare the pants off a bloke doing that! I nearly had a flaming heart attack! What the bloody hell do you dickheads think you're doing?'

'I'm sorry,' I say, recovering myself. 'We thought you were someone else.'

Australian Death gives a hollow laugh. 'Too many people do, mate,' he says and he turns once more towards the sea.

It's a half hour later and we are climbing the path to the cliff walk. Diesel and Lauren, still watching through the telescope on the West Cliff, are sure they've just seen Ros struggling up here. She's long been out of view but they reckon that if we hurry, we might just catch her. For goths, the path leads to only one place, Esmerelda's Lookout. There is a legend that in the first years of the nineteenth century, a local girl of good parentage had a fling (a dalliance they would have called it) with a handsome officer of the Royal Navy, who served on the frigate HMS Typhoon. His ship patrolled the Eastern coast and often put in to Whitby for supplies.

Whether he intended to marry Esmerelda or whether she was only a sailor's plaything was never established, but when Esmerelda, as she wrote in her diary, found herself 'quick with child' she began to watch for his ship from this lonely spot on the cliff walk. Only his return and their speedy marriage could save her reputation, could save her, in fact, from being rejected by the whole community. Esmerelda waited and waited.

For weeks she was seen on this cliff top, a lone figure who stood for hours in all weathers, awaiting the return of her lover. But Esmerelda wasn't to know that the captain of HMS Typhoon had received a signal while at sea, ordering his ship to join the fleet at Spithead: Britain was once again at war with France. Esmerelda waited and waited, with the child growing bigger inside her and her predicament beginning to show. And then one day, the lonely figure was seen walking up the hill towards her cliff-top lookout but no one saw her coming down. Esmerelda was gone, never to be seen again.

I learn all this from Teresa as we hurry up the path, hearing the incoming tide crashing upon the shore far below. Teresa says Ros has always been fascinated by the story and has visited Esmerelda's Lookout many times before. It's her hope and mine that she is only paying the place one more visit and has nothing more dreadful on her troubled mind. The place is a well-known tourist spot for moody Goths, but none is there now and nor is Rosalind. We look about, down towards distant trees and back towards the town but we can see no sign of her. Teresa sends Faruk in one direction and Clive in the other. Then she finds something in the grass, a single black glove. 'Oh, God,' she's saying. 'Please, God, no.'

She goes towards the edge of the cliff.

'I can't look,' she says.

But I do. I stand on the edge of the cliff with the wind blowing hard and a fine salty spray slapping my face and peer down upon the shingly shore below, which is fast disappearing under the racing tide. At first, I can't make out much, just a lot of black stones, half-submerged by swirling water. But at least there's no Ros and the faintest of hope begins to fill my veins – until I spot something ominous between two big rocks. It's the shape of a black cloak, which is already being attacked by the fast-encroaching sea.

I point and Teresa screams.

I don't remember deciding to descend the cliff but I do, making quickly for a place where climbing down might just be practicable, if still dangerous. This isn't something I would have attempted in any other circumstances. But I'm not thinking, I'm just seeing the stones slipping away under my feet, concentrating on grabbing at handholds as I slip and stumble down a vertiginous slope towards the shore below. I won't know that I have cuts to my face and hands until much later. Now, bruised and confused at the bottom of the cliff, I can just hear Teresa shouting from far above me, but the noise down here drowns all but the top notes.

I stumble over wet shingle and then wade knee-deep in swirling water, pushing against the force of the tide, until finally I can see the lumpy, sodden cloth bundle only yards ahead. I'm calling Ros's name but the bundle lies inert, all but submerged by the water. I struggle on and can now see, with heart-stopping certainty, the familiar death's head brooch, the one that Ros wears on dresses but must have been using now as a clasp for her cloak. It's her, I say to myself, my heart sinking fast. I so don't want to lift the cloak and find Ros's body, drowned or smashed by the fall. I don't want to do this, but I see now that it has to be done. And so, steeling myself for the worst, I kneel in the water and lift the heavy hem of the cloak.

She is not there. The cloak covers only another black rock. But there's small relief in that. The cloak is Ros's, I'm sure. And if the cloak is here but Ros is not, then the inescapable and terrible conclusion is that she has already been swept out to sea. However, I search the narrowing strip of shore beyond the sea's reach, scan the dark and choppy waters on which I can make out nothing but the occasional breaking wave and then, with dragging reluctance, begin a difficult and painful climb back up the cliff. It seems to take hours, my hands hurt so much and my mind is in turmoil over what on earth I am to tell her best friend and protector, Teresa? But, after slipping and sliding and eating considerable amounts of dirt, I make the top, where I roll over, dead beat, upon the grass, and then slowly, very slowly, get to my knees, hardly daring to look up at Teresa, who will immediately know the worst from the look on my face.

But it's Teresa who speaks first.

'Well, bugger me,' she says. 'If it isn't Yorkshire's very own Spiderman.'

This is not the reaction I'm expecting. Nor was I reckoning on the peel of laughter that rings in my ears as I stagger to my feet and see Faruk and Clive with Teresa, all looking like they've tremendously enjoyed the spectacle I have just provided. Faruk is already playing back the footage on his iPhone for Clive. But I'm surprised I notice such insignificant details, when there is a much bigger surprise awaiting. There's Teresa, grinning at me like an idiot, a very pretty idiot, and with her, dressed not in her black gothy clothes, but in a light-coloured summer dress and a cardigan, and wearing no makeup, gothy or otherwise, is Rosalind. Rosalind Chandler, the girl who was dead and washed far out to sea, as far as I knew, only minutes ago. 'I don't understand,' I say.

This is so unnecessary. The look on my face – which Faruk caught with his phone, that look of total, brainless bewilderment which has since proved such an amazingly popular image with the readers of *Smeg!!* – said all of that and more.

And as we all walk back to town, having called Diesel and Lauren with our news, I hear that Ros has had what is called an epiphany, a revelation. She had it on the way to Whitby. A bit like St Paul's on the way to Damascus, only this was about her goth image. What she realised was that in Whitby, she was no longer different, she was just a goth among goths. Even the townsfolk were used to goths in Whitby and were as likely to say, 'Morning, rotten weather we're having!' to a corpse in a top hat smoking a big spliff as they were to Mrs Ryan, who wears a greasy apron and only smokes kippers.

She had to change, she thought. It was time to end it all, she had said, meaning her phase as a goth. In Whitby she would better stand out dressed as she is now than she would in her run-of-the-mill scary stuff and when she had left the hotel, it was only to find a shop which sold clothing which wasn't black. And there could be no more symbolic place to put her past as a goth behind her than at Esmerelda's Lookout, where she had cast her cloak and various other items, into the sea.

I watch her as she walks on ahead, with Teresa. She looks so different, though still attractive, with her dark hair brushed out and her quite nice legs on show, but I am not at all convinced that this is the girl I have spent so much time and energy pursuing. Her mood, I'm glad to see, has lifted entirely and the girls are chatting about a 'drop-dead gorgeous' boy who had helped her find her purse when she had to retrace her footsteps to the Lookout, just now. I hear that Ros has arranged to meet him for a drink later this evening. This is news that would have sent me plunging into my own bleak mood only yesterday, but not tonight. I am just so relieved that Ros is okay and that I did my bit to make sure of it. And, I think, I'm also kind of pleased with the look Teresa gave me when I finally reappeared at the top of the cliff.

Everyone is talking at once and I can hardly hear a word. 'Yes, yes, I'm fine,' I'm saying, loudly.

Faruk is telling Diesel about my exploits earlier this evening.

Lauren is talking to Clive about the shops she's found here in Whitby.

Ros is laughing at something Teresa has said and I think it might be about me as she keeps casting quick looks in my direction. We're sitting at a table in a pub garden. The sun has set and the beer garden is lit up by colourful hanging lanterns. Between the toilets and the door to the kitchen, I can see the tiny lights of a ship, far out at sea. I'm excited by everything that's going on around me, by having all my best friends together at the same time in one really cool place and I'm exchanging grins and glances with Teresa while trying to talk to my dad on my mobile.

'He's done what?' I say, suddenly brought to earth as I grasp what Dad is saying.

He's telling me that GD has broken his leg. It's not a bad break, Dad is saying, but he'll be stuck at home for a while and might need some shopping doing.

'How is Nana?' I ask him and learn that she took a turn for the worse and had to go back to hospital. She seems better now, I'm so relieved to hear, though the doctors want to keep her in for a spell.

But it's okay, I can help. I don't have exams to worry about now and I'll happily make time to do GD's shopping and I'll look in on Nana at the hospital whenever I can. I'll take her some flowers from her garden, she'll like that. And now Dad's telling me to enjoy myself but not to do anything he wouldn't do (there's no answer to that) and something about how much Roger admires his garden. He comes over to ours quite a lot now, apparently and talks a lot about his 'fiance' – the one he hasn't yet met. I pocket my phone and we eat our dinners, pub lasagne with chips and salad (no chips for the girls) and it's all so very nearly perfect.

In fact I think it would be perfect, a memory I could treasure forever, were it not for the sad and secretive gaze I see Lauren giving Diesel, when he's looking somewhere else. I wonder what's on her mind and think I see trouble brewing there, but I've no idea what it might be. Meanwhile, Teresa has leaned over the table and asked for a word with me, in private. We say we're just going to look at the sea and because it's a moonlit night, our departure is accompanied by some not unexpected catcalls and whistles.

When we're alone, and we do indeed have the kind of moonlit view and warm, balmy evening that backdrops the stomach-turning slushy bits in so many rom-coms (or so I'm told), Teresa says, 'I have some bad news for you, BJ.'

I hate it when people say this. Why can't they just come straight out with it and then you know the worst there and then, without this horrible wait?

'What is it?'

'It's Ros. I've spoken to her about you.'

'What do you mean?'

'I've asked her how she feels about you. I hope you don't mind too much. I said you might be interested in her.'

'I see,' I say. I wish she hadn't done that. Soo embarrassing.

'The thing is, BJ,' Teresa continues, 'I asked her and she's said that she's not interested in you at all. In fact she finds the idea quite funny. She says you're just so not her type.'

'Not her type?' I say. I'm amazed, or maybe the word is appalled, after all the effort I've put in, trying to make sure I was her type. 'But I've read Kerouac and Kafka and I know she reads them because I saw them in her bag.'

Teresa tries to suppress a laugh, but can't quite do it.

'Oh, Brian,' she says. 'Those were my books. Ros was taking them back to the local library for me – it's on her way home. I hope you enjoyed them, anyway.'

'I'm not sure, now,' I say.

'Ah, well,' Teresa says. 'At least it's only incompatibility. Nothing to do with you having her stomach pumped.'

'That's a relief,' I say. And maybe everything she's just told me is a relief too, I'm not sure. The way Ros has changed and learning her real feelings about me is all a lot of stuff I need to sort out in my head. I can't say that I feel particularly upset, though, which must be a good thing. Not with Teresa standing so close to me, here by the moonlit sea, my senses completely overpowered by her proximity and her perfume.

'But hey, never mind,' she says, turning towards me and, totally unexpectedly, resting her long, slender wrists, which smell of jasmine and honeysuckle, on my caped shoulders. 'You're still my hero.' And then she seems much closer, in fact she is much closer and then our lips meet, hers warm and wet and tasting of cherries, mine of chips and cheap grease paint, I suspect, but we are kissing, Teresa Davenport and me, Brian Johnson. It's a sight seen countless times along the seafront at Whitby, just one more girl kissing one more vampire, but it's special for me and, as I feel Teresa's tongue dart into my mouth,

I think it might be special for her, too. And when she has finished eating me alive, she says, oh, so memorably, 'Come back to my room, later. There's something I want to show you.'

CHAPTER 18

Love Hurts

Roger is sitting on the compactor in his red Speedos, telling me how he met Poon Tang at the airport. He's completely given up on trying to pronounce her real name now and Pao-Pei will, in Laurel Gardens at least, forever be Poon Tang. He is as happy as Larry, probably much happier; I doubt if this Larry ever went about with such a goofy grin spread across his chops. By the side of Roger, said Larry would be a miserable character, incapable of raising a smile or enjoying a chuckle. Roger Dyson is where happiness is at, right now.

He looks like he hasn't got a care in the world and any menace I might have imagined about him has vanished completely. He doesn't give a monkey's about Clive's failure to score at Whitby, despite his footing of most of the bill for our trip. 'Clive will sort himself out when he's good and ready,' Roger says.

'You can lead a horse to water,' I say, unwisely.

'Like I said before,' Roger says quickly. 'No whores.'

I have never seen him like this, grinning away as he sits in the sun, one hand down his Speedos, scratching his balls. In fact, I don't think I've ever seen anyone quite this happy. It's unnatural. And all because of the delightful young lady in a blue and pink sarong who has just now served us with long glasses of ice cold beer. She is as striking as her photographs. Tall, lean and angular, not much of a top deck, I notice, but that doesn't worry Roger, who professes to be a leg man anyway. And Poon Tang has legs, he says, which reach all the way to the ground. He watches her bottom jiggle under the silk as she sashays back to the house, casting a last quick smile over her shapely shoulder.

'I can't tell you how that woman has changed my life,' Roger says. 'Life without her was meaningless, empty. But now, it's as if

the sun has come out and chased every grey cloud from the sky.'
Ee-yuk, I'm thinking, this man is in love.

He tells me how Poon Tang has taken over the house, deep
cleaning the kitchen and sorting all the other forgotten places too
and how her cooking is 'just out of this world'. He tells me that
it's an added bonus that Clive and Poon Tang get on like a house
on fire. But I've seen that already, when they got off the bus
outside the bungalow earlier on, giggling like a pair of schoolgirls. Clive has talked of no one else since Roger drove down to
Heathrow and picked her up, last week.

Poon Tang has taken over Clive's room for the time being;
Clive sleeps on the sofa in the living room. This is in accordance
with a custom which Poon Tang insists on maintaining, which is
that a betrothed couple mustn't share a bed until a month before
the wedding. After initial resistance, Roger has gone along with
his beloved's wishes and is only glad that he doesn't have to wait
until after the wedding itself.

'She is a paragon of womankind,' Roger says. 'She is more
beautiful, much sexier and far superior in every respect to any
other woman on God's earth. She is, you know. And she's mine,
Brian, all mine. Can you believe that?'

I've become a little bored with loved-up Roger and my mind
has drifted somewhere else. I might just be thinking of someone
who outdoes Roger's Poon Tang on all these counts and several
more. But Roger interprets my distraction in his own way and
says, 'But don't get me wrong, son. Your mother is a lovely lady
too and your father is very lucky indeed to have her. The
gorgeous Violet is a wonderful woman. It's just that she hasn't
got that little extra something which I think my Poon Tang's got.
You know what I mean?'

I don't, not just then, anyway.

Clive and Poon Tang come out of the house bearing trays of
snacks and more drinks. Clive and Poon Tang sit on a seat
together. It's only a rough plank on two piles of bricks but neither

seem to mind that at all. Roger beams at Poon Tang, then at Clive and then me. Then once again, he slips his hand under the elastic of his trunks and sighs deeply and contentedly as he adjusts the lie of his tackle.

Before Chris Evans took over Radio 2's breakfast slot, Mum would listen to Terry Wogan. She listened religiously, from the until 9.30, when the show ended. She would have 'listened in' from 7.00, but there was Dad's breakfast to make and his shirt to iron and a list of complaints, usually about Roger, to pretend to listen to. She had a signed photograph of Terry himself in a drawer in her sewing room and unbeknownst to Dad, sometimes wore her TOGS sweatshirt around the house when he wasn't there. Under the pseudonym of Crazy Daisy, I'm amazed to learn, Mum's made regular contributions to the show. And she knows all Terry's catchphrases, often retiring to bed muttering something about being banjaxed. The one I've heard her most use has been, Is it me? For years I thought this was a very silly and meaningless expression. It says you're realising that though the world mightn't be crazy after all, you are. And now I've been using it myself.

Is it me? I'm thinking as I see Dad going off late to work with his face unshaven and his tie left on the breakfast table. He's late because instead of the bowl of All-Bran he's had every breakfast of his life as far as I know, Dad's had a big fry up, which he cooked himself and shared with Mum. It's the culmination of a week in which everything he's done could be termed out of character. Yesterday, Sunday, he was out in the garden wearing baggy trousers and a smiley tee shirt, both of which items must date from about 1989 and look like he wore them once and put them away forever. And he wasn't gardening, either, but rolling out the lines for a badminton court. The net was up by mid-afternoon and he and Mum and Roger and Poon Tang were enjoying a noisy knockabout shortly afterwards. It's unsettling.

Mum, I should say in the interests of fairness, has also been acting oddly, which of course, brings me back to the, *Is it me?* thing. But she really has been a different person these past few days. For instance, I've never heard Mum make a disparaging remark about anyone, not even about Mrs Shaw across the road, who's rumoured to supplement her housekeeping with 'personal services', but Mum's been surprisingly sharp-tongued about Roger's intended. According to Mum, Poon Tang is 'no better than she should be' and while I don't know exactly what that means, I don't think it's a compliment. And she, Mum, has been wearing brighter clothes, might even have bought some new ones and I think she's been using a little makeup, too.

I'm wondering if this has anything to do with Dad passing on what I'd told him. He did it out in his greenhouse, where she'd brought him a cup of tea. I could see them both from the house, Dad's hands describing his surprise and relief at discovering the missing piece of his life's jigsaw. And I saw Mum take it all in and then turn her gaze towards the house. They were there for ages and must have talked about more than Dad's adoption and it's my guess that he told her something of his future plans. That might explain the strange, faraway smile that crosses Mum's face these days, when she thinks no one's looking. To me, it's the smile of someone realising that life isn't set in stone after all and that other possibilities might still be open.

Today the changes in the Johnson household moved up a gear and they began with my unshaven Dad driving off to work thirty-one minutes late. He didn't appear to care, either. And then, as he passed the breakfast table, I had the bizarre idea that he was humming something by The Smiths. I looked at Mum for reassurance but she only shrugged and stirred something in a pan, saying she was going to take something hot round for Roger – goodness knew what that new girl was giving him. I was still pondering all this, trying to identify the song Dad was singing and even considering the possibility that I'd been overdoing things recently – maybe if I had a nice long sleep, everything would seem more normal when I woke up. But then, just before lunch, Dad's car swings back into the driveway and my world does a backflip.

That's what I'm thinking as I stand in the kitchen with Mum, listening to Dad – my dad, the wage slave and probable company "yes" man – describing in excited tones how he's told the manager of his department store to do one. I'm gobsmacked. My dad's actually told the Victoria where they can stick their crappy job. He's finally stood up to the machine which has been grinding him down, year after year. Go, Dad! I stand in the kitchen looking at him in a whole new light, the shockwaves still bouncing about the room: I don't think Mum or I think for one minute about what we'd all do about the salary he'd just lost.

No one says 'language, Brian!' as I sit down at the kitchen table, muttering fuck me, over and over again. Mum doesn't say anything, not just then. She smiles at Dad and at me too, like she knows that somehow, everything's going to be fine, that Dad chucking his job is the best thing that could have happened. Dad must have stopped off somewhere to buy pastries and popping these on a plate, he makes a pot of coffee. Sitting across the table from Mum, he tells us that this is indeed all for the best. Now, he says, is the time for us all to take stock. Then he gets all philosophical.

'The way we've been living has been safe and secure,' he says. 'But it's also been dull and, um, perhaps devoid of the brilliant bursts of happiness which should punctuate a well-rounded existence.' Wow. Where did that come from? Has Dad been at his Readers' Digests again? And there's more. 'I've only lately realised,' he says, 'that the pursuit of happiness itself is not a selfish idea and that if we are all to find our own, then now is the time to start looking.' While Mum and I are digesting this, he says he knows what he himself needs to do to find happiness and he'd like to talk to Violet about it later. He thinks she'll see that his way will be best for all of us. And while he makes his plans, he's going to cash in the lump sum of his pension, which will give us more than we need for our present difficulties. Mum and I sit there, stunned, frozen, flakes from the pastries left unbrushed from our lips.

Mum recovers first and a very neat recovery it is too, mentioning that the corner shop down by the Co-op is empty now, the one that had been a tobacconist's, and saying what a nice florist's it would make. Dad swallows too much of his Danish and tries not to splutter. Then he thinks for a moment, comes quickly to a decision and says he'll see how much is in his pension fund, but that Mum should start costing it out now. Dad says he won't need much to live on, not for the life he's got planned. It sounds to me like Mum and himself might go their separate ways and I want to ask what's going on? And what about me? But Mum's already talking about wholesale flower dealers

I'm wondering if she knew this was coming.

And I'm just sitting there thinking, *Is it me?*

Mum may be fine with all this. I'm sure she has enough reason to be, but I'm a little shaken, to tell the truth. To restore just a little order in the only way I know how, I spend the whole of the afternoon not just tidying, but actually cleaning my room. You heard right, bubba. And this gives me plenty of time to think. As I carefully extract about a hundred used tissues from behind the headboard and tear off a second bin liner for crushed Diet Coke tins, empty bottles of Smirnoff Ice, half-finished bottles of cobalt-coloured WKD and some hard, green and long-forgotten slices of pizza, I come around to thinking that okay, these changes have had their positive sides, too. They may all be positive – I won't know until I've seen where they're taking us. But definitely on the plus side has been Dad's much-improved attitude towards GD and Nana. Now that he knows for certain that he isn't their natural son and understands how he was rescued from an orphanage by their kindness, it seems he can't do enough to make up for what he considers to be his own inattentiveness. And Mum's clearly much happier, even excited about the future. So I'm thinking something new: if my parents actually split, would that have to be a bad thing?

Dad has driven me over to see GD, who has been as much surprised in the transformations in Charlie as I've been. But GD has had no reservations about this, he's been delighted and might have leapt off his chair to hug his adopted son, had his lower leg not been encased in a pottery cast which has already been autographed by about a hundred friends.

This afternoon, we are having a heart to heart, at Narnia, GD, Charlie and me. (Dad actually prefers to be called Charlie now, even by me – how weird is that?) GD is telling us how he comes to be chair-bound, when he should be at Nana's side. He's saying that when Nana suddenly got worse and she had to go into hospital, not being able to be with her was almost more than he could bear. He talked to the doctors and while they tried to say the right things, it was clear enough to him that they weren't holding out a lot of hope. GD visited her twice daily but coming home from one of these visits, he had been close to despair.

'If I couldn't be with Ruth, then there was only one place I wanted to be,' he tells us.

'Nana's Rock,' I say.

'That's the big granite overhang on the tops,' Dad says.

'So you do know, Charlie,' GD says, evidently pleased.

'Where you proposed to Ruth. To Mum, I mean.'

'Right again. So there I was, sitting on what BJ here calls Nana's Rock, plumbing the depths of despair. I didn't know what I could do for the best. I saw that all the plans we had made to give her a good death were really only to distract and comfort me. I'm not one to feel sorry for myself, you both know that. I'd sooner take my disappointments and frustrations out on a piece of wood in my workshop. But right then, I have to say, I saw no future. Not a glimmer of hope, nothing. All I wanted, was to be with Ruth.'

I am choked up and I can see that Dad's upset too. Dad says, 'So you jumped, then. You jumped from the rock. You tried to end it all. Well, under these circumstances, it's hard to blame you. Even if you would have left Mum on her own for who knows how many more days or weeks. I can't say I approve of what you tried to do. But I want you to know that I understand.'

Dad pats the pot on GD's leg: it's going to take them a while to get touchy-feely. But I'm with Dad on this. What GD attempted is a terrible thing, but I can almost understand what's driven him to it.

But GD is smiling, the first time I've seen him break into a smile in days. In fact, he's laughing.

'You think I tried to kill myself?' he says, as if that's an idea he finds wildly funny. 'No one needs to do that. Death will come to us all soon enough without hurrying it along. No, I didn't jump off Nana's Rock. Of course I didn't.' He pauses, now looking a little uncomfortable. 'I might, um, have fallen off it, though'

'How?' That's Dad and me, together.

GD is looking sheepish, as if he's about to say something he'd rather not, not in front of Charlie, anyway. But he can see we want an answer. 'Well, you know how I like the odd smoke when I'm up on the rock?'

'Yes,' I say and get a look from Dad.

'Odd smoke?' he says.

'You know what I'm talking about, Charlie. You didn't grow up within these walls without recognising the smell of a decent block of Red Leb burning in a hash pipe.'

Dad sighs now. 'I suppose not,' he says. 'I tried to pretend we were normal. I wanted us to be normal. I can see why, now. I think that my hankering for a so-called normality was some surviving vestige of the life I'd lived before the car crash.'

There is a moment's silence as GD considers this. Then he says, with a wink at me, 'Bugger me, Charlie, but your real parents must have been straight as coat hangers!'

No one says anything. The record that's been playing quietly on the turntable reaches the end of its side and begins to click repetitively. I'm thinking GD has just insulted the fragile half-memory which is all that survives of Dad's biological parents. But then it's Dad himself who breaks the silence, cracking up in a long burst of seemingly uncontrollable laughter. My dad, laughing until tears shine in his eyes, here at Narnia, with me. And he's laughing about GD smoking dope.

Is it me?

'Well, I have to admit that I only have myself to blame,' GD says, gravely. 'These injuries are, I confess it now, the result of reefer madness. No, it's true. I realise now that my own parents were quite right to have warned me off the stuff. The scare stories in the tabloids were right, after all. Cannabis is dangerous, no question about it. Just look at what smoking it has done to my leg!'

Dad and GD are laughing their socks off and it looks like it's doing them both the world of good. I'm finding it just as hilarious but I'd still like to know how GD broke his leg. At last, GD is sufficiently composed to continue. 'The fact is,' he says, 'there's been no decent hash to be had in town for bloody eons and all Magic Mick's been able to get me is the ubiquitous skunk and pretty heinous it is, too. I'm used to a quality high, not this wicked stuff. I'm sure I had no more than two or three joints that night, in fact, I'm certain of it. But when I tried to get up, I couldn't. It was like my legs had turned to rubber. And then, when I did get up, I walked straight off the edge. If I landed on the rocks instead of thick bracken, I'd probably would have killed myself.'

'You idiot,' my dad says. 'I'm not your keeper, Arthur, but I don't want to see you smoking that stuff again. Not up on Nana's

Rock, anyway.'

And now it's my turn to laugh like a drain.

In the Casablanca, Faruk is having one of his frequent blazing rows with Deniz, in the kitchen. Deniz is reminding Faruk of what a world of worry he is causing their parents, him not having a clue what he wants to do with his life. Diesel and I have interrupted our conversation, and Diesel's late lunch, to listen in. We hear something smash against a wall and Deniz shouting at her brother, 'Be realistic, for once in your life, Faruk! You can't be an airline pilot, it's just not possible!' and Faruk saying, 'Why's it not possible?' and Deniz replying, 'You're afraid of heights, for one thing. Diesel shakes his head. 'Women,' he says and goes on forking sausage, egg, beans, chips and mushrooms until he's finished. Then, in response to Deniz shouting, 'You're not big enough to be a fireman,' Diesel says, 'Women' again and mournfully mops up his ketchup with his 'slice on the side'.

'How's it going?' I ask. We both know what I'm talking about.

'She won't listen to me,' Diesel says. 'She's having the kid and that's that.'

'And you're not going to leave her?'

'No,' he says.

'So what will you do?'

'I'll do what every other Dad has done since Eve told Adam there was a sprog on the way. I'll get married and I'll go out to work and when I get home, I'll help bath the kid and put it to bed and read it a story and fall asleep in a chair. And the next day I'll get up and do it all over again. And on Saturdays I won't be going out with you lot, not unless you happen to be going down the swings in the park. Or possibly McDonald's.'

'It won't all be like that,' I say, because I know nothing about these things. Through the big window I can see Clive and his 22-year-old prospective step-mother crossing the road, each clutching two or three shopping bags. Pao-Pei, oh, fuck it, Poon

Tang, whispers something in Clive's ear and Clive laughs.

'It'll be exactly like that,' Diesel says, but he's not talking about Clive and Poon Tang as he stirs the contents of five sachets of sugar into his cup of tea. 'She's already got me one of those papoose things so I can carry it in a sling.'

'Oh my God,' I say, because I've seen fathers in those and they don't look cool.

'I'm doomed,' Diesel's telling me, as Clive and Poon Tang, smirking conspiratorially, slide into the booth, Clive next to Diesel, Poon Tang next to me. Faruk comes over and squeezes on to the end of the plastic-covered seat, next to Poon Tang, leaving Deniz standing at the counter, arms folded, a warning of slow service to come. Clive and Poon Tang are chattering like they've known each other for years. I relay Diesel's worries to everyone, hoping that they can offer more in the way of consoling thoughts than I've been able to.

'You're fucked, mate,' Faruk says. Very helpful.

'You won't be able to come down the Queen's Head with us anymore,' Clive says. 'You'll be stuck indoors listening to the baby alarm.'

'No more skating,' Faruk says.

'I was crap at that, anyway,' Diesel says and looks out the window. Faruk's brother is working on the Green Dragon in the garage across the road.

'No more smoking weed on the roof of the library.'

'Obviously,' says Diesel.

'No more Poon Tang,' says Poon Tang and giggles. 'At least only from wife!'

We're going to have to watch this Poon Tang, I see.

'It'll be all right, really, Deez,' I say. 'We'll help you out, babysit for you, won't we?'

There's some ambiguous nodding and a lot of coughing and Diesel rolls his eyes and watches as Abdullah slams the bonnet of our car with a loud bang and gives a tyre a savage kick with his boot. We've been so engrossed in Diesel's appalling situation that we haven't noticed the Casablanca's other regulars, the girls from the Upper School, piling into the next booth. To be strictly accurate, it's only Faruk and I who have been appalled. Clive and Poon Tang seem to think it's as funny as they're finding everything else, these days. Clive is holding Poon Tang's hand and asking where she's had her nails done.

Carole, the big one with the dirty laugh and the range of colourful thongs, spots this immediately and brings it to the attention of the two slightly dumpy blondes and the cute little red head. She says something to Clive, which I miss, as I'm saying something consoling to Diesel, but I'm fairly sure it's an observation highlighting the anomaly of Clive's lifestyle choice being at odds with the attention he's paying to a member of the opposite sex.

'What's the matter?' Carole asks him. 'Your boyfriends over there not giving you enough cock?'

Carole's cronies think this is very funny. One of the dumpy blondes says, 'Couldn't find an English girl to do it with, could he?' and they all erupt again, squawking like agitated parrots. Faruk is clearly angry, but like me, isn't sure how to react when the tormentor is a woman.

Clive has gone scarlet but his 'Fuck off, you slags' sounds neither witty nor intimidating. It's looking like a clear victory for the mouthy schoolgirls, when Poon Tang grabs Diesel's tomato-shaped ketchup dispenser and the plastic bottle of mayo too. I think I know what's coming but I still can't quite believe it when she aims both bottles at the blondes and squeezes hard.

The blondes both scream and stare down at their sauce-splattered tops and scream some more. The cute little redhead escapes under the table and bolts for the door. But Carole's not having this, not from some 'foreign slapper' and she stuffs her chocolate éclair with extra whipped cream down Poon Tang's blouse. The girls scratch and they grapple, nails break, seams

split and plates smash while, variously, we – watch apprecia-
tively (Diesel), shout at Faruk to bloody well do something
(Clive), or just sit there screaming (the two blondes). Me, I'm the
detached observer, crushed against the window, outside which
there's a growing crowd of interested spectators.

By the time the combatants have at last been forcibly
separated by a furious Deniz, Poon Tang has ruined her clothes
and will have to go shopping again, the girls will have a lot of
explaining to do when they get home and Faruk will be cleaning
the caff until this time next month, I expect. It has not been an
elevating afternoon. But as I leave a larger than usual tip on my
saucer and get up to go. I'm thinking that Diesel has at least been
well and truly cheered up. For the moment, at least.

CHAPTER 19

Take Me Bak 'Ome

It's not hard to see why Big Noddy Liversage is called Noddy when his proper name is Nigel. Not if you've seen videos of Slade in their heyday. Roger Dyson has the lot, by the way, everything from *Gudbuy T' Jane*, to *Mama, Weer All Crayzee Now*. It's not that Noddy Liversage is the dead spit of Noddy Holder, but rather that he tries really hard to be. And as you enter the public bar through the big old swing doors like me, Diesel, Lauren, Clive and Faruk did earlier tonight, the chances are that your ears will be assaulted by damagingly loud renditions of *Get Down And Get With It* or *'Coz I Luv You* (there's nothing on the juke box later than 1974), and the first thing your eyes will fix on will be Noddy's own gigantic physique and balloon-red face, which is curtained by enormous mutton-chop sideburns.

If you're lucky, the landlord of the Queen's Head will be wearing his replica Noddy Holder top hat, the one with the little round mirrors and his tartan suit – though he prizes this and generally only gets it out for special occasions: Noddy Holder's birthday, the anniversary of the first time Dave Hill wore that silver outfit with the stacked heel boots and so on. But that's just the landlord. Look around you in the public bar of the Queen's Head and you'll see that the whole place is a time capsule. The decor hasn't changed in decades, the Wurlitzer plays vinyl 45s and Roger reckons you can still get Aztec chocolate bars and hedgehog flavour crisps from behind the bar.

'Orrlroight, ow-er Broy-yan,' Noddy says as I return our glasses to the bar. 'Foo-arr moo-er points of Krownenbee-urg for yow, eez eet?'

I tell Noddy that I think his Black Country accent is coming along a real treat. It's Noddy's ambition to be able to talk just like

231

his heroes, who define a 'kipper tie' as a hot drink with milk and two sugars. I tell him that I think his accent is so good, in fact, that it's probably safe for him to try it out in Wolverhampton itself: I'm almost certain he won't get beaten up this time. His pub might be a museum piece with hygiene standards and a blocked toilet which both pre-date the Health and Safety at Work Act, but it's the one place in town which doesn't ask for ID from obvious minors. 'Oi can't be bothid with all that,' Noddy says. 'Them's orrl forged on the int-init innywhy.' Which is why the Queen's Head has been the pub of choice for the Four Horsemen this last year.

We're here tonight at Diesel's instigation. Lauren's not drinking, of course, but Diesel is letting his hair down – not drinking like every pint might be his last, which is probably what I would do, but drinking like he has something to celebrate. The mood is infectious. Clive is knocking back dusty bottles of Cherry B and Babycham and going on about Poon Tang, whom Roger has taken out tonight. Lauren has never looked happier and we discover she can be very nice and quite funny, when you let her.

It's when Diesel and I go for a quick spliff in what Noddy calls the toilets and his customers call the Fatal Swamp, that I find out what this is all about. 'She's all right, isn't she?' Diesel says, skinning up on the broken hand-dryer. There's only a single low-wattage bulb in here and it's all a bit gloomy. But Diesel isn't. I can see he's smiling from the way his teeth glow in the yellow light. I'm saying, sure she is, Lauren's a nice girl and wondering what's brought about Diesel's change of mood.

'It's not going to be easy, I know that,' Diesel says now. 'I've talked with people who've got kids and I know pretty much what to expect. Basically, when you have a kid, you're no longer the centre of your own universe. You're just a satellite orbiting around Planet Kid. And it's a full time job. And there will be a struggle with money and it's all going to be stressful for the first few years and I won't get to do loads of the stuff I wanted to. But you know what?'

'No?'

'I'm cool with all that.'

'You are?'

'I am,' Diesel says, and passes me the spliff. 'I mean, can you imagine me and Little Diesel kicking a ball in the park, me passing on all my old skills...'

'What skills?'

'Don't be funny. And taking him for his first Big Mac? And watching all my old DVDs with him? He'll be watching *Back to the Future* like it's new. And going fishing with him?'

'You don't fish.'

'Not yet I don't, but there's going to be so much stuff I'll want to do just so I can share it with him.'

'Or her?'

'I'm just saying. Of course, or her. Little girls these days, they like the same stuff anyway. And hey, what about the first time I take him in a pub? And he buys his old man a pint? How cool will that be?'

And, over the noise of a man with amazingly long hair hawking phlegm as he noisily uses the urinal, Diesel tells me what Lauren nearly did which made him see his predicament in an entirely new light. Partly, it was his fault, too. He should never have given her that leaflet about terminating a pregnancy, he says. Perhaps I've noticed, he says, that Lauren hasn't been her usual, bubbly self these past few weeks.

'Neither have you,' I remind him. 'You've been a right miserable twat, in fact.'

'He's got a point,' the long-haired man says as he zips up and stumbles back to the bar.

'There is a kernel of truth in what you say,' Diesel says. 'And Lauren saw I was miserable and I suppose she saw that this was never going to work, not if I always thought I'd been forced into a life of fatherhood. I'd resent it, she told me. She said that sooner or later, I'd resent her. Which is why she set the ball rolling to have our baby terminated.'

'What?' I can't believe Lauren would do such a thing. We talked of it as a possibility, as you do, but the reality is too terrible even to consider. 'But she was dead set on having a kid,' I say.

'She was dead set on us being happy together, too,' Diesel says. 'And so was I. But the baby was coming between us. So that mad little brain of hers decides that the time just isn't right. She'll get rid of this baby and we'll try again further down the line, when we're settled and more...'

'Mature?'

'Yes.'

'So what happened?'

'I found out what was happening when some idiot from the clinic left a message on the call minder. I should've been happy. It was what I'd wanted her to do from the start. But now that it was actually going to happen, everything changed. All those plans she'd made, the ones I thought I was only going along with very reluctantly. All the stuff we'd bought, the cute mobile with the frogs on it that I'd chosen myself. I don't know, BJ, I don't really know what happened. All I do know is that I suddenly realized that I'd been wrong and that what I wanted more than anything, was for us to have that kid.'

'Wow. I suppose one of us had to grow up sooner or later. Just glad it wasn't me.'

We talk about the anticipated joys of fatherhood for a while longer, finish the spliff and go inside, where Noddy is offering an impromptu a cappella version of *Take Me Bak 'Ome*, while Faruk stumbles about the place, slurring his words and telling other customers that he really, really loves them. This week, I found out that he really, really loves Rashida, the other half of the marriage arranged for him when he was ten. This year, determined to resolve the confusion he felt about the matter, he started corresponding with Rashida online, meaning to tell her how he felt and see if there was a way out. He wasn't expecting to fall in love with her, he just did, he says. She's going to come and see him later this summer. But now, he says, if they are ever going to get married, it will be on their terms and at a time of their choosing.

Diesel sits down next to Lauren and drapes his podgy arm around her shoulders. 'This won't stop us going out,' he says. 'Lauren says the secret to a happy marriage is that we both get on with our own social lives. She's got her friends and I've got you lot.' Which, we all agree, is just how it should be. It's been one of those evenings I know even now that I'll look back on and think, those were the days, when we had real friends, when we all stuck together and were four against the world. That or some similar bollocks. This is what I'm thinking just before Someone notices that I am enjoying myself and the phone in my pocket starts buzzing.

'Suup?' I say, slightly drunkenly. And then realise it's Dad.

'It's your grandmother,' I hear Dad saying. 'I'm sorry, Brian, but she's not good. She's unconscious. I think this might be it.'

'Oh, fuck, no,' I say.

'What?' Dad says.

'Where is she?'

'She's in the hospital. But that's not where she should be. I do understand that now.'

'Can't we get her out of there? Back to Narnia? GD must be going mental.'

'I've spoken to the doctors and they won't release her. It's not in the best interests of the patient, they're saying. So unless we do something, she'll die in hospital while Arthur probably dies of grief in his chair.'

'Unless we do something?'

'Wait there,' Dad says. 'I'm coming to get you.'

We stop the camper van in a pick-up point across from the bright glare of the hospital entrance. Faruk is to stay with the van and be ready for us when we come out. He keeps the engine idling and tries not to look like a getaway driver outside a bank. Garcia, who had jumped aboard when Dad wasn't looking, is curled up in the well of the passenger seat. The hospital's automatic doors whoosh open and Dad and I cross the newly waxed lobby, where an officious old man in a shabby dressing gown is loudly complaining to the nurses at reception. 'This is not good enough,' he's saying. 'This will not do.' He's telling the nurses what isn't good enough and what will not do while a tired-looking woman in a supermarket tunic waits patiently behind him with her two children, who are both in their pyjamas. A porter wheeling cylinders of gas crosses the path of two young female doctors who are heading towards the food court.

Dad walks briskly across the open space, like a man with a purpose. We both know where we're going, but never having visited Nana at such a late hour, and coming on such an unusual errand, the hospital feels strange and not a little threatening. We pass down a corridor where most of the side wards are in darkness, though there's a reading light on here and there and hooded lamps on the ward desks. Dad, surprising me again, has swiped a clipboard from an empty bed and stuck it under his arm. When we see anyone approaching, a tired ward sister in one case, an over-worked doctor in another, he taps it with a pen and tells me quite loudly to take care of myself and not to go overdoing it in future. With his old suit on and a row of pens in his pockets, he can just about pass for a doctor, though not a doctor who can afford a stethoscope, or a good suit.

The lift Dad used on his previous visit is out of order, so we walk quickly down a long corridor until we find another, which we take to the fourth floor. Before the doors open, we've run over the plan of action one more time. Dad tells me that though he made it clear that he now wanted to take Nana home, some prick of a registrar bluntly refused, telling him that to remove her now could have the most serious consequences for Nana's health. Dad argued with him, pointed at her unconscious form and demanded to know just how much more serious it got than that? Luck appears to be on our side as we approach the mixed ward in which Nana's bed is parked. The other patients seem to be asleep and there are no doctors or nurses. We draw the curtains around her bed and switch on the bedside light. She looks terrible, her skin a bluey grey in the artificial light, lying there with the cardiograph beeping and a tube up her nose. Dad looks at me and I nod. He switches off the machine, carefully removes the tube and then the patches on her arms and chest. I empty her bedside cabinet of the few items GD had sent with her: the photograph of them as young people, a book of her poems, her spectacles, toothbrush and a spare nightdress, and put everything in a carrier bag.

'All ready?' Dad says.

I nod and take the brakes off the wheels of the bed. We hear a pair of heels clicking down the corridor and wait until whoever is wearing them has gone. Then Dad pops his head from between the curtains, sees the coast is clear and quietly draws them back. I start to push the bed out into the corridor. Then my heart stops. There's a disturbance behind me, as a lamp clicks on. I'm ready to run, bed and all, but it's only another patient, an old man who seems to be smiling at us. 'Good luck!' he whispers, with a wink. The bed creaks and the wheels squeak like a labful of tormented mice as I push the bed slowly towards the swing doors at the end of the passage. I'm trying to look like I do this all the time and it's all a bit of a chore and I'm looking forward to my break and a cup of tea. Halfway down the corridor, we pass a nurses' station which looks onto a small side ward.

The nurse on duty puts down her magazine. She regards us with some surprise, or is it suspicion? A doctor she's never seen before is removing a patient against the express wishes of Mr Ryan, the registrar. And the new porter isn't wearing his coat. But before she can turn any such thinking into questions, Dad has demanded her name, inspected her desk, said that it's a wonder she can find anything on it and told her that efficiency depends on order – and might he suggest she brings some to it without delay? While the flustered nurse bustles about the desk, we arrive at the end of the corridor only to find that the lift is out of order. It's the wrong lift, an easy mistake to make in the circumstances, but one which could ruin everything. Awkwardly, we now have to pass the nurse at the desk one more time. I can't read her expression as she watches us approach – the game may be up. But Dad stops by the desk again and points out a crisp packet stuffed in an open drawer. He tells the nurse to remind maintenance about that broken lift. I'm quietly impressed.

On the ground floor, we slide the bed into a bay where there's an empty stretcher on wheels, which Dad had pointed out earlier. There's no way we can take a bed across the lobby without inviting questions, he says, but a gurney might just be heading towards the ambulance station. And so, with great care, we lift Nana from her bed. She is much lighter than I expect and seems to feel nothing as we lie her down on the stretcher and cover her with a sheet. The corridor is empty, apart from a patient in pyjamas who shuffles by, wheeling an intravenous drip bag on a stand. 'Now,' Dad says.

I push the stretcher out into the lobby towards the front entrance. Dad looks at his clipboard, I watch the chequered tiles passing under my feet. We're almost at the doors when a voice behind us calls out, 'Doctor!' It's one of the nurses at the desk. 'I've no paperwork on this patient?'

'That's quite all right, nurse,' Dad says, waving his clipboard. 'All taken care of, all under control.' And then we're out in the warm summer night. Faruk is waiting with the van doors open. The inside has been configured as a bed which will accommodate Nana nicely. She gives a little moan as we transfer her to the van. Dad jumps in the passenger seat while I squeeze in next to Nana. The nurse from reception is at the doors waving at us as Faruk guns the engine and the campervan lurches forward. Faruk drives off, checking his mirror like he thinks we might be followed.

I hold Nana's hand as the caravan leaves the hospital grounds, swings through the outskirts of town and joins a ribbon of traffic heading in the general direction of Derbyshire. I'm still bursting with adrenaline but I can't help smiling. Dad turns around in his seat and asks how Nana's doing? I tell him I don't know, but she looks comfortable. As we pass under a streetlight, I can see he's grinning at me and now (he knows how to do this?) he offers me a high five. Amazing!

Faruk's driving is amazing too – we really should let him do this more often. He drives quickly but every corner is smoothly taken and if there are potholes, Faruk avoids them. Soon, he's backing the van carefully up to Nana's front door, where GD is standing, draped on a pair of crutches, the light from the coach lamp illuminating a worried face. We take Nana inside and settle her upon the day bed under the stairs. The village doctor, a friend of my grandparents, is on hand to take a look at her. He can't offer hope but he tells GD that she would have been no better off in the hospital, which seems to offer GD relief of a kind, anyway. He leaves painkillers with instructions and tells us to call him if she gets worse. Nana is unconscious still, unaware of what we have done, but her face no longer looks so awful and she appears peaceful. GD makes us all a hot drink, but no one wants anything to eat. We sit and talk quietly until it's late. Faruk has fallen asleep in his chair and GD, Dad and I take turns to watch Nana and grab some sleep ourselves.

Throughout the next day, a succession of Nana's friends drop in to pay their respects. Villagers stay only long enough to leave flowers or some other small gift and sit briefly with Nana, who seems unchanged since last might, though GD has cleaned her face with a damp cloth and gently brushed her hair. A nurse is in and out all day. Other friends have come from further afield and room will have to be found for some of them to sleep over. I remember some of these people from my visit to Narnia as a child: Paul the professor of literature who used to have a yellow pony tail and wear a leather hat; Leo the guitarist has a grey mane now, while Samantha, an artist and teacher who tried to teach me to paint, looks just the same.

More visitors arrive and GD calls in favours and finds rooms for them in the village, some at B&B's, but others courtesy of helpful friends and neighbours. They speak to Nana as if she is fully conscious, wishing her well and sometimes remembering days they had shared together. And then they drift out into the sunny garden, where they can talk without disturbing her.

Faruk is talking to Magic Mick and an American from San Francisco who says he knew GD many years ago. GD himself is dividing his time between talking to his friends and going inside to check on Nana. Dad's here too, looking out of place in his business suit but getting along well with everyone just the same. Old friends are reunited and memories unearthed. There's a lot of talk about Nana and about her poetry too. I didn't realise that in some circles, Nana is almost famous. Someone has provided a picnic lunch, cold chicken, salad, glasses of white wine and after this, GD reads aloud one of Nana's poems and we all raise a glass to her.

Then Faruk is calling from the house, where he's gone to get Garcia a drink. 'It's your nana,' he calls to me. Everyone tries to enter the house at once but GD asks his friends to stay in the garden while Dad and I follow him to Nana's bed. She is lying quite still, with her head sunk deeply into the soft pillow, over which spills her silver-grey hair. Her eyes are open. She tries to say something, but it comes out as a croak. GD raises her head and helps her to take a sip from a glass of water. She is saying, 'This is wonderful,' as her eyes drink in every detail of the familiar room in the home she loves.

People have started to drift in, despite what GD has said. Nana nods as she recognizes familiar faces, smiles at others.

People settle themselves about the room, on furniture, floor and window seats and some upon the stairs. GD wants everyone to be quiet at least and let Nana rest but Nana says no, she wants to hear her friends talking. She squeezes GD's hand and whispers, 'This is just how it should be.' Leo takes up his guitar and sings a song softly. It's *The Attics of My Life*, an old favourite in this house. People join in. I join in, because GD has played it so often that I know all the words. Nana lies peacefully upon her bed listening to the songs and chatter. If she's in any pain, she hides it well. No one notices when Nana dies. GD is at her side, still holding her hand and talking about old times. He looks up to reply to something his friend Paul is saying and when he turns back to Nana, she is gone.

In a place between the ring of standing stones and Nana's Rock, a place which would command a widescreen view of the hills and dales of the Derbyshire countryside had not the sun gone down, we stand in a circle around the carefully laid logs and branches which make an enormous stack which must be nine or ten feet high. We hold hands, me, Mum and Dad, Magic Mick, Paul, Leo, Sam and many others who came to see Nana's body as she lay on her bed, which was soon surrounded by flowers. Lauren and Diesel are over on the other side with Faruk and Clive. Ros is here too, brought along by Teresa, whose hot hand is in mine.

Magic Mick had organised everything the day before, directing Faruk and me and a lot of other helpers to collect together piles of wood and big logs he had already chopped which would only have to be dragged out from the nearby copse and assembled when a flashing torch from across the valley signalled that all was ready (mobile reception is pretty flaky here). Mum had arrived earlier in the day and with the help of a neighbour, had put Nana in her favourite blouse and skirt and arranged her hair.

People made their way to Nana's Rock by car or on foot and by the time the camper van arrived bearing a bundle wrapped in a blue silk cloth, some fifty or sixty people were already waiting by the pyre. They are solemn faced now, as Magic Mick and Paul mount ladders and the long bundle is gently passed up to them. I have a queasy feeling in my stomach. A cremation isn't something I have ever wanted to see firsthand. I can hear other expressions of doubt and concern too, but this is what Nana wanted. The cremations she saw in India seemed more like joyous celebrations of a life than mournful leave-takings and that was the way she'd like to go, Nana had told GD, if only that were possible.

I still think this isn't right somehow, but I know I must respect her wishes and those of GD too, so I stand quietly as GD says a few words before lighting the fire. He tells us how happy she was to see her old friends on the day she died and of how pleased she would be to see so many of us here tonight. He tells us a little about her life, her travels in India, about the work she did for orphanages there and the contented life they have enjoyed together at their cottage in the hills. He says he doesn't quite know what he will do without her, but intends to treat this not as an ending but as a new beginning, because that is what Ruth would have wanted. And with that, he sets light to paper and brushwood and stands back as the fire takes hold.

I am a little shocked, somehow, to find that joints are being passed hand to hand around the circle. But no one else seems to mind and even Dad takes a hit before passing it on. Now I have seen everything, I think. The fire blossoms and spreads and soon the bundle in blue is lost among the leaping flames and billowing smoke. The heat is tremendous and we all step back. Teresa gives my hand a squeeze. Ros mutters, 'This is amazing.'

Somewhere in the crowd a lone female voice has begun singing her own version of something by Joni Mitchell, Nana's favourite singer, and the song is taken up by others, until all I can hear are beautiful harmonies and the crackling of the burning wood. Tears are winding down GD's cheeks, but he's smiling at the same time. I can see Diesel and Lauren are smiling too. Across the valley, we can see a tiny flashing blue light and a siren. It's a pity there's an ugly green Ford Escort with three flat tyres abandoned in the middle of the narrow lane down there.

It's a month or so after Dad left and we're gathered around the television in our front room. Mum, wearing a bright new dress, is sitting with Roger on the sofa while Clive and Poon Tang make use of big cushions on the floor. Clive's hand rests on Poon Tang's leg, just below the hem of her worryingly short skirt. We're watching Roger and Clive's appearance on *Bargain Search*: presenter Tom Honeypott mugs to the camera as he informs viewers that the Dysons, a father and son team from Sheffield, like nothing better than bagging a bargain! Actually, there's a long list of things they enjoy more, but they're not really suitable for exposure on daytime television. As I watch the Blue team rooting through the stalls of an antiques market near Peterborough, I can see that Roger was quite right about the blue fleeces – some people can carry them off, but Roger and Clive look like a pair of Smurfs.

The final edit makes it appear that Roger spent the whole of his allotted hour arguing with both Clive and his antiques expert but at last, the Blue team settles on a Clarice Cliff plate, a Toby jug and a brace of duelling pistols. A little later, the auctioneer reveals that the Clarice Cliff isn't a Clarice Cliff, the Toby Jug has been inexpertly repaired and the pistols are fakes and by the end of the auction, the Dysons are minus two hundred and eighty pounds, which Tom Honeypott says might be a winning score, but it isn't, of course.

'What do I know about old plates and jugs?' Roger's grumbling. 'I'm more Bauhaus, me.'

'Not to worry,' Mum says, giving Roger a quick, passionate

kiss on the lips. 'I'll be your bargain.'

From which little cameo, you'll gather that there have been one or two more changes at this end of Laurel Gardens. The first comes about four weeks before the date that Roger and Poon Tang have set for their wedding. Roger has taken Poon Tang out to a Thai restaurant, where they both have too much to drink and they no sooner get home than Poon Tang and Roger are dragging each other off to the bedroom. Sex, she has told already him, in a matter of fact way as they ate their desserts, is now permissible.

Clive watches their bedroom door close with some misgivings. He sits on his bed in his room, which Poon Tang has lately been using as her own, and waits. He counts on his fingers. 'Any second...now,' is what he's saying when there's an anguished scream from the other room and it isn't from Poon Tang.

Roger, bollock-naked and clutching his tackle in his hands, flies out of his room, down the hall and into Clive's, where he slams and bolts the door. 'It's her, Poon Tang!' he gibbers. 'She's got a whatsit, a thing, down there.' He gestures at his own genital area.

'You mean a cock?' Clive says to his father. 'I thought you knew.'

Clive didn't think that at all but he didn't much fancy telling Nutter Dyson that he had very nearly married a ladyboy. Even if he was his father.

'Yes, a cock,' Roger says, still shaking. 'And it's bigger than mine.'

Clive's news hasn't come as a complete surprise to me. I thought I'd seen something when Poon Tang was fighting with Carole, in the Casablanca. But when a bird flashes what looks a lot like a pair of balls and big cock it's very easy to think you're seeing things. It did come as a complete surprise to Roger, though. She had kissed him on the lips and slipped off her top, revealing what Clive assures me are the most perfectly formed pair of tits. Not big ones, but very sexy all the same. The erection Roger got when he saw them hadn't quite subsided when he burst into his son's room in a state of shock. Poon Tang seemed to think Roger knew all about her little, or not so little, secret and had wriggled out of her panties and hoisted her skirt without a thought. Which was when Roger had screamed, leapt off the bed and claimed refuge in Clive's bedroom.

It took Roger a little while to adjust to the new state of things. It didn't take him long to cancel the wedding, though. Poon Tang understood and was very good about it, admitting that ladyboys weren't everyone's cup of chai. According to Poon Tang, men who suddenly discover they have inadvertently gone to bed with a transsexual either are horrified like Roger was or reckon they've got double bubble and get stuck in, though she might not actually have said 'double bubble'. As far as Poon Tang was concerned, things had worked out for the best. She had soon realised that she wasn't in love with Roger, but she rather thought she might be love with his son, Clive. And there was no doubt that Clive was in love with Poon Tang and would certainly have declared his love earlier if he didn't think it might queer his dad's pitch, he says.

Roger was in two minds about Poon Tang taking up with his boy. It wasn't only because of the embarrassment she'd caused him. It was just that as a man and a Millwall supporting man at that, you have to have your doubts when your boy starts dating a girl with nice breasts and a big cock. But by this time, Roger was more worried about Clive coming home with a bloke. And, as Clive cannily pointed out, half a girlfriend was better than none. And so Clive was finally fixed up, if not to his father's complete satisfaction. Which left Roger free and single once again, but not for long.

It was about this time that Dad had revealed the big change that would affect us all. As I'd suspected and had at first feared, my parents were going to split up. And because I thought I'd seen it coming, it wasn't the shock it might have been a year ago, when it would have rocked the Richter scale. But it was still sad and very strange. Weeks after it actually happened, I was still finding it disconcerting to come home in the evenings and find only Mum at home – if she wasn't still out at her flower shop. Dad had left soon after she had signed the lease, going off like some latent hippie, to find himself.

After learning the facts about his life, Dad came to see his past existence as what he called a living lie. The real Charlie wasn't the department store drudge who holidayed in garden centres, he told me. The real Charlie had been smothered by fear and suspicion and it was high time he found him again – and much as he loved Mum and me, he wasn't going to do that in Laurel Gardens. He was leaving the next morning, he told me, crushing any idea I might be having that this was only a pipe dream. He was sure that sooner or later we would understand. Mum, he was convinced, already did. He kissed me goodnight and closed the door, leaving me to my thoughts and maybe one or two tears. He was gone before Mum or I had got up. I was woken by the familiar splutter and fart of the campervan driving off and knew that though we would surely see him again, as a member of our family, Dad was gone for good.

The campervan? I forgot to mention that in another, enormous departure from reality, Dad had accepted GD's offer of the rusting heap of nuts and bolts he'd complained about for so long, for which GD had no further use, he said, not now that Nana was gone. And that is how Dad went, setting off on his strange quest in the unlikeliest of transport. I think of him all the time, driving relentlessly onward in that psychedelically painted microbus, looking for the man he might have been. He had wanted his leaving to be as painless as possible. He didn't want to hurt Mum and perhaps he had already seen a future for her with Roger. It was obvious to anyone that Mum liked Roger – I don't think I heard her laugh until he showed up. And I know Roger liked my mum, but I never knew how much until he turned up on our doorstep soon after Dad had left, dressed like Russell Crowe in *Gladiator*, with a bunch of flowers in one hand and a Roman short sword in the other. Within weeks, Roger had moved in. It's on the cards that once Mum and Dad get a divorce, Roger will become my stepdad and Clive my stepbrother. I really don't know how Poon Tang will fit into all this.

Mum has a real Russell Crowe now, or as real as she'll get without having the real real thing, so to speak. She doesn't have Russell Crowe the shop window mannequin any more. That Russell disappeared some weeks back and she's been rather evasive about what's happened to him. Possibly he came a cropper in one of Mum and Roger's disturbingly noisy sex games and was decapitated by Roger's sword, but I sometimes wonder if there is any truth in the rumour I've heard that Nana wasn't cremated, but buried quietly in a lovely woodland site and that something else was put on top of the pyre. That way GD would have found a fitting way of marking her passing without the risk of some terrible mishap or unwanted trouble with the authorities. It's a thought.

Roger's not been living here long but already there have been changes. For one thing, he's sold the house next door, having first found a new site for his business, which now sits on an industrial estate five miles away. The last thing he wants, he tells Mum, is to live next door to a bleedin' scrapyard. He keeps up Dad's garden, but it's much less formal than before and we make good use of it, especially when my friends come round for barbecues, like the one we're enjoying this evening.

Lauren's here and her pregnancy is really showing now and the father, dressed in an apron decorated with enormous cartoon breasts as he prods and turns the sausages, couldn't be prouder. He couldn't be much happier, either. Magic Mick has been so pleased with the improvements Diesel's made in the running of the shop that he's made him a partner in the business, effective as soon as he leaves school and Diesel has big plans for the place. Lauren has heard all about the road trip we're still planning to mark the end of school next year and has said that Diesel must go with us, or she'll never hear the last it. She's actually a good sort, is Lauren.

Faruk is eating a hamburger, which is dribbling ketchup down his shirt, and talking to Roger about his new venture. His latest interest is motor racing and it might just be something he's good at. We only discovered how good a driver he is when he helped us rescue Nana from the hospital. Just lately, he's been trying to persuade Abdullah to start up their own Team Casablanca, racing a certain Ford Escort and though it sounds like just one more of Faruk's pipe dreams, who knows, with Allah on their side, they might just do it.

Now everyone's talking of nothing else but the road trip. We don't know where we'll be going, not exactly, but we do know we're going to have a high old time getting there, as GD would say. He's here too, sitting in Dad's old deckchair and probably thinking about Nana. What he'll do in the future, I don't know. It's hard to imagine him being happy again now that Nana has gone, but he has his own weird philosophies and though he's not religious in the conventional sense, I think he sees Nana as having gone to some better place. I think, or better still, I believe, that he'll be okay.

And what about me, I hope you're thinking. Have I changed?

Oh, come on! You mean to say you haven't noticed a new confidence in my attitude, a decisiveness in my actions and a cocky swagger in my walk? Really?

Well, let me fill you in on what's been going down.

The above-listed qualities are all born on the night that Teresa Davenport invites me back to her room on our last night in Whitby, saying she has something to show me. You've got to be ahead of me here, because what she shows me – and oh, so expertly – is what I've been wanting a woman to show me for longer than I can remember and show me she surely does. She takes off my clothes, piece by piece and then she takes me in hand, so to speak.

And then it happens and it is actually, amazingly, better than I had ever imagined – and I've done a lot of imagining. She can be quite dominating, I'm thinking, as I lie on my back and stare up in wonder at her small yet beautifully formed breasts bouncing quickly up and down while she fucks me – she's actually fucking me, I'm having SEX! – but she's dominating in – a – really – really – nice – way. And I'm trying to think of anything, anything at all, which will stop – me – from – coming – too – soon – as – I – want – this – to – last – for – ever.

Teresa continues to bounce up and down.

I start thinking of all the stupid, fun stuff the Four Horsemen have done together, about Prom night, when Diesel got Lauren pregnant, about The Party to End All Parties, about weirdly Gothic Whitby and the road trip which might now actually happen and I'm thinking of how Teresa looked at me just now, when she pulled off my Spiderman pants and dropped them onto the floor and how she didn't appear to think that I had a small cock at all, an idea borne out by the low moan she made as she sank herself down upon me. She didn't actually stop what she was doing and say, 'Oh My God, that is HUGE', which I must admit, I would have rather liked, but just got on with what we were about to do like she hadn't even noticed how big or how small it was.

It's enough to make me wonder if I hadn't got this thing out of proportion. Could it be that I'm not spectacularly big or minisculely small but boringly average? And is that something I should worry about too? And another thing I'm wondering is how I could possibly have wasted so much time chasing the wrong girl when any idiot could have seen immediately that Teresa Davenport is much smarter, far prettier and so much sexier than Rosalind Chandler. Teresa must be much better in bed too. Because surely, I'm thinking, as Teresa groans and squeezes me and tells me I'm giving her just what she wants – and I can't take it one second longer and we climax together, noisily, warmly, wetly on our very first time – it can't get any better than this? Can it?

**LODESTONE
BOOKS**

Lodestone Books is a new imprint, which offers a broad
spectrum of subjects in YA/NA literature. Compelling reading,
the Teen/Young/New Adult reader is sure to find something
edgy, enticing and innovative. From dystopian societies, through
a whole range of fantasy, horror, science fiction and paranormal
fiction, all the way to the other end of the sphere, historical
drama, steam-punk adventure, and everything in between.
You'll find stories of crime, coming of age and contemporary
romance. Whatever your preference you will discover it here.